A JOURNEY TO THE CENTER OF THE EARTH

PAPER MILL PRESS CLASSICS

The Arabian Nights	Andrew Lang
Black Beauty	Anna Sewell
Dracula	Bram Stoker
Great Expectations	Charles Dickens
Oliver Twist	Charles Dickens
A Tale of Two Cities	Charles Dickens
Jane Eyre	Charlotte Bronte
Robinson Crusoe	Daniel Defoe
Wuthering Heights	Emily Bronte
The Great Gatsby	F. Scott Fitzgerald
The Secret Garden	Frances Hodgson Burnett
The Phantom of the Opera	Gaston Leroux
Madame Bovary	Gustave Flaubert
Moby Dick	Herman Melville
The Call of the Wild	Jack London
The Last of the Mohicans	James Fenimore Cooper
Emma	Jane Austen
Persuasion	Jane Austen
Pride and Prejudice	Jane Austen
Sense and Sensibility	Jane Austen
Gulliver's Travels	Jonathan Swift
A Journey to the Center of the Earth	Jules Verne
Around the World in Eighty Days	Jules Verne
20000 Leagues Under the Sea	Jules Verne
The Wonderful Wizard of Oz	L. Frank Baum
Alice's Adventures in Wonderland	Lewis Carroll
Little Women	Louisa May Alcott
The Adventures of Huckleberry Finn	Mark Twain
The Adventures of Tom Sawyer	Mark Twain
The Prince and the Pauper	Mark Twain
Frankenstein	Mary Shelley
The Scarlet Letter	Nathaniel Hawthorne
The Picture of Dorian Gray	Oscar Wilde
Treasure Island	Robert Louis Stevenson
The Jungle Book	Rudyard Kipling
The Adventures of Sherlock Holmes	Sir Arthur Conan Doyle

Jules Verne

A JOURNEY TO THE CENTER OF THE EARTH

PAPER
MILL
PRESS

PAPER
MILL
PRESS

Paper Mill Press
Published by Book Depot, Inc.
67 Front Street North
Thorold, ON L2V 1X3

This 2019 Book Depot, Inc. edition
published by arrangement with Atlantic Publishing.

Cover and endpaper design by Yvonne Fetig Roehler

ISBN: 978-1-7740-2173-6

Printed and Bound in China
23 22 21 20 19 • 5 4 3 2 1

CONTENTS

CHAPTER 1

MY UNCLE MAKES A GREAT DISCOVERY

Looking back to all that has occurred to me since that eventful day, I am scarcely able to believe in the reality of my adventures. They were truly so wonderful that even now I am bewildered when I think of them.

My uncle was a German, having married my mother's sister, an Englishwoman. Being very much attached to his fatherless nephew, he invited me to study under him in his home in the fatherland. This home was in a large town, and my uncle a professor of philosophy, chemistry, geology, mineralogy, and many other ologies.

One day, after passing some hours in the laboratory—my uncle being absent at the time—I suddenly felt the necessity of renovating the tissues—*i.e.*, I was hungry, and was about to rouse up our old French cook, when my uncle, Professor Von Hardwigg, suddenly opened the street door, and came rushing upstairs.

Now Professor Hardwigg, my worthy uncle, is by no means a bad sort of man; he is, however, choleric and original. To bear with him means to obey; and scarcely had his heavy feet resounded within our joint domicile than he shouted for me to attend upon him.

"Harry—Harry—Harry—"

I hastened to obey, but before I could reach his room, jumping three steps at a time, he was stamping his right foot upon the landing.

"Harry!" he cried, in a frantic tone, "are you coming up?"

Now to tell the truth, at that moment I was far more interested in the question as to what was to constitute our dinner than in any problem of science; to me soup was more interesting than soda, an omelette more tempting than arithmetic, and an artichoke of ten times more value than any amount of asbestos.

But my uncle was not a man to be kept waiting; so adjourning therefore all minor questions, I presented myself before him.

He was a very learned man. Now most persons in this category supply themselves with information, as peddlers do with goods, for the benefit of others, and lay up stores in order to diffuse them abroad for the benefit of society in general. Not so my excellent uncle, Professor Hardwigg; he studied, he consumed the midnight oil, he pored over heavy tomes, and digested huge quartos and folios in order to keep the knowledge acquired to himself.

There was a reason, and it may be regarded as a good one, why my uncle objected to display his learning more than was absolutely necessary: he stammered; and when intent upon explaining the phenomena of the heavens, was apt to find himself at fault, and allude in such a vague way to sun, moon, and stars that few were able to comprehend his meaning. To tell the honest truth, when the right word would not come, it was generally replaced by a very powerful adjective.

In connection with the sciences there are many almost unpronounceable names—names very much resembling those of Welsh villages; and my uncle being very fond of using them, his habit of stammering was not thereby improved. In fact, there were periods in his discourse when he would finally give up and swallow his discomfiture—in a glass of water.

As I said, my uncle, Professor Hardwigg, was a very learned man; and I now add a most kind relative. I was bound to him by the double ties of affection and interest. I took deep interest in all his doings, and hoped some day to be almost as learned myself. It was a rare thing for me to be absent from his lectures. Like him, I preferred mineralogy to all the other sciences. My anxiety was to gain real *knowledge of the earth*. Geology and mineralogy were to us the sole objects of life, and in connection with these studies many a fair specimen of stone, chalk, or metal did we break with our hammers.

Steel rods, loadstones, glass pipes, and bottles of various acids were oftener before us than our meals. My uncle Hardwigg was once known to classify six hundred different geological specimens by their weight, hardness, fusibility, sound, taste, and smell.

He corresponded with all the great, learned, and scientific men of the age. I was, therefore, in constant communication with, at all events the letters of, Sir Humphry Davy, Captain Franklin, and other great men.

But before I state the subject on which my uncle wished to confer with me, I must say a word about his personal appearance. Alas! my readers will see a very different portrait of him at a future time, after he has gone through the fearful adventures yet to be related.

My uncle was fifty years old; tall, thin, and wiry. Large spectacles hid, to a certain extent, his vast, round, and goggle eyes, while his nose was irreverently compared to a thin file. So much indeed did it resemble that useful article, that a compass was said in his presence to have made considerable N (Nasal) deviation.

The truth being told, however, the only article really attracted to my uncle's nose was tobacco.

Another peculiarity of his was, that he always stepped a yard at a time, clenched his fists as if he were going to hit you, and was, when in one of his peculiar humors, very far from a pleasant companion.

It is further necessary to observe that he lived in a very nice house, in that very nice street, the Konigstrasse at Hamburg. Though lying in the centre of a town, it was perfectly rural in its aspect—half wood, half bricks, with old-fashioned gables—one of the few old houses spared by the great fire of 1842.

When I say a nice house, I mean a handsome house—old, tottering, and not exactly comfortable to English notions: a house a little off the perpendicular and inclined to fall into the neighboring canal; exactly the house for a wandering artist to depict; all the more that you could scarcely see it for ivy and a magnificent old tree which grew over the door.

My uncle was rich; his house was his own property, while he had a considerable private income. To my notion the best part of his possessions was his god-daughter, Gretchen. And the old cook, the young lady, the Professor and I were the sole inhabitants.

I loved mineralogy, I loved geology. To me there was nothing like pebbles—and if my uncle had been in a little less of a fury, we should have been the happiest of families. To prove the excellent Hardwigg's impatience, I solemnly declare that when the flowers in the drawing-room pots began to grow, he rose every morning at four o'clock to make them grow quicker by pulling the leaves!

Having described my uncle, I will now give an account of our interview.

He received me in his study; a perfect museum, containing every natural curiosity that can well be imagined—minerals, however, predominating. Every one was familiar to me, having been catalogued by my own hand. My uncle, apparently oblivious of the fact that he had summoned me to his presence, was absorbed in a book. He was particularly fond of early editions, tall copies, and unique works.

"Wonderful!" he cried, tapping his forehead. "Wonderful—wonderful!"

It was one of those yellow-leaved volumes now rarely found on stalls, and to me it appeared to possess but little value. My uncle, however, was in raptures.

He admired its binding, the clearness of its characters, the ease with which it opened in his hand, and repeated aloud, half a dozen times, that it was very, very old.

To my fancy he was making a great fuss about nothing, but it was not my province to say so. On the contrary, I professed considerable interest in the subject, and asked him what it was about.

"It is the Heims-Kringla of Snorre Tarleson," he said, "the celebrated Icelandic author of the twelfth century—it is a true and correct account of the Norwegian princes who reigned in Iceland."

My next question related to the language in which it was written. I hoped at all events it was translated into German. My uncle was indignant at the very thought, and declared he wouldn't give a penny for a translation. His delight was to have found the original work in the Icelandic tongue, which he declared to be one of the most magnificent and yet simple idioms in the world—while at the same time its grammatical combinations were the most varied known to students.

"About as easy as German?" was my insidious remark.

My uncle shrugged his shoulders.

"The letters at all events," I said, "are rather difficult of comprehension."

"It is a Runic manuscript, the language of the original population of Iceland, invented by Odin himself," cried my uncle, angry at my ignorance.

I was about to venture upon some misplaced joke on the subject, when a small scrap of parchment fell out of the leaves. Like a hungry man snatching at a morsel of bread the Professor seized it. It was about five inches by three and was scrawled over in the most extraordinary fashion.

The lines shown here are an exact facsimile of what was written on the venerable piece of parchment—and have wonderful importance, as they induced my uncle to undertake the most wonderful series of adventures which ever fell to the lot of human beings.

My uncle looked keenly at the document for some moments and then declared that it was Runic. The letters were similar to those in the book, but then what did they mean? This was exactly what I wanted to know.

Now as I had a strong conviction that the Runic alphabet and dialect were simply an invention to mystify poor human nature, I was delighted to find that my uncle knew as much about the matter as I did—which was nothing. At all events the tremulous motion of his fingers made me think so.

"And yet," he muttered to himself, "it is old Icelandic, I am sure of it."

And my uncle ought to have known, for he was a perfect polyglot dictionary in himself. He did not pretend, like a certain learned pundit, to speak the two thousand languages and four thousand idioms made use of in different parts of the globe, but he did know all the more important ones.

It is a matter of great doubt to me now, to what violent measures my uncle's impetuosity might have led him, had not the clock struck two, and our old French cook called out to let us know that dinner was on the table.

"Bother the dinner!" cried my uncle.

But as I was hungry, I sallied forth to the dining room, where I took up my usual quarters. Out of politeness I waited three minutes, but no sign of my uncle, the Professor. I was surprised. He was not usually so blind to the pleasure of a good dinner. It was the acme of German luxury—parsley soup, a ham omelette with sorrel trimmings, an oyster of veal stewed with prunes, delicious fruit, and sparkling Moselle. For the sake of poring over this musty old piece of parchment, my uncle forbore to share our meal. To satisfy my conscience, I ate for both.

The old cook and housekeeper was nearly out of her mind. After taking so much trouble, to find her master not appear at dinner was to her a sad disappointment—which, as she occasionally watched the havoc I was making on the viands, became also alarm. If my uncle were to come to table after all?

Suddenly, just as I had consumed the last apple and drunk the last glass of wine, a terrible voice was heard at no great distance. It was my uncle roaring for me to come to him. I made very nearly one leap of it—so loud, so fierce was his tone.

Chapter 2

THE MYSTERIOUS PARCHMENT

"I declare," cried my uncle, striking the table fiercely with his fist, "I declare to you it is Runic—and contains some wonderful secret, which I must get at, at any price."

I was about to reply when he stopped me.

"Sit down," he said, quite fiercely, "and write to my dictation."

I obeyed.

"I will substitute," he said, "a letter of our alphabet for that of the Runic: we will then see what that will produce. Now, begin and make no mistakes."

The dictation commenced with the following incomprehensible result:

mm.rnlls esruel seecJde
sgtssmf unteief niedrke
kt,samn atrateS Saodrrn
emtnaeI nuaect rrilSa
Atvaar .nscrc ieaabs
ccdrmi eeutul frantu
dt,iac oseibo KediiY

Scarcely giving me time to finish, my uncle snatched the document from my hands and examined it with the most rapt and deep attention.

"I should like to know what it means," he said, after a long period.

I certainly could not tell him, nor did he expect me to—his conversation being uniformly answered by himself.

"I declare it puts me in mind of a cryptograph," he cried, "unless, indeed, the letters have been written without any real meaning; and yet why take so much trouble? Who knows but I may be on the verge of some great discovery?"

My candid opinion was that it was all rubbish! But this opinion I kept carefully to myself, as my uncle's choler was not pleasant to bear. All this time he was comparing the book with the parchment.

"The manuscript volume and the smaller document are written in different hands," he said, "the cryptograph is of much later date than the book; there is an undoubted proof of the correctness of my surmise. [An irrefragable proof I took it to be.] The first letter is a double M, which was only added to the Icelandic language in the twelfth century—this makes the parchment two hundred years posterior to the volume."

The circumstances appeared very probable and very logical, but it was all surmise to me.

"To me it appears probable that this sentence was written by some owner of the book. Now who was the owner, is the next important question. Perhaps by great good luck it may be written somewhere in the volume."

With these words Professor Hardwigg took off his spectacles, and, taking a powerful magnifying glass, examined the book carefully.

On the fly leaf was what appeared to be a blot of ink, but on examination proved to be a line of writing almost effaced by time. This was what he sought; and, after some considerable time, he made out these letters:

"Arne Saknussemm!" he cried in a joyous and triumphant tone, "that is not only an Icelandic name, but of a learned professor of the sixteenth century, a celebrated alchemist."

I bowed as a sign of respect"These alchemists," he continued, "Avicenna, Bacon, Lully, Paracelsus, were the true, the only learned men of the day. They made surprising discoveries. May not this Saknussemm, nephew mine, have hidden on this bit of parchment some astounding invention? I believe the cryptograph to have a profound meaning—which I must make out."

My uncle walked about the room in a state of excitement almost impossible to describe.

"It may be so, sir," I timidly observed, "but why conceal it from posterity, if it be a useful, a worthy discovery?"

"Why—how should I know? Did not Galileo make a secret of his discoveries in connection with Saturn? But we shall see. Until I discover the meaning of this sentence I will neither eat nor sleep."

"My dear uncle—" I began.

"Nor you neither," he added.

It was lucky I had taken double allowance that day.

"In the first place," he continued, "there must be a clue to the meaning. If we could find that, the rest would be easy enough."

I began seriously to reflect. The prospect of going without food and sleep was not a promising one, so I determined to do my best to solve the mystery. My uncle, meanwhile, went on with his soliloquy.

"The way to discover it is easy enough. In this document there are one hundred and thirty-two letters, giving seventy-nine consonants to fifty-three vowels. This is about the proportion found in most southern languages, the idioms of the north being much more rich in consonants. We may confidently predict, therefore, that we have to deal with a southern dialect."

Nothing could be more logical.

"Now," said Professor Hardwigg, "to trace the particular language."

"As Shakespeare says, 'that is the question,'" was my rather satirical reply.

"This man Saknussemm," he continued, "was a very learned man: now as he did not write in the language of his birthplace, he probably, like most learned men of the sixteenth century, wrote in Latin. If, however, I prove wrong in this guess, we must try Spanish, French, Italian, Greek, and even Hebrew. My own opinion, though, is decidedly in favor of Latin."

This proposition startled me. Latin was my favorite study, and it seemed sacrilege to believe this gibberish to belong to the country of Virgil.

"Barbarous Latin, in all probability," continued my uncle, "but still Latin."

"Very probably," I replied, not to contradict him.

"Let us see into the matter," continued my uncle; "here you see we have a series of one hundred and thirty-two letters, apparently thrown pell-mell upon paper, without method or organization. There are words which are composed wholly of consonants, such as *mm.rnlls*, others which are nearly all vowels, the fifth, for instance, which is unteief, and one of the last oseibo. This appears an extraordinary combination. Probably we shall find that the phrase is arranged according to some mathematical plan. No doubt a certain sentence has been written out and then jumbled up—some plan to which some figure is the clue. Now, Harry, to show your English wit—what is that figure?"

I could give him no hint. My thoughts were indeed far away. While he was speaking I had caught sight of the portrait of my cousin Gretchen, and was wondering when she would return.

We were affianced, and loved one another very sincerely. But my uncle, who never thought even of such sublunary matters, knew nothing of this. Without noticing my abstraction, the Professor began reading the puzzling cryptograph all sorts of ways, according to some theory of his own. Presently, rousing my wandering attention, he dictated one precious attempt to me.

I mildly handed it over to him. It read as follows:

mmessunkaSenrA.icefdoK.segnittamurtn
ecertserrette,rotaivsadua,ednecsedsadne
lacartniiilrJsiratracSarbmutabiledmek
meretarcsilucoYsleffenSnI.

I could scarcely keep from laughing, while my uncle, on the contrary, got in a towering passion, struck the table with his fist, darted out of the room, out of the house, and then taking to his heels was presently lost to sight.

Chapter 3

AN ASTOUNDING DISCOVERY

"What is the matter?" cried the cook, entering the room; "when will master have his dinner?"

"Never."

"And, his supper?"

"I don't know. He says he will eat no more, neither shall I. My uncle has determined to fast and make me fast until he makes out this abominable inscription," I replied.

"You will be starved to death," she said.

I was very much of the same opinion, but not liking to say so, sent her away, and began some of my usual work of classification. But try as I might, nothing could keep me from thinking alternately of the stupid manuscript and of the pretty Gretchen.

Several times I thought of going out, but my uncle would have been angry at my absence. At the end of an hour, my allotted task was done. How to pass the time? I began by lighting my pipe. Like all other students, I delighted in tobacco; and, seating myself in the great armchair, I began to think.

Where was my uncle? I could easily imagine him tearing along some solitary road, gesticulating, talking to himself, cutting the air with his cane, and still thinking of the absurd bit of hieroglyphics. Would he hit upon some clue? Would he come home in better humor? While these thoughts were passing through my brain, I mechanically took up the execrable puzzle and tried every imaginable way of grouping the letters. I put them together by twos, by threes, fours, and fives—in vain. Nothing intelligible came out, except that the fourteenth, fifteenth, and sixteenth made *ice* in English; the eighty-fourth, eighty-fifth, and eighty-sixth, the word *sir*; then at last I seemed to find the Latin words *rota, mutabile, ira, nec, atra.*

"Ha! there seems to be some truth in my uncle's notion," thought I.

Then again I seemed to find the word *luco*, which means sacred wood. Then in the third line I appeared to make out *labiled*, a perfect Hebrew word, and at the last the syllables mere, are, mer, which were French.

It was enough to drive one mad. Four different idioms in this absurd phrase. What connection could there be between ice, sir, anger, cruel, sacred wood, changing, mother, are, and sea? The first and the last might, in a sentence connected with Iceland, mean sea of ice. But what of the rest of this monstrous cryptograph?

I was, in fact, fighting against an insurmountable difficulty; my brain was almost on fire; my eyes were strained with staring at the parchment; the whole absurd collection of letters appeared to dance before my vision in a number of black little groups. My mind was possessed with temporary hallucination—I was stifling. I wanted air. Mechanically I fanned myself with the document, of which now I saw the back and then the front.

Imagine my surprise when glancing at the back of the wearisome puzzle, the ink having gone through, I clearly made out Latin words, and among others craterem and terrestre.

I had discovered the secret!

It came upon me like a flash of lightning. I had got the clue. All you had to do to understand the document was to read it backwards. All the ingenious ideas of the Professor were realized; he had dictated it rightly to me; by a mere accident I had discovered what he so much desired.

My delight, my emotion may be imagined, my eyes were dazzled and I trembled so that at first I could make nothing of it. One look, however, would tell me all I wished to know.

"Let me read," I said to myself, after drawing a long breath.

I spread it before me on the table, I passed my finger over each letter, I spelled it through; in my excitement I read it out.

What horror and stupefaction took possession of my soul. I was like a man who had received a knock-down blow. Was it possible that I really read the terrible secret, and it had really been accomplished! A man had dared to do—what?

No living being should ever know.

"Never!" cried I, jumping up. "Never shall my uncle be made aware of the dread secret. He would be quite capable of undertaking the terrible journey. Nothing would check him, nothing stop him. Worse, he would compel me to accompany him, and we should be lost forever. But no; such folly and madness cannot be allowed."

I was almost beside myself with rage and fury.

"My worthy uncle is already nearly mad," I cried aloud. "This would finish him. By some accident he may make the discovery; in which case, we are both lost. Perish the fearful secret—let the flames forever bury it in oblivion."

I snatched up book and parchment, and was about to cast them into the fire, when the door opened and my uncle entered.

I had scarcely time to put down the wretched documents before my uncle was by my side. He was profoundly absorbed. His thoughts were evidently bent on the terrible parchment. Some new combination had probably struck him while taking his walk.

He seated himself in his armchair, and with a pen began to make an algebraical calculation. I watched him with anxious eyes. My flesh crawled as it became probable that he would discover the secret.

His combinations I knew now were useless, I having discovered the one only clue. For three mortal hours he continued without speaking a word, without raising his head, scratching, rewriting, calculating over and over again. I knew that in time he must hit upon the right phrase. The letters of every alphabet have only a certain number of combinations. But then years might elapse before he would arrive at the correct solution.

Still time went on; night came, the sounds in the streets ceased—and still my uncle went on, not even answering our worthy cook when she called us to supper.

I did not dare to leave him, so waved her away, and at last fell asleep on the sofa.

When I awoke my uncle was still at work. His red eyes, his pallid countenance, his matted hair, his feverish hands, his hectically flushed cheeks, showed how terrible had been his struggle with the impossible, and what fearful fatigue he had undergone during that long sleepless night. It made me quite ill to look at him. Though he was rather severe with me, I loved him, and my heart ached at his sufferings. He was so overcome by one idea that he could not even get in a passion! All his energies were focused on one point. And I knew that by speaking one little word all this suffering would cease. I could not speak it.

My heart was, nevertheless, inclining towards him. Why, then, did I remain silent? In the interest of my uncle himself.

"Nothing shall make me speak," I muttered. "He will want to follow in the footsteps of the other! I know him well. His imagination is a perfect volcano, and to make discoveries in the interests of geology he would sacrifice his life. I will therefore be silent and strictly keep the secret I have discovered. To reveal it would be suicidal. He would not only rush, himself, to destruction, but drag me with him."

I crossed my arms, looked another way and smoked—resolved never to speak.

When our cook wanted to go out to market, or on any other errand, she found the front door locked and the key taken away. Was this done purposely or not? Surely Professor Hardwigg did not intend the old woman and myself to become martyrs to his obstinate will. Were we to be starved to death? A frightful recollection came to my mind. Once we had fed on bits and scraps for a week while he sorted some curiosities. It gave me the cramp even to think of it!

I wanted my breakfast, and I saw no way of getting it. Still my resolution held good. I would starve rather than yield. But the cook began to take me seriously to task. What was to be done? She could not go out; and I dared not.

My uncle continued counting and writing; his imagination seemed to have translated him to the skies. He neither thought of eating nor drinking. In this way twelve o'clock came round. I was hungry, and there was nothing in the house. The cook had eaten the last bit of bread. This could not go on. It did, however, until two, when my sensations were terrible. After all, I began to think the document very absurd. Perhaps it might only be a gigantic hoax. Besides, some means would surely be found to keep my uncle back from attempting any such absurd expedition. On the other hand, if he did attempt anything so quixotic, I should not be compelled to accompany him. Another line of reasoning partially decided me. Very likely he would make the discovery himself when I should have suffered starvation for nothing. Under the influence of hunger this reasoning appeared admirable. I determined to tell all.

The question now arose as to how it was to be done. I was still dwelling on the thought, when he rose and put on his hat.

What! go out and lock us in? Never!

"Uncle," I began.

He did not appear even to hear me.

"Professor Hardwigg," I cried.

"What," he retorted, "did you speak?"

"How about the key?"

"What key—the key of the door?"

"No—of these horrible hieroglyphics?"

He looked at me from under his spectacles, and started at the odd expression of my face. Rushing forward, he clutched me by the arm and keenly examined my countenance. His very look was an interrogation.

I simply nodded.

With an incredulous shrug of the shoulders, he turned upon his heel. Undoubtedly he thought I had gone mad.

"I have made a very important discovery."

His eyes flashed with excitement. His hand was lifted in a menacing attitude. For a moment neither of us spoke. It is hard to say which was most excited.

"You don't mean to say that you have any idea of the meaning of the scrawl?"

"I do," was my desperate reply. "Look at the sentence as dictated by you."

"Well, but it means nothing," was the angry answer.

"Nothing if you read from left to right, but mark, if from right to left—"

"Backwards!" cried my uncle, in wild amazement. "Oh most cunning Saknussemm; and I to be such a blockhead!"

He snatched up the document, gazed at it with haggard eye, and read it out as I had done.

It read as follows:

In Sneffels Yoculis craterem kem delibat
umbra Scartaris Julii intra calendas descende,
audas viator, et terrestre centrum attinges.
Kod feci. Arne Saknussemm

Which dog Latin being translated, reads as follows:

Descend into the crater of Yocul of Sneffels, which the shade of Scartaris caresses, before the kalends of July, audacious traveler, and you will reach the centre of the earth. I did it.

ARNE SAKNUSSEMM

My uncle leaped three feet from the ground with joy. He looked radiant and handsome. He rushed about the room wild with delight and satisfaction. He knocked over tables and chairs. He threw his books about until at last, utterly exhausted, he fell into his armchair.

"What's o'clock?" he asked.

"About three."

"My dinner does not seem to have done me much good," he observed. "Let me have something to eat. We can then start at once. Get my portmanteau ready."

"What for?"

"And your own," he continued. "We start at once."

My horror may be conceived. I resolved however to show no fear. Scientific reasons were the only ones likely to influence my uncle. Now, there were many against this terrible journey. The very idea of going down to the centre of the earth was simply absurd. I determined therefore to argue the point after dinner.

My uncle's rage was now directed against the cook for

having no dinner ready. My explanation however satisfied him, and having gotten the key, she soon contrived to get sufficient to satisfy our voracious appetites.

During the repast my uncle was rather gay than otherwise. He made some of those peculiar jokes which belong exclusively to the learned. As soon, however, as dessert was over, he called me to his study. We each took a chair on opposite sides of the table.

"Henry," he said, in a soft and winning voice; "I have always believed you ingenious, and you have rendered me a service never to be forgotten. Without you, this great, this wondrous discovery would never have been made. It is my duty, therefore, to insist on your sharing the glory."

"He is in a good humor," thought I; "I'll soon let him know my opinion of glory."

"In the first place," he continued, "you must keep the whole affair a profound secret. There is no more envious race of men than scientific discoverers. Many would start on the same journey. At all events, we will be the first in the field."

"I doubt your having many competitors," was my reply.

"A man of real scientific acquirements would be delighted at the chance. We should find a perfect stream of pilgrims on the traces of Arne Saknussemm, if this document were once made public."

"But, my dear sir, is not this paper very likely to be a hoax?" I urged.

"The book in which we find it is sufficient proof of its authenticity," he replied.

"I thoroughly allow that the celebrated Professor wrote the lines, but only, I believe, as a kind of mystification," was my answer.

Scarcely were the words out of my mouth, when I was sorry I had uttered them. My uncle looked at me with a dark and gloomy scowl, and I began to be alarmed for the results of our conversation. His mood soon changed, however, and a smile took the place of a frown.

"We shall see," he remarked, with decisive emphasis.

"But see, what is all this about Yocul, and Sneffels, and this Scartaris? I have never heard anything about them."

"The very point to which I am coming. I lately received from my friend Augustus Peterman, of Leipzig, a map. Take down the third atlas from the second shelf, series Z, plate 4."

I rose, went to the shelf, and presently returned with the volume indicated.

"This," said my uncle, "is one of the best maps of Iceland. I believe it will settle all your doubts, difficulties and objections."

With a grim hope to the contrary, I stooped over the map.

Chapter 4

WE START ON THE JOURNEY

"You see, the whole island is composed of volcanoes," said the Professor, "and remark carefully that they all bear the name of Yocul. The word is Icelandic, and means a glacier. In most of the lofty mountains of that region the volcanic eruptions come forth from icebound caverns. Hence the name applied to every volcano on this extraordinary island."

"But what does this word Sneffels mean?"

To this question I expected no rational answer. I was mistaken.

"Follow my finger to the western coast of Iceland, there you see Reykjavik, its capital. Follow the direction of one of its innumerable fjords or arms of the sea, and what do you see below the sixty-fifth degree of latitude?"

"A peninsula—very like a thighbone in shape."

"And in the centre of it—?"

"A mountain."

"Well, that's Sneffels."

I had nothing to say.

"That is Sneffels—a mountain about five thousand feet in height, one of the most remarkable in the whole island, and certainly doomed to be the most celebrated in the world, for through its crater we shall reach the centre of the earth."

"Impossible!" cried I, startled and shocked at the thought.

"Why impossible?" said Professor Hardwigg in his severest tones.

"Because its crater is choked with lava, by burning rocks—by infinite dangers."

"But if it be extinct?"

"That would make a difference."

"Of course it would. There are about three hundred volcanoes on the whole surface of the globe—but the greater number are extinct. Of these Sneffels is one. No eruption has occurred since 1219—in fact it has ceased to be a volcano at all."

After this what more could I say? Yes,—I thought of another objection.

"But what is all this about Scartaris and the kalends of July—?"

My uncle reflected deeply. Presently he gave forth the result of his reflections in a sententious tone. "What appears obscure to you, to me is light. This very phrase shows how particular Saknussemm is in his directions. The Sneffels mountain has many craters. He is careful therefore to point the exact one which is the highway into the Interior of the Earth. He lets us know, for this purpose, that about the end of the month of June, the shadow of Mount Scartaris falls upon the one crater. There can be no doubt about the matter."

My uncle had an answer for everything.

"I accept all your explanations" I said, "and Saknussemm is right. He found out the entrance to the bowels of the earth, he has indicated correctly, but that he or anyone else ever followed up the discovery is madness to suppose."

"Why so, young man?"All scientific teaching, theoretical and practical, shows it to be impossible."

"I care nothing for theories," retorted my uncle.

"But is it not well-known that heat increases one degree for every seventy feet you descend into the earth? Which gives a fine idea of the central heat. All the matters which compose the globe are in a state of incandescence; even gold, platinum, and the hardest rocks are in a state of fusion. What would become of us?"

"Don't be alarmed at the heat, my boy."

"How so?"

"Neither you nor anybody else know anything about the real state of the earth's interior. All modern experiments tend to explode the older theories. Were any such heat to exist, the upper crust of the earth would be shattered to atoms, and the world would be at an end."

A long, learned and not uninteresting discussion followed, which ended in this wise:

"I do not believe in the dangers and difficulties which you, Henry, seem to multiply; and the only way to learn, is like Arne Saknussemm, to go and see."

"Well," cried I, overcome at last, "let us go and see. Though how we can do that in the dark is another mystery."

"Fear nothing. We shall overcome these, and many other difficulties. Besides, as we approach the centre, I expect to find it luminous—"

"Nothing is impossible."

"And now that we have come to a thorough understanding, not a word to any living soul. Our success depends on secrecy and dispatch."

Thus ended our memorable conference, which roused a perfect fever in me. Leaving my uncle, I went forth like one possessed. Reaching the banks of the Elbe, I began to think. Was all I had heard really and truly possible? Was my uncle in his sober senses, and could the interior of the earth be reached? Was I the victim of a madman, or was he a discoverer of rare courage and grandeur of conception?

To a certain extent I was anxious to be off. I was afraid my enthusiasm would cool. I determined to pack up at once. At the end of an hour, however, on my way home, I found that my feelings had very much changed.

"I'm all abroad," I cried; "'tis a nightmare—I must have dreamed it."

At this moment I came face to face with Gretchen, whom I warmly embraced.

"So you have come to meet me," she said; "how good of you. But what is the matter?"

Well, it was no use mincing the matter, I told her all. She listened with awe, and for some minutes she could not speak.

"Well?" I at last said, rather anxiously.

"What a magnificent journey. If I were only a man! A journey worthy of the nephew of Professor Hardwigg. I should look upon it as an honor to accompany him."

"My dear Gretchen, I thought you would be the first to cry out against this mad enterprise."

"No; on the contrary, I glory in it. It is magnificent, splendid—an idea worthy of my father. Henry Lawson, I envy you."

This was, as it were, conclusive. The final blow of all.

When we entered the house we found my uncle surrounded by workmen and porters, who were packing up. He was pulling and hauling at a bell.

"Where have you been wasting your time? Your portmanteau is not packed—my papers are not in order—the precious tailor has not brought my clothes, nor my gaiters—the key of my carpet bag is gone!"

I looked at him stupefied. And still he tugged away at the bell.

"We are really off, then?" I said.

"Yes—of course, and yet you go out for a stroll, unfortunate boy!"

"And when do we go?"

"The day after tomorrow, at daybreak."

I heard no more; but darted off to my little bedchamber and locked myself in. There was no doubt about it now. My uncle had been hard at work all the afternoon. The garden was full of ropes, rope ladders, torches, gourds, iron clamps, crowbars, alpenstocks, and pickaxes—enough to load ten men.

I passed a terrible night. I was called early the next day to learn that the resolution of my uncle was unchanged and irrevocable. I also found my cousin and affianced wife as warm on the subject as was her father.

Next day, at five o'clock in the morning, the post chaise was at the door. Gretchen and the old cook received the keys of the house; and, scarcely pausing to wish anyone good-by, we started on our adventurous journey into the centre of the earth.

Chapter 5

FIRST LESSONS IN CLIMBING

At Altona, a suburb of Hamburg, is the Chief Station of the Kiel railway, which was to take us to the shores of the Belt. In twenty minutes from the moment of our departure we were in Holstein, and our carriage entered the station. Our heavy luggage was taken out, weighed, labeled, and placed in a huge van. We then took our tickets, and exactly at seven o'clock were seated opposite each other in a firstclass railway carriage.

My uncle said nothing. He was too busy examining his papers, among which of course was the famous parchment, and some letters of introduction from the Danish consul which were to pave the way to an introduction to the Governor of Iceland. My only amusement was looking out of the window. But as we passed through a flat though fertile country, this occupation was slightly monotonous. In three hours we reached Kiel, and our baggage was at once transferred to the steamer.

We had now a day before us, a delay of about ten hours. Which fact put my uncle in a towering passion. We had nothing to do but to walk about the pretty town and bay. At length, however, we went on board, and at half past ten were steaming down the Great Belt. It was a dark night, with a strong breeze and a rough sea, nothing being visible but the occasional fires on shore, with here and there a lighthouse. At seven in the morning we left Korsor, a little town on the western side of Seeland.

Here we took another railway, which in three hours brought us to the capital, Copenhagen, where, scarcely taking time for refreshment, my uncle hurried out to present one of his letters of introduction. It was to the director of the Museum of Antiquities, who, having been informed that we were tourists bound for Iceland, did all he could to assist us. One wretched hope sustained me now. Perhaps no vessel was bound for such distant parts.

Alas! a little Danish schooner, the *Valkyrie*, was to sail on the second of June for Reykjavik. The captain, M. Bjarne, was on board, and was rather surprised at the energy and cordiality with which his future passenger shook him by the hand. To him a voyage to Iceland was merely a matter of course. My uncle, on the other hand, considered the event of sublime importance. The honest sailor took advantage of the Professor's enthusiasm to double the fare.

"On Tuesday morning at seven o'clock be on board," said M. Bjarne, handing us our receipts.

"Excellent! Capital! Glorious!" remarked my uncle as we sat down to a late breakfast; "refresh yourself, my boy, and we will take a run through the town."

Our meal concluded, we went to the Kongens-Nye-Torw; to the king's magnificent palace; to the beautiful bridge over the canal near the Museum; to the immense cenotaph of Thorwaldsen with its hideous naval groups; to the castle of Rosenberg; and to all the other lions of the place-none of which my uncle even saw, so absorbed was he in his anticipated triumphs.

But one thing struck his fancy, and that was a certain

singular steeple situated on the Island of Amak, which is the southeast quarter of the city of Copenhagen. My uncle at once ordered me to turn my steps that way, and accordingly we went on board the steam ferry boat which does duty on the canal, and very soon reached the noted dockyard quay.

In the first instance we crossed some narrow streets, where we met numerous groups of galley slaves, with particolored trousers, grey and yellow, working under the orders and the sticks of severe taskmasters, and finally reached the Vor-Frelser's-Kirk.

This church exhibited nothing remarkable in itself; in fact, the worthy Professor had only been attracted to it by one circumstance, which was, that its rather elevated steeple started from a circular platform, after which there was an exterior staircase, which wound round to the very summit.

"Let us ascend," said my uncle.

"But I never could climb church towers," I cried, "I am subject to dizziness in my head."

"The very reason why you should go up. I want to cure you of a bad habit."

"But, my good sir—"

"I tell you to come. What is the use of wasting so much valuable time?"

It was impossible to dispute the dictatorial commands of my uncle. I yielded with a groan. On payment of a fee, a verger gave us the key. He, for one, was not partial to the ascent. My uncle at once showed me the way, running up the steps like a schoolboy. I followed as well as I could, though no sooner was I outside the tower, than my head began to swim. There was nothing of the eagle about me. The earth was enough for me, and no ambitious desire to soar ever entered my mind. Still things did not go badly until I had ascended 150 steps, and was near the platform, when I began to feel the rush of cold air. I could scarcely stand, when clutching the railings, I looked upwards. The railing was frail enough, but nothing to those which skirted the terrible winding staircase, that appeared, from where I stood, to ascend to the skies.

"Now then, Henry."

"I can't do it!" I cried, in accents of despair.

"Are you, after all, a coward, sir?" said my uncle in a pitiless tone. "Go up, I say!"

To this there was no reply possible. And yet the keen air acted violently on my nervous system; sky, earth, all seemed to swim round, while the steeple rocked like a ship. My legs gave way like those of a drunken man. I crawled upon my hands and knees; I hauled myself up slowly, crawling like a snake. Presently I closed my eyes, and allowed myself to be dragged upwards.

"Look around you," said my uncle in a stern voice, "heaven knows what profound abysses you may have to look down. This is excellent practice."

Slowly, and shivering all the while with cold, I opened my eyes. What then did I see? My first glance was upwards at the cold fleecy clouds, which as by some optical delusion appeared to stand still, while the steeple, the weathercock, and our two selves were carried swiftly along. Far away on one side could be seen the grassy plain, while on the other lay the sea bathed in translucent light. The Sund, or Sound as we call it, could be discovered beyond the point of Elsinore, crowded with white sails, which, at that distance looked like the wings of seagulls; while to the east could be made out the far-off coast of Sweden. The whole appeared a magic panorama.

But faint and bewildered as I was, there was no remedy for it. Rise and stand up I must. Despite my protestations my first lesson lasted quite an hour. When, nearly two hours later, I reached the bosom of mother earth, I was like a rheumatic old man bent double with pain.

"Enough for one day," said my uncle, rubbing his hands, "we will begin again tomorrow."

There was no remedy. My lessons lasted five days, and at the end of that period, I ascended blithely enough, and found myself able to look down into the depths below without even winking, and with some degree of pleasure.

Chapter 6

OUR VOYAGE TO ICELAND

The hour of departure came at last. The night before, the worthy Mr. Thompson brought us the most cordial letters of introduction for Baron Trampe, Governor of Iceland, for M. Pictursson, coadjutor to the bishop, and for M. Finsen, mayor of the town of Reykjavik. In return, my uncle nearly crushed his hands, so warmly did he shake them.

On the second of the month, at two in the morning, our precious cargo of luggage was taken on board the good ship *Valkyrie*. We followed, and were very politely introduced by the captain to a small cabin with two standing bed places, neither very well ventilated nor very comfortable. But in the cause of science men are expected to suffer.

"Well, and have we a fair wind?" cried my uncle, in his most mellifluous accents.

"An excellent wind!" replied Captain Bjarne; "we shall leave the Sound, going free with all sails set."

A few minutes afterwards, the schooner started before the wind, under all the canvas she could carry, and entered the channel. An hour later, the capital of Denmark seemed to sink into the waves, and we were at no great distance from the coast of Elsinore. My uncle was delighted; for myself, moody and dissatisfied, I appeared almost to expect a glimpse of the ghost of Hamlet.

"Sublime madman," thought I, "you doubtless would

approve our proceedings. You might perhaps even follow us to the centre of the earth, there to resolve your eternal doubts."

But no ghost or anything else appeared upon the ancient walls. The fact is, the castle is much later than the time of the heroic prince of Denmark. It is now the residence of the keeper of the Strait of the Sound, and through that Sound more than fifteen thousand vessels of all nations pass every year.

The castle of Kronborg soon disappeared in the murky atmosphere, as well as the tower of Helsinborg, which raises its head on the Swedish Bank. And here the schooner began to feel in earnest the breezes of the Kattegat. The *Valkyrie* was swift enough, but with all sailing boats there is the same uncertainty. Her cargo was coal, furniture, pottery, woolen clothing, and a load of corn. As usual, the crew was small, five Danes doing the whole of the work.

"How long will the voyage last?" asked my uncle.

"Well, I should think about ten days," replied the skipper, "unless, indeed, we meet with some northeast gales among the Faroe Islands."

"At all events, there will be no very considerable delay," cried the impatient Professor.

"No, Mr. Hardwigg," said the captain, "no fear of that. At all events, we shall get there some day."

Towards evening the schooner doubled Cape Skagen, the northernmost part of Denmark, crossed the Skagerrak during the night—skirted the extreme point of Norway through the gut of Cape Lindesnes, and then reached the Northern Seas. Two days later we were not far from the coast of Scotland, somewhere near what Danish sailors call Peterhead, and then the *Valkyrie* stretched out direct for the Faroe Islands, between Orkney and Shetland. Our vessel now felt the full force of the ocean waves, and the wind shifting, we with great difficulty made the Faroe Isles. On the eighth day, the captain made out Myganness, the westernmost of the isles, and from that moment headed direct for Portland, a cape on the southern shores of the singular island for which we were bound.

The voyage offered no incident worthy of record. I bore it very well, but my uncle to his great annoyance, and even shame, was remarkably seasick! This mal de mer troubled him the more that it prevented him from questioning Captain Bjarne as to the subject of Sneffels, as to the means of communication, and the facilities of transport. All these explanations he had to adjourn to the period of his arrival. His time, meanwhile, was spent lying in bed groaning, and dwelling anxiously on the hoped—for termination of the voyage. I didn't pity him.

On the eleventh day we sighted Cape Portland, over which towered Mount Myrdals Yokul, which, the weather being clear, we made out very readily. The cape itself is nothing but a huge mount of granite standing naked and alone to meet the Atlantic waves. The *Valkyrie* kept off the coast, steering to the westward. On all sides were to be seen whole "schools" of whales and sharks. After some hours we came in sight of a solitary rock in the ocean, forming a mighty vault, through which the foaming waves poured with intense fury. The islets of Westman appeared to leap from the ocean, being so low in the water as scarcely to be seen until you were right upon them. From that moment the schooner was steered to the westward in order to round Cape Reykjanes, the western point of Iceland.

My uncle, to his great disgust, was unable even to crawl on deck, so heavy a sea was on, and thus lost the first view of the Land of Promise. Forty-eight hours later, after a storm which drove us far to sea under bare poles, we came once more in sight of land, and were boarded by a pilot, who, after three hours of dangerous navigation, brought the schooner safely to an anchor in the bay of Faxa before Reykjavik.

My uncle came out of his cabin pale, haggard, thin, but full of enthusiasm, his eyes dilated with pleasure and satisfaction. Nearly the whole population of the town was on foot to see us land. The fact was, that scarcely any one of them but expected some goods by the periodical vessel.

Professor Hardwigg was in haste to leave his prison, or rather as he called it, his hospital; but before he attempted to do so, he caught hold of my hand, led me to the quarterdeck of the schooner, took my arm with his left hand, and pointed inland with his right, over the northern part of the bay, to where rose a high two-peaked mountain—a double cone covered with eternal snow.

"Behold he whispered in an awe-stricken voice, behold—Mount Sneffels!"

Then without further remark, he put his finger to his lips, frowned darkly, and descended into the small boat which awaited us. I followed, and in a few minutes we stood upon the soil of mysterious Iceland!

Scarcely were we fairly on shore when there appeared before us a man of excellent appearance, wearing the costume of a military officer. He was, however, but a civil servant, a magistrate, the governor of the island—Baron Trampe. The Professor knew whom he had to deal with. He therefore handed him the letters from Copenhagen, and a brief conversation in Danish followed, to which I of course was a stranger, and for a very good reason, for I did not know the language in which they conversed. I afterwards heard, however, that Baron Trampe placed himself entirely at the beck and call of Professor Hardwigg.

My uncle was most graciously received by M. Finsen, the mayor, who as far as costume went, was quite as military as the governor, but also from character and occupation quite as pacific. As for his coadjutor, M. Pictursson, he was absent on an episcopal visit to the northern portion of the diocese. We were therefore compelled to defer the pleasure of being presented to him. His absence was, however, more than compensated by the presence of M. Fridriksson, professor of natural science in the college of Reykjavik, a man of invaluable ability. This modest scholar spoke no languages save Icelandic and Latin. When, therefore, he addressed himself to me in the language of Horace, we at once came to understand one another. He was, in fact, the only person that I did thoroughly understand during the whole period of my residence in this benighted island.

Out of three rooms of which his house was composed, two were placed at our service, and in a few hours we were installed with all our baggage, the amount of which rather astonished the simple inhabitants of Reykjavik.

"Now, Harry," said my uncle, rubbing his hands, "an goes well, the worse difficulty is now over."

"How the worse difficulty over?" I cried in fresh amazement.

"Doubtless. Here we are in Iceland. Nothing more remains but to descend into the bowels of the earth."

"Well, sir, to a certain extent you are right. We have only to go down—but, as far as I am concerned, that is not the question. I want to know how we are to get up again."

"That is the least part of the business, and does not in any way trouble me. In the meantime, there is not an hour to lose. I am about to visit the public library. Very likely I may find there some manuscripts from the hand of Saknussemm. I shall be glad to consult them."

"In the meanwhile," I replied, "I will take a walk through the town. Will you not likewise do so?"

"I feel no interest in the subject," said my uncle. "What for me is curious in this island, is not what is above the surface, but what is below."

I bowed by way of reply, put on my hat and furred cloak, and went out.

It was not an easy matter to lose oneself in the two streets of Reykjavik; I had therefore no need to ask my way. The town lies on a flat and marshy plain, between two hills. A vast field of lava skirts it on one side, falling away in terraces towards the sea. On the other hand is the large bay of Faxa, bordered on the north by the enormous glacier of Sneffels, and in which bay the *Valkyrie* was then the only vessel at anchor. Generally there were one or two English or French gunboats, to watch and protect the fisheries in the offing. They were now, however, absent on dutyThe longest of the streets of Reykjavik runs parallel to the shore. In this street the merchants and traders live in wooden huts made with beams of wood, painted red—mere log huts, such as you find in the wilds of America. The other street, situated more to the west, runs toward a little lake between the residences of the bishop and the other personages not engaged in commerce.

I had soon seen all I wanted of these weary and dismal thoroughfares. Here and there was a strip of discolored turf, like an old worn-out bit of woolen carpet; and now and then a bit of kitchen garden, in which grew potatoes, cabbage, and lettuce, almost diminutive enough to suggest the idea of Lilliput.

In the centre of the new commercial street, I found the public cemetery, enclosed by an earthen wall. Though not very large, it appeared not likely to be filled for centuries. From hence I went to the house of the Governor—a mere hut in comparison with the Mansion House of Hamburg—but a palace alongside the other Icelandic houses. Between the little lake and the town was the church, built in simple Protestant style, and composed of calcined stones, thrown up by volcanic action. I have not the slightest doubt that in high winds its red tiles were blown out, to the great annoyance of the pastor and congregation. Upon an eminence close at hand was the national school, in which were taught Hebrew, English, French, and Danish.

In three hours my tour was complete. The general impression upon my mind was sadness. No trees, no vegetation, so to speak—on all sides volcanic peaks—the huts of turf and earth—more like roofs than houses. Thanks to the heat of these residences, grass grows on the roof, which grass is carefully cut for hay. I saw but few inhabitants during my excursion, but I met a crowd on the beach, drying, salting and loading codfish, the principal article of exportation. The men appeared robust but heavy; fair-haired like Germans, but of pensive mien—exiles of a higher scale in the ladder of humanity than the Eskimos, but, I thought, much more unhappy, since with superior perceptions they are compelled to live within the limits of the Polar Circle.

Sometimes they gave vent to a convulsive laugh, but by no chance did they smile. Their costume consists of a coarse capote of black wool, known in Scandinavian countries as the "vadmel," a broad-brimmed hat, trousers of red serge, and a piece of leather tied with strings for a shoe—a coarse kind of moccasin. The women, though sad-looking and mournful, had rather agreeable features, without much expression. They wear a bodice and petticoat of somber vadmel. When unmarried they wear a little brown knitted cap over a crown of plaited hair; but when married, they cover their heads with a colored handkerchief, over which they tie a white scarf.

Chapter 7

CONVERSATION AND DISCOVERY

When I returned, dinner was ready. This meal was devoured by my worthy relative with avidity and voracity. His shipboard diet had turned his interior into a perfect gulf. The repast, which was more Danish than Icelandic, was in itself nothing, but the excessive hospitality of our host made us enjoy it doubly.

The conversation turned upon scientific matters, and M. Fridriksson asked my uncle what he thought of the public library.

"Library, sir?" cried my uncle; "it appears to me a collection of useless odd volumes, and a beggarly amount of empty shelves."

"What!" cried M. Fridriksson; "why, we have eight thousand volumes of most rare and valuable works—some in the Scandinavian language, besides all the new publications from Copenhagen."

"Eight thousand volumes, my dear sir—why, where are they?" cried my uncle.

"Scattered over the country, Professor Hardwigg. We are very studious, my dear sir, though we do live in Iceland. Every farmer, every laborer, every fisherman can both read and write—and we think that books instead of being locked up in cupboards, far from the sight of students, should be distributed as widely as possible. The books of our library are therefore passed from hand to hand without returning to the library shelves perhaps for years."

"Then when foreigners visit you, there is nothing for them to see?"

"Well, sir, foreigners have their own libraries, and our first consideration is, that our humbler classes should be highly educated. Fortunately, the love of study is innate in the Icelandic people. In 1816 we founded a Literary Society and Mechanics' Institute; many foreign scholars of eminence are honorary members; we publish books destined to educate our people, and these books have rendered valuable services to our country. Allow me to have the honor, Professor Hardwigg, to enroll you as an honorary member?"

My uncle, who already belonged to nearly every literary and scientific institution in Europe, immediately yielded to the amiable wishes of good M. Fridriksson.

"And now," he said, after many expressions of gratitude and good will, "if you will tell me what books you expected to find, perhaps I may be of some assistance to you."

I watched my uncle keenly. For a minute or two he hesitated, as if unwilling to speak; to speak openly was, perhaps, to unveil his projects. Nevertheless, after some reflection, he made up his mind.

"Well, M. Fridriksson," he said in an easy, unconcerned kind of way, "I was desirous of ascertaining, if among other valuable works, you had any of the learned Arne Saknussemm."

"Arne Saknussemm!" cried the Professor of Reykjavik; "you speak of one of the most distinguished scholars of the sixteenth century, of the great naturalist, the great alchemist, the great traveler."

"Exactly so."

"One of the most distinguished men connected with Icelandic science and literature."

"As you say, sir—"

"A man illustrious above all."

"Yes, sir, all this is true, but his works?"

"We have none of them."

"Not in Iceland?"

"There are none in Iceland or elsewhere," answered the other, sadly.

"Why so?"

"Because Arne Saknussemm was persecuted for heresy, and in 1573 his works were publicly burnt at Copenhagen, by the hands of the common hangman."

"Very good! capital!" murmured my uncle, to the great astonishment of the worthy Icelander.

"You said, sir—"

"Yes, yes, all is clear, I see the link in the chain; everything is explained, and I now understand why Arne Saknussemm, put out of court, forced to hide his magnificent discoveries, was compelled to conceal beneath the veil of an incomprehensible cryptograph, the secret—"

"What secret?"

"A secret—which," stammered my uncle.

"Have you discovered some wonderful manuscript?" cried M. Fridriksson.

"No! no, I was carried away by my enthusiasm. A mere supposition."

"Very good, sir. But, really, to turn to another subject, I hope you will not leave our island without examining into its mineralogical riches."

"Well, the fact is, I am rather late. So many learned men have been here before me."

"Yes, yes, but there is still much to be done," cried M. Fridriksson.

"You think so," said my uncle, his eyes twinkling with hidden satisfaction.

"Yes, you have no idea how many unknown mountains, glaciers, volcanoes there are which remain to be studied. Without moving from where we sit, I can show you one. Yonder on the edge of the horizon, you see Sneffels."

"Oh yes, Sneffels," said my uncle.

"One of the most curious volcanoes in existence, the crater of which has been rarely visited."

"Extinct?"

"Extinct, any time these five hundred years," was the ready reply.

"Well," said my uncle, who dug his nails into his flesh, and pressed his knees tightly together to prevent himself leaping up with joy. "I have a great mind to begin my studies with an examination of the geological mysteries of this Mount Seffel—Feisel—what do you call it?"

"Sneffels, my dear sir."

This portion of the conversation took place in Latin, and I therefore understood all that had been said. I could scarcely keep my countenance when I found my uncle so cunningly concealing his delight and satisfaction. I must confess that his artful grimaces, put on to conceal his happiness, made him look like a new Mephistopheles.

"Yes, yes," he continued, "your proposition delights me. I will endeavor to climb to the summit of Sneffels, and, if possible, will descend into its crater."

"I very much regret," continued M. Fridriksson, "that my occupation will entirely preclude the possibility of my accompanying you. It would have been both pleasurable and profitable if I could have spared the time."

"No, no, a thousand times no," cried my uncle. "I do not wish to disturb the serenity of any man. I thank you, however, with all my heart. The presence of one so learned as yourself, would no doubt have been most useful, but the duties of your office and profession before everything."

In the innocence of his simple heart, our host did not perceive the irony of these remarks.

"I entirely approve your project," continued the Icelander after some further remarks. "It is a good idea to begin by examining this volcano. You will make a harvest of curious observations. In the first place, how do you propose to get to Sneffels?"

"By sea. I shall cross the bay. Of course that is the most rapid route."

"Of course. But still it cannot be done."

"Why?"

"We have not an available boat in all Reykjavik," replied the other.

"What is to be done?"

"You must go by land along the coast. It is longer, but much more interesting."

"Then I must have a guide."

"Of course; and I have your very man."

"Somebody on whom I can depend."

"Yes, an inhabitant of the peninsula on which Sneffels is situated. He is a very shrewd and worthy man, with whom you will be pleased. He speaks Danish like a Dane."

"When can I see him—today?"

"No, tomorrow; he will not be here before."

"Tomorrow be it," replied my uncle, with a deep sigh.

The conversation ended by compliments on both sides. During the dinner my uncle had learned much as to the history of Arne Saknussemm, the reasons for his mysterious and hieroglyphical document. He also became aware that his host would not accompany him on his adventurous expedition, and that next day we should have a guide.

Chapter 8

THE EIDER-DOWN HUNTER—OFF AT LAST

That evening I took a brief walk on the shore near Reykjavik, after which I returned to an early sleep on my bed of coarse planks, where I slept the sleep of the just. When I awoke I heard my uncle speaking loudly in the next room. I rose hastily and joined him. He was talking in Danish with a man of tall stature, and of perfectly Herculean build. This man appeared to be possessed of very great strength. His eyes, which started rather prominently from a very large head, the face belonging to which was simple and naive, appeared very quick and intelligent. Very long hair, which even in England would have been accounted exceedingly red, fell over his athletic shoulders. This native of Iceland was active and supple in appearance, though he scarcely moved his arms, being in fact one of those men who despise the habit of gesticulation common to southern people.

Everything in this man's manner revealed a calm and phlegmatic temperament. There was nothing indolent about him, but his appearance spoke of tranquillity. He was one of those who never seemed to expect anything from anybody, who liked to work when he thought proper, and whose philosophy nothing could astonish or trouble.

I began to comprehend his character, simply from the way in which he listened to the wild and impassioned verbiage of my worthy uncle. While the excellent Professor spoke sentence after sentence, he stood with folded arms, utterly still, motionless to all my uncle's gesticulations. When he wanted to say No he moved his head from left to right; when he acquiesced he nodded, so slightly that you could scarcely see the undulation of his head. This economy of motion was carried to the length of avarice.

Judging from his appearance I should have been a long time before I had suspected him to be what he was, a mighty hunter. Certainly his manner was not likely to frighten the game. How, then, did he contrive to get at his prey?

My surprise was slightly modified when I knew that this tranquil and solemn personage was only a hunter of the eider duck, the down of which is, after all, the greatest source of the Icelanders' wealth.

In the early days of summer, the female of the eider, a pretty sort of duck, builds its nest amid the rocks of the fjords—the name given to all narrow gulfs in Scandinavian countries—with which every part of the island is indented. No sooner has the eider duck made her nest than she lines the inside of it with the softest down from her breast. Then comes the hunter or trader, taking away the nest, the poor bereaved female begins her task over again, and this continues as long as any eider down is to be found.

When she can find no more the male bird sets to work to see what he can do. As, however, his down is not so soft, and has therefore no commercial value, the hunter does not take the trouble to rob him of his nest lining. The nest is accordingly finished, the eggs are laid, the little ones are born, and next year the harvest of eider down is again collected.

Now, as the eider duck never selects steep rocks or aspects to build its nest, but rather sloping and low cliffs near to the sea, the Icelandic hunter can carry on his trade operations without much difficulty. He is like a farmer who has neither to plow, to sow, nor to harrow, only to collect his harvest.

This grave, sententious, silent person, as phlegmatic as an Englishman on the French stage, was named Hans Bjelke. He had called upon us in consequence of the recommendation of M. Fridriksson. He was, in fact, our future guide. It struck me that had I sought the world over, I could not have found a greater contradiction to my impulsive uncle.

They, however, readily understood one another. Neither of them had any thought about money; one was ready to take all that was offered him, the other ready to offer anything that was asked. It may readily be conceived, then, that an understanding was soon come to between them.

Now, the understanding was, that he was to take us to the village of Stapi, situated on the southern slope of the peninsula of Sneffels, at the very foot of the volcano. Hans, the guide, told us the distance was about twenty-two miles, a journey which my uncle supposed would take about two days.

But when my uncle came to understand that they were Danish miles, of eight thousand yards each, he was obliged to be more moderate in his ideas, and, considering the horrible roads we had to follow, to allow eight or ten days for the journey.

Four horses were prepared for us, two to carry the baggage, and two to bear the important weight of myself and uncle. Hans declared that nothing ever would make him climb on the back of any animal. He knew every inch of that part of the coast, and promised to take us the very shortest way.

His engagement with my uncle was by no means to cease with our arrival at Stapi; he was further to remain in his service during the whole time required for the completion of his scientific investigations, at the fixed salary of three rix-dollars a week, being exactly fourteen shillings and twopence, minus one farthing, English currency. One stipulation, however, was made by the guide—the money was to be paid to him every Saturday night, failing which, his engagement was at an end.

The day of our departure was fixed. My uncle wished to hand the eider-down hunter an advance, but he refused in one emphatic word—

"Efter."

Which being translated from Icelandic into plain English means—"After."

The treaty concluded, our worthy guide retired without another word.

"A splendid fellow," said my uncle; "only he little suspects the marvelous part he is about to play in the history of the world."

"You mean, then," I cried in amazement, "that he should accompany us?"

"To the interior of the earth, yes," replied my uncle. "Why not?"

There were yet forty-eight hours to elapse before we made our final start. To my great regret, our whole time was taken up in making preparations for our journey. All our industry and ability were devoted to packing every object in the most advantageous manner—the instruments on one side, the arms on the other, the tools here and the provisions there. There were, in fact, four distinct groups.

The instruments were of course of the best manufacture:

1. A centigrade thermometer of Eigel, counting up to 150 degrees, which to me did not appear half enough—or too much. Too hot by half, if the degree of heat was to ascend so high—in

which case we should certainly be cooked—not enough, if we wanted to ascertain the exact temperature of springs or metal in a state of fusion.

2. A manometer worked by compressed air, an instrument used to ascertain the upper atmospheric pressure on the level of the ocean. Perhaps a common barometer would not have done as well, the atmospheric pressure being likely to increase in proportion as we descended below the surface of the earth.

3. A first-class chronometer made by Boissonnas, of Geneva, set at the meridian of Hamburg, from which Germans calculate, as the English do from Greenwich, and the French from Paris.

4. Two compasses, one for horizontal guidance, the other to ascertain the dip.

5. A night glass.

6. Two Ruhmkorff coils, which, by means of a current of electricity, would ensure us a very excellent, easily carried, and certain means of obtaining light.

7. A voltaic battery on the newest principle.

Our arms consisted of two rifles, with two revolving six-shooters. Why these arms were provided it was impossible for me to say. I had every reason to believe that we had neither wild beasts nor savage natives to fear. My uncle, on the other hand, was quite as devoted to his arsenal as to his collection of instruments, and above all was very careful with his provision of fulminating or gun cotton, warranted to keep in any climate, and of which the expansive force was known to be greater than that of ordinary gunpowder.

Our tools consisted of two pickaxes, two crowbars, a silken ladder, three iron-shod Alpine poles, a hatchet, a hammer, a dozen wedges, some pointed pieces of iron, and a quantity of strong rope. You may conceive that the whole made a tolerable parcel, especially when I mention that the ladder itself was three hundred feet long!

Then there came the important question of provisions. The hamper was not very large but tolerably satisfactory, for I knew that in concentrated essence of meat and biscuit there was enough to last six months. The only liquid provided by my uncle was Schiedam. Of water, not a drop. We had, however, an ample supply of gourds, and my uncle counted on finding water, and enough to fill them, as soon as we commenced our downward journey. My remarks as to the temperature, the quality, and even as to the possibility of none being found, remained wholly without effectTo make up the exact list of our traveling gear—for the guidance of future travelers—add, that we carried a medicine and surgical chest with all apparatus necessary for wounds, fractures and blows; lint, scissors, lancets—in fact, a perfect collection of horrible looking instruments; a number of vials containing ammonia, alcohol, ether, Goulard water, aromatic vinegar, in fact, every possible and impossible drug—finally, all the materials for working the Ruhmkorff coil!

My uncle had also been careful to lay in a goodly supply of tobacco, several flasks of very fine gunpowder, boxes of tinder, besides a large belt crammed full of notes and gold. Good boots rendered watertight were to be found to the number of six in the tool box.

"My boy, with such clothing, with such boots, and such general equipment," said my uncle, in a state of rapturous delight, "we may hope to travel far."

It took a whole day to put all these matters in order. In the evening we dined with Baron Trampe, in company with the Mayor of Reykjavik, and Doctor Hyaltalin, the great medical man of Iceland. M. Fridriksson was not present, and I was afterwards sorry to hear that he and the governor did not agree on some matters connected with the administration of the island. Unfortunately, the consequence was, that I did not understand a word that was said at dinner—a kind of semiofficial reception. One thing I can say, my uncle never left off speaking.

The next day our labor came to an end. Our worthy host delighted my uncle, Professor Hardwigg, by giving him a good map of Iceland, a most important and precious document for a mineralogist.

Our last evening was spent in a long conversation with M. Fridriksson, whom I liked very much—the more that I never expected to see him or anyone else again. After this agreeable way of spending an hour or so, I tried to sleep. In vain; with the exception of a few dozes, my night was miserable.

At five o'clock in the morning I was awakened from the only real half hour's sleep of the night by the loud neighing of horses under my window. I hastily dressed myself and went down into the street. Hans was engaged in putting the finishing stroke to our baggage, which he did in a silent, quiet way that won my admiration, and yet he did it admirably well. My uncle wasted a great deal of breath in giving him directions, but worthy Hans took not the slightest notice of his words.

At six o'clock all our preparations were completed, and M. Fridriksson shook hands heartily with us. My uncle thanked him warmly, in the Icelandic language, for his kind hospitality, speaking truly from the heart.

As for myself I put together a few of my best Latin phrases and paid him the highest compliments I could. This fraternal and friendly duty performed, we sallied forth and mounted our horses.

As soon as we were quite ready, M. Fridriksson advanced, and by way of farewell, called after me in the words of Virgil—

words which appeared to have been made for us, travelers starting for an uncertain destination:

"Et quacunque viam dederit fortuna sequamur."

("And whichsoever way thou goest, may fortune follow!")

Chapter 9

OUR START— WE MEET WITH ADVENTURES BY THE WAY

The weather was overcast but settled, when we commenced our adventurous and perilous journey. We had neither to fear fatiguing heat nor drenching rain. It was, in fact, real tourist weather.

As there was nothing I liked better than horse exercise, the pleasure of riding through an unknown country caused the early part of our enterprise to be particularly agreeable to me.

I began to enjoy the exhilarating delight of traveling, a life of desire, gratification and liberty. The truth is, that my spirits rose so rapidly, that I began to be indifferent to what had once appeared to be a terrible journey.

"After all," I said to myself, "what do I risk? Simply to take a journey through a curious country, to climb a remarkable mountain, and if the worst comes to the worst, to descend into the crater of an extinct volcano."

There could be no doubt that this was all this terrible Saknussemm had done. As to the existence of a gallery, or of subterraneous passages leading into the interior of the earth, the idea was simply absurd, the hallucination of a distempered imagination. All, then, that may be required of me I will do cheerfully, and will create no difficulty.

It was just before we left Reykjavik that I came to this decision.

Hans, our extraordinary guide, went first, walking with a steady, rapid, unvarying step. Our two horses with the luggage followed of their own accord, without requiring whip or spur. My uncle and I came behind, cutting a very tolerable figure upon our small but vigorous animals.

Iceland is one of the largest islands in Europe. It contains thirty thousand square miles of surface, and has about seventy thousand inhabitants. Geographers have divided it into four parts, and we had to cross the southwest quarter which in the vernacular is called Sudvestr Fjordungr.

Hans, on taking his departure from Reykjavik, had followed the line of the sea. We took our way through poor and sparse meadows, which made a desperate effort every year to show a little green. They very rarely succeed in a good show of yellow.

The rugged summits of the rocky hills were dimly visible on the edge of the horizon, through the misty fogs; every now and then some heavy flakes of snow showed conspicuous in the morning light, while certain lofty and pointed rocks were first lost in the grey low clouds, their summits clearly visible above, like jagged reefs rising from a troublous sea.

Every now and then a spur of rock came down through the arid ground, leaving us scarcely room to pass. Our horses, however, appeared not only well acquainted with the country, but by a kind of instinct, knew which was the best road. My uncle had not even the satisfaction of urging forward his steed by whip, spur, or voice. It was utterly useless to show any signs of impatience. I could not help smiling to see him look so big on his little horse; his long legs now and then touching the ground made him look like a six-footed centaur.

"Good beast, good beast," he would cry. "I assure you, that I begin to think no animal is more intelligent than an Icelandic horse. Snow, tempest, impracticable roads, rocks, icebergs—nothing stops him. He is brave; he is sober; he is safe; he never makes a false step; never glides or slips from his path. I dare to say that if any river, any fjord has to be crossed—and I have no doubt there will be many—you will see him enter the water without hesitation like an amphibious animal, and reach the opposite side in safety. We must not, however, attempt to hurry him; we must allow him to have his own way, and I will undertake to say that between us we shall do our ten leagues a day."

"We may do so," was my reply, "but what about our worthy guide?"

"I have not the slightest anxiety about him: that sort of people go ahead without knowing even what they are about. Look at Hans. He moves so little that it is impossible for him to become fatigued. Besides, if he were to complain of weariness, he could have the loan of my horse. I should have a violent attack of the cramp if I were not to have some sort of exercise. My arms are right—but my legs are getting a little stiff."

All this while we were advancing at a rapid pace. The country we had reached was already nearly a desert. Here and there could be seen an isolated farm, some solitary bur, or Icelandic house, built of wood, earth, fragments of lava—looking like beggars on the highway of life. These wretched and miserable huts excited in us such pity that we felt half disposed to leave alms at every door. In this country there are no roads, paths are nearly unknown, and vegetation, poor as it was, slowly as it reached perfection, soon obliterated all traces of the few travelers who passed from place to place.

Nevertheless, this division of the province, situated only a few miles from the capital, is considered one of the best cultivated and most thickly peopled in all Iceland. What, then, must be the state of the less known and more distant parts of the island? After traveling fully half a Danish mile, we had met neither a farmer at the door of his hut, nor even a wandering shepherd with his wild and savage flock.

A few stray cows and sheep were only seen occasionally. What, then, must we expect when we come to the upheaved regions—to the districts broken and roughened from volcanic eruptions and subterraneous commotions?

We were to learn this all in good time. I saw, however, on consulting the map, that we avoided a good deal of this rough country, by following the winding and desolate shores of the sea. In reality, the great volcanic movement of the island, and all its attendant phenomena, are concentrated in the interior of the island; there, horizontal layers or strata of rocks, piled one upon the other, eruptions of basaltic origin, and streams of lava, have given this country a kind of supernatural reputation.

Little did I expect, however, the spectacle which awaited us when we reached the peninsula of Sneffels, where agglomerations of nature's ruins form a kind of terrible chaos.

Some two hours or more after we had left the city of Reykjavik, we reached the little town called Aoalkirkja, or the principal church. It consists simply of a few houses—not what in England or Germany we should call a hamlet.

Hans stopped here one half hour. He shared our frugal breakfast, answered Yes, and No to my uncle's questions as to the nature of the road, and at last when asked where we were to pass the night was as laconic as usual.

"Gardar!" was his one-worded reply.

I took occasion to consult the map, to see where Gardar was to be found. After looking keenly I found a small town of that name on the borders of the Hvalfjord, about four miles from Reykjavik. I pointed this out to my uncle, who made a very energetic grimace.

"Only four miles out of twenty-two? Why it is only a little walk."

He was about to make some energetic observation to the guide, but Hans, without taking the slightest notice of him, went in front of the horses, and walked ahead with the same imperturbable phlegm he had always exhibited.

Three hours later, still traveling over those apparently interminable and sandy prairies, we were compelled to go round the Kollafjord, an easier and shorter cut than crossing the gulfs. Shortly after we entered a place of communal jurisdiction called Ejulberg, and the clock of which would then have struck twelve, if any Icelandic church had been rich enough to possess so valuable and useful an article. These sacred edifices are, however, very much like these people, who do without watches—and never miss them.

Here the horses were allowed to take some rest and refreshment, then following a narrow strip of shore between high rocks and the sea, they took us without further halt to the Aoalkirkja of Brantar, and after another mile to Saurboer Annexia, a chapel of ease, situated on the southern bank of the Hvalfjord.

It was four o'clock in the evening and we had traveled four Danish miles, about equal to twenty English.

The fjord was in this place about half a mile in width. The sweeping and broken waves came rolling in upon the pointed rocks; the gulf was surrounded by rocky walls—a mighty cliff, three thousand feet in height, remarkable for its brown strata, separated here and there by beds of tufa of a reddish hue. Now, whatever may have been the intelligence of our horses, I had not the slightest reliance upon them, as a means of crossing a stormy arm of the sea. To ride over salt water upon the back of a little horse seemed to me absurd.

"If they are really intelligent," I said to myself, "they will certainly not make the attempt. In any case, I shall trust rather to my own intelligence than theirs."

But my uncle was in no humor to wait. He dug his heels into the sides of his steed, and made for the shore. His horse went to the very edge of the water, sniffed at the approaching wave and retreated.

My uncle, who was, sooth to say, quite as obstinate as the beast he bestrode, insisted on his making the desired advance. This attempt was followed by a new refusal on the part of the horse which quietly shook his head. This demonstration of rebellion was followed by a volley of words and a stout application of whipcord; also followed by kicks on the part of the horse, which threw its head and heels upwards and tried to throw his rider. At length the sturdy little pony, spreading out his legs, in a stiff and ludicrous attitude, got from under the Professor's legs, and left him standing, with both feet on a separate stone, like the Colossus of Rhodes.

"Wretched animal!" cried my uncle, suddenly transformed into a foot passenger—and as angry and ashamed as a dismounted cavalry officer on the field of battle.

"Farja," said the guide, tapping him familiarly on the shoulder.

"What, a ferry boat!"

"Der," answered Hans, pointing to where lay the boat in question—"there."

"Well," I cried, quite delighted with the information; "so it is."

"Why did you not say so before," cried my uncle; "why not start at once?"

"Tidvatten," said the guide.

"What does he say?" I asked, considerably puzzled by the delay and the dialogue.

"He says tide," replied my uncle, translating the Danish word for my information.

"Of course I understand—we must wait till the tide serves."

"For bida?" asked my uncle.

"Ja," replied Hans.

My uncle frowned, stamped his feet and then followed the horses to where the boat lay.

I thoroughly understood and appreciated the necessity for waiting, before crossing the fjord, for that moment when the sea at its highest point is in a state of slack water. As neither the ebb nor flow can then be felt, the ferry boat was in no danger of being carried out to sea, or dashed upon the rocky coast.

The favorable moment did not come until six o'clock in the evening. Then my uncle, myself, and guide, two boatmen and the four horses got into a very awkward flat-bottom boat. Accustomed as I had been to the steam ferry boats of the Elbe, I found the long oars of the boatmen but sorry means of locomotion. We were more than an hour in crossing the fjord; but at length the passage was concluded without accident.

Half an hour later we reached Gardar.

Chapter 10

TRAVELING IN ICELAND

It ought, one would have thought, to have been night, even in the sixty-fifth parallel of latitude; but still the nocturnal illumination did not surprise me. For in Iceland, during the months of June and July, the sun never sets.

The temperature, however, was very much lower than I expected. I was cold, but even that did not affect me so much as ravenous hunger. Welcome indeed, therefore, was the hut which hospitably opened its doors to us.

It was merely the house of a peasant, but in the matter of hospitality, it was worthy of being the palace of a king. As we alighted at the door the master of the house came forward, held out his hand, and without any further ceremony, signaled to us to follow him.

We followed him, for to accompany him was impossible. A long, narrow, gloomy passage led into the interior of this habitation, made from beams roughly squared by the ax. This passage gave ingress to every room. The chambers were four in number—the kitchen, the workshop, where the weaving was carried on, the general sleeping chamber of the family, and the best room, to which strangers were especially invited. My uncle, whose lofty stature had not been taken into consideration when the house was built, contrived to knock his head against the beams of the roof.

We were introduced into our chamber, a kind of large room

with a hard earthen floor, and lighted by a window, the panes of which were made of a sort of parchment from the intestines of sheep—very far from transparent.

The bedding was composed of dry hay thrown into two long red wooden boxes, ornamented with sentences painted in Icelandic. I really had no idea that we should be made so comfortable. There was one objection to the house, and that was, the very powerful odor of dried fish, of macerated meat, and of sour milk, which three fragrances combined did not at all suit my olfactory nerves.

As soon as we had freed ourselves from our heavy traveling costume, the voice of our host was heard calling to us to come into the kitchen, the only room in which the Icelanders ever make any fire, no matter how cold it may be.

My uncle, nothing loath, hastened to obey this hospitable and friendly invitation. I followed.

The kitchen chimney was made on an antique model. A large stone standing in the middle of the room was the fireplace; above, in the roof, was a hole for the smoke to pass through. This apartment was kitchen, parlor and dining room all in one.

On our entrance, our worthy host, as if he had not seen us before, advanced ceremoniously, uttered a word which means "be happy," and then kissed both of us on the cheek.

His wife followed, pronounced the same word, with the same ceremonial, then the husband and wife, placing their right hands upon their hearts, bowed profoundly.

This excellent Icelandic woman was the mother of nineteen children, who, little and big, rolled, crawled, and walked about in the midst of volumes of smoke arising from the angular fireplace in the middle of the room. Every now and then I could see a fresh white head, and a slightly melancholy expression of countenance, peering at me through the vapor.

Both my uncle and myself, however, were very friendly with the whole party, and before we were aware of it, there were three or four of these little ones on our shoulders, as many on our boxes, and the rest hanging about our legs. Those who could speak kept crying out saellvertu in every possible and impossible key. Those who did not speak only made all the more noise.

This concert was interrupted by the announcement of supper. At this moment our worthy guide, the eider-duck hunter, came in after seeing to the feeding and stabling of the horses—which consisted in letting them loose to browse on the stunted green of the Icelandic prairies. There was little for them to eat, but moss and some very dry and innutritious grass; next day they were ready before the door, some time before we were.

"Welcome," said Hans.

Then tranquilly, with the air of an automaton, without any more expression in one kiss than another, he embraced the host and hostess and their nineteen children.

This ceremony concluded to the satisfaction of all parties, we all sat down to table, that is twenty-four of us, somewhat crowded. Those who were best off had only two juveniles on their knees.

As soon, however, as the inevitable soup was placed on the table, the natural taciturnity, common even to Icelandic babies, prevailed over all else. Our host filled our plates with a portion of lichen soup of Iceland moss, of by no means disagreeable flavor, an enormous lump of fish floating in sour butter. After that there came some skyr, a kind of curds and whey, served with biscuits and juniper-berry juice. To drink, we had blanda, skimmed milk with water. I was hungry, so hungry, that by way of dessert I finished up with a basin of thick oaten porridge.

As soon as the meal was over, the children disappeared, whilst the grown people sat around the fireplace, on which was placed turf, heather, cow dung and dried fish-bones. As soon as everybody was sufficiently warm, a general dispersion took place, all retiring to their respective couches. Our hostess offered to pull off our stockings and trousers, according to the custom of the country, but as we graciously declined to be so honored, she left us to our bed of dry fodder.

Next day, at five in the morning, we took our leave of these hospitable peasants. My uncle had great difficulty in making them accept a sufficient and proper remuneration.

Hans then gave the signal to start.

We had scarcely got a hundred yards from Gardar, when the character of the country changed. The soil began to be marshy and boggy, and less favorable to progress. To the right, the range of mountains was prolonged indefinitely like a great system of natural fortifications, of which we skirted the glacis. We met with numerous streams and rivulets which it was necessary to ford, and that without wetting our baggage. As we advanced, the deserted appearance increased, and yet now and then we could see human shadows flitting in the distance. When a sudden turn of the track brought us within easy reach of one of these specters, I felt a sudden impulse of disgust at the sight of a swollen head, with shining skin, utterly without hair, and whose repulsive and revolting wounds could be seen through his rags. The unhappy wretches never came forward to beg; on the contrary, they ran away; not so quick, however, but that Hans was able to salute them with the universal saellvertu.

"Spetelsk," said he"A leper," explained my uncle.

The very sound of such a word caused a feeling of repulsion. The horrible affliction known as leprosy, which has almost vanished before the effects of modern science, is common in Iceland. It is not contagious but hereditary, so that marriage is strictly prohibited to these unfortunate creatures.

These poor lepers did not tend to enliven our journey, the scene of which was inexpressibly sad and lonely. The very last tufts of grassy vegetation appeared to die at our feet. Not a tree was to be seen, except a few stunted willows about as big as blackberry bushes. Now and then we watched a falcon soaring in the grey and misty air, taking his flight towards warmer and sunnier regions. I could not help feeling a sense of melancholy come over me. I sighed for my own Native Land, and wished to be back with Gretchen.

We were compelled to cross several little fjords, and at last came to a real gulf. The tide was at its height, and we were able to go over at once, and reach the hamlet of Alftanes, about a mile farther.

That evening, after fording the Alfa and the Heta, two rivers rich in trout and pike, we were compelled to pass the night in a deserted house, worthy of being haunted by all the fays of Scandinavian mythology. The King of Cold had taken up his residence there, and made us feel his presence all night.

The following day was remarkable by its lack of any particular incidents. Always the same damp and swampy soil; the same dreary uniformity; the same sad and monotonous aspect of scenery. In the evening, having accomplished the half of our projected journey, we slept at the Annexia of Krosolbt.

For a whole mile we had under our feet nothing but lava. This disposition of the soil is called *hraun*: the crumbled lava on the surface was in some instances like ship cables stretched out horizontally, in others coiled up in heaps; an immense field of lava came from the neighboring mountains, all extinct volcanoes, but whose remains showed what once they had been. Here and there could be made out the steam from hot water springs.

There was no time, however, for us to take more than a cursory view of these phenomena. We had to go forward with what speed we might. Soon the soft and swampy soil again appeared under the feet of our horses, while at every hundred yards we came upon one or more small lakes. Our journey was now in a westerly direction; we had, in fact, swept round the great bay of Faxa, and the twin white summits of Sneffels rose to the clouds at a distance of less than five miles.

The horses now advanced rapidly. The accidents and difficulties of the soil no longer checked them. I confess that fatigue began to tell severely upon me; but my uncle was as firm and as hard as he had been on the first day. I could not help admiring both the excellent Professor and the worthy guide; for they appeared to regard this rugged expedition as a mere walk!

On Saturday, the 20th June, at six o'clock in the evening, we reached Budir, a small town picturesquely situated on the shore of the ocean; and here the guide asked for his money. My uncle settled with him immediately. It was now the family of Hans himself, that is to say, his uncles, his cousins—german, who offered us hospitality. We were exceedingly well received, and without taking too much advantage of the goodness of these worthy people, I should have liked very much to have rested with them after the fatigues of the journey. But my uncle, who did not require rest, had no idea of anything of the kind; and despite the fact that next day was Sunday, I was compelled once more to mount my steed.

The soil was again affected by the neighborhood of the mountains, whose granite peered out of the ground like tops of an old oak. We were skirting the enormous base of the mighty volcano. My uncle never took his eyes from off it; he could not keep from gesticulating, and looking at it with a kind of sullen defiance as much as to say "That is the giant I have made up my mind to conquer."

After four hours of steady traveling, the horses stopped of themselves before the door of the presbytery of Stapi.

Chapter 11

WE REACH MOUNT SNEFFELS—THE "REYKIR"

Stapi is a town consisting of thirty huts, built on a large plain of lava, exposed to the rays of the sun, reflected from the volcano. It stretches its humble tenements along the end of a little fjord, surrounded by a basaltic wall of the most singular character.

Basalt is a brown rock of igneous origin. It assumes regular forms, which astonish by their singular appearance. Here we found Nature proceeding geometrically, and working quite after a human fashion, as if she had employed the plummet line, the compass and the rule. If elsewhere she produces grand artistic effects by piling up huge masses without order or connection—if elsewhere we see truncated cones, imperfect pyramids, with an odd succession of lines; here, as if wishing to give a lesson in regularity, and preceding the architects of the early ages, she has erected a severe order of architecture, which neither the splendors of Babylon nor the marvels of Greece ever surpassed.

I had often heard of the Giant's Causeway in Ireland, and of Fingal's Cave in one of the Hebrides, but the grand spectacle of a real basaltic formation had never yet come before my eyes.

This at Stapi gave us an idea of one in all its wonderful beauty and grace.

The wall of the fjord, like nearly the whole of the peninsula, consisted of a series of vertical columns, in height about thirty feet. These upright pillars of stone, of the finest proportions, supported an archivault of horizontal columns which formed a kind of half-vaulted roof above the sea. At certain intervals, and below this natural basin, the eye was pleased and surprised by the sight of oval openings through which the outward waves came thundering in volleys of foam. Some banks of basalt, torn from their fastenings by the fury of the waves, lay scattered on the ground like the ruins of an ancient temple—ruins eternally young, over which the storms of ages swept without producing any perceptible effect!

This was the last stage of our journey. Hans had brought us along with fidelity and intelligence, and I began to feel somewhat more comfortable when I reflected that he was to accompany us still farther on our way.

When we halted before the house of the Rector, a small and incommodious cabin, neither handsome nor more comfortable than those of his neighbors, I saw a man in the act of shoeing a horse, a hammer in his hand, and a leathern apron tied round his waist.

"Be happy," said the eider-down hunter, using his national salutation in his own language.

"God dag—good day!" replied the former, in excellent Danish.

"Kyrkoherde," cried Hans, turning round and introducing him to my uncle.

"The Rector," repeated the worthy Professor; "it appears, my dear Harry, that this worthy man is the Rector, and is not above doing his own work."

During the speaking of these words the guide intimated to

the Kyrkoherde what was the true state of the case. The good man, ceasing from his occupation, gave a kind of halloo, upon which a tall woman, almost a giantess, came out of the hut. She was at least six feet high, which in that region is something considerable.

My first impression was one of horror. I thought she had come to give us the Icelandic kiss. I had, however, nothing to fear, for she did not even show much inclination to receive us into her house.

The room devoted to strangers appeared to me to be by far the worst in the presbytery; it was narrow, dirty and offensive. There was, however, no choice about the matter. The Rector had no notion of practicing the usual cordial and antique hospitality. Far from it. Before the day was over, I found we had to deal with a blacksmith, a fisherman, a hunter, a carpenter, anything but a clergyman. It must be said in his favor that we had caught him on a weekday; probably he appeared to greater advantage on the Sunday.

These poor priests receive from the Danish Government a most ridiculously inadequate salary, and collect one quarter of the tithe of their parish—not more than sixty marks current, or about L3 10s. sterling. Hence the necessity of working to live. In truth, we soon found that our host did not count civility among the cardinal virtues.

My uncle soon became aware of the kind of man he had to deal with. Instead of a worthy and learned scholar, he found a dull ill-mannered peasant. He therefore resolved to start on his great expedition as soon as possible. He did not care about fatigue, and resolved to spend a few days in the mountains.

The preparations for our departure were made the very next day after our arrival at Stapi; Hans now hired three Icelanders to take the place of the horses—which could no longer carry our luggage. When, however, these worthy islanders had reached the bottom of the crater, they were to go back and leave us to ourselves. This point was settled before they would agree to start.

On this occasion, my uncle partly confided in Hans, the eider-duck hunter, and gave him to understand that it was his intention to continue his exploration of the volcano to the last possible limits.

Hans listened calmly, and then nodded his head. To go there, or elsewhere, to bury himself in the bowels of the earth, or to travel over its summits, was all the same to him! As for me, amused and occupied by the incidents of travel, I had begun to forget the inevitable future; but now I was once more destined to realize the actual state of affairs. What was to be done? Run away? But if I really had intended to leave Professor Hardwigg to his fate, it should have been at Hamburg and not at the foot of Sneffels.

One idea, above all others, began to trouble me: a very terrible idea, and one calculated to shake the nerves of a man even less sensitive than myself.

"Let us consider the matter," I said to myself; "we are going to ascend the Sneffels mountain. Well and good. We are about to pay a visit to the very bottom of the crater. Good, still. Others have done it and did not perish from that course.

"That, however, is not the whole matter to be considered. If a road does really present itself by which to descend into the dark and subterraneous bowels of Mother Earth, if this thrice unhappy Saknussemm has really told the truth, we shall be most certainly lost in the midst of the labyrinth of subterraneous galleries of the volcano. Now, we have no evidence to prove that Sneffels is really extinct. What proof have we that an eruption is not shortly about to take place? Because the monster has slept soundly since 1219, does it follow that he is never to wake?

"If he does wake what is to become of us?"

These were questions worth thinking about, and upon them I reflected long and deeply. I could not lie down in search of sleep without dreaming of eruptions. The more I thought, the more I objected to be reduced to the state of dross and ashes.

I could stand it no longer; so I determined at last to submit the whole case to my uncle, in the most adroit manner possible, and under the form of some totally irreconcilable hypothesis.

I sought him. I laid before him my fears, and then drew back in order to let him get his passion over at his ease.

"I have been thinking about the matter," he said, in the quietest tone in the world.

What did he mean? Was he at last about to listen to the voice of reason? Did he think of suspending his projects? It was almost too much happiness to be true.

I however made no remark. In fact, I was only too anxious not to interrupt him, and allowed him to reflect at his leisure. After some moments he spoke out.

"I have been thinking about the matter," he resumed. "Ever since we have been at Stapi, my mind has been almost solely occupied with the grave question which has been submitted to me by yourself—for nothing would be unwiser and more inconsistent than to act with imprudence."

"I heartily agree with you, my dear uncle," was my somewhat hopeful rejoinder.

"It is now six hundred years since Sneffels has spoken, but though now reduced to a state of utter silence, he may speak again. New volcanic eruptions are always preceded by perfectly well-known phenomena. I have closely examined the inhabitants of this region; I have carefully studied the soil, and I beg to tell you emphatically, my dear Harry, there will be no eruption at present."

As I listened to his positive affirmations, I was stupefied and could say nothing.

"I see you doubt my word," said my uncle; "follow me."

I obeyed mechanically.

Leaving the presbytery, the Professor took a road through an opening in the basaltic rock, which led far away from the sea. We were soon in open country, if we could give such a name to a place all covered with volcanic deposits. The whole land seemed crushed under the weight of enormous stones—of trap, of basalt, of granite, of lava, and of all other volcanic substances.

I could see many spouts of steam rising in the air. These white vapors, called in the Icelandic language "reykir," come from hot water fountains, and indicate by their violence the volcanic activity of the soil. Now the sight of these appeared to justify my apprehension. I was, therefore, all the more surprised and mortified when my uncle thus addressed me.

"You see all this smoke, Harry, my boy?"

"Yes, sir."

"Well, as long as you see them thus, you have nothing to fear from the volcano."

"How can that be?"

"Be careful to remember this," continued the Professor. "At the approach of an eruption these spouts of vapor redouble their activity—to disappear altogether during the period of volcanic eruption; for the elastic fluids, no longer having the necessary tension, seek refuge in the interior of the crater, instead of escaping through the fissures of the earth. If, then, the steam remains in its normal or habitual state, if their energy does not increase, and if you add to this, the remark that the wind is not replaced by heavy atmospheric pressure and dead calm, you may be quite sure that there is no fear of any immediate eruption."

"But—"

"Enough, my boy. When science has sent forth her fiat—it is only to hear and obey."

I came back to the house quite downcast and disappointed. My uncle had completely defeated me with his scientific arguments. Nevertheless, I had still one hope, and that was, when once we were at the bottom of the crater, that it would be impossible in default of a gallery or tunnel, to descend any deeper; and this, despite all the learned Saknussemms in the world.

I passed the whole of the following night with a nightmare on my chest! and, after unheard-of miseries and tortures, found myself in the very depths of the earth, from which I was suddenly launched into planetary space, under the form of an eruptive rock!

Next day, June 23rd, Hans calmly awaited us outside the presbytery with his three companions loaded with provisions, tools, and instruments. Two iron-shod poles, two guns, and two large game bags, were reserved for my uncle and myself. Hans, who was a man who never forgot even the minutest precautions, had added to our baggage a large skin full of water, as an addition to our gourds. This assured us water for eight days.

It was nine o'clock in the morning when we were quite ready. The rector and his huge wife or servant, I never knew which, stood at the door to see us off. They appeared to be about to inflict on us the usual final kiss of the Icelanders. To our supreme astonishment their adieu took the shape of a formidable bill, in which they even counted the use of the pastoral house, really and truly the most abominable and dirty place I ever was in. The worthy couple cheated and robbed us like a Swiss innkeeper, and made us feel, by the sum we had to pay, the splendors of their hospitality.

My uncle, however, paid without bargaining. A man who had made up his mind to undertake a voyage into the Interior of the Earth, is not the man to haggle over a few miserable rix-dollars.

This important matter settled, Hans gave the signal for departure, and some few moments later we had left Stapi.

Chapter 12

THE ASCENT OF MOUNT SNEFFELS

The huge volcano which was the first stage of our daring experiment is above five thousand feet high. Sneffels is the termination of a long range of volcanic mountains, of a different character to the system of the island itself. One of its peculiarities is its two huge pointed summits. From whence we started it was impossible to make out the real outlines of the peak against the grey field of sky. All we could distinguish was a vast dome of white, which fell downwards from the head of the giant.

The commencement of the great undertaking filled me with awe. Now that we had actually started, I began to believe in the reality of the undertaking!

Our party formed quite a procession. We walked in single file, preceded by Hans, the imperturbable eider-duck hunter. He calmly led us by narrow paths where two persons could by no possibility walk abreast. Conversation was wholly impossible. We had all the more opportunity to reflect and admire the awful grandeur of the scene around.

Beyond the extraordinary basaltic wall of the fjord of Stapi we found ourselves making our way through fibrous turf, over which grew a scanty vegetation of grass, the residuum of the ancient vegetation of the swampy peninsula. The vast mass of this combustible, the field of which as yet is utterly unexplored, would suffice to warm Iceland for a whole century. This mighty turf pit, measured from the bottom of certain ravines, is often not less than seventy feet deep, and presents to the eye the view of successive layers of black burned-up rocky detritus, separated by thin streaks of porous sandstone.

The grandeur of the spectacle was undoubted, as well as its arid and deserted air.

As a true nephew of the great Professor Hardwigg, and despite my preoccupation and doleful fears of what was to come, I observed with great interest the vast collection of mineralogical curiosities spread out before me in this vast museum of natural history. Looking back to my recent studies, I went over in thought the whole geological history of Iceland.

This extraordinary and curious island must have made its appearance from out of the great world of waters at a comparatively recent date. Like the coral islands of the Pacific, it may, for aught we know, be still rising by slow and imperceptible degrees.

If this really be the case, its origin can be attributed to only one cause—that of the continued action of subterranean fires.

This was a happy thought.

If so, if this were true, away with the theories of Sir Humphry Davy; away with the authority of the parchment of Arne Saknussemm; the wonderful pretensions to discovery on the part of my uncle—and to our journey!

All must end in smoke.

Charmed with the idea, I began more carefully to look about me. A serious study of the soil was necessary to negative or confirm my hypothesis. I took in every item of what I saw, and I began to comprehend the succession of phenomena which had preceded its formation.

Iceland, being absolutely without sedimentary soil, is composed exclusively of volcanic tufa; that is to say, of an agglomeration of stones and of rocks of a porous texture. Long before the existence of volcanoes, it was composed of a solid body of massive trap rock lifted bodily and slowly out of the sea, by the action of the centrifugal force at work in the earth.

The internal fires, however, had not as yet burst their bounds and flooded the exterior cake of Mother Earth with hot and raging lava.

My readers must excuse this brief and somewhat pedantic geological lecture. But it is necessary to the complete understanding of what follows.

At a later period in the world's history, a huge and mighty fissure must, reasoning by analogy, have been dug diagonally from the southwest to the northeast of the island, through which by degrees flowed the volcanic crust. The great and wondrous phenomenon then went on without violence—the outpouring was enormous, and the seething fused matter, ejected from the bowels of the earth, spread slowly and peacefully in the form of vast level plains, or what are called mamelons or mounds.

It was at this epoch that the rocks called feldspars, syenites, and porphyries appearedBut as a natural consequence of this overflow, the depth of the island increased. It can readily be believed what an enormous quantity of elastic fluids were piled up within its centre, when at last it afforded no other openings, after the process of cooling the crust had taken place.

At length a time came when despite the enormous thickness and weight of the upper crust, the mechanical forces of the combustible gases below became so great, that they actually upheaved the weighty back and made for themselves huge and gigantic shafts. Hence the volcanoes which suddenly arose through the upper crust, and next the craters, which burst forth at the summit of these new creations.

It will be seen that the first phenomena in connection with the formation of the island were simply eruptive; to these, however, shortly succeeded the volcanic phenomena.

Through the newly formed openings, escaped the marvelous mass of basaltic stones with which the plain we were now crossing was covered. We were trampling our way over heavy rocks of dark grey color, which, while cooling, had been moulded into six-sided prisms. In the "back distance" we could see a number of flattened cones, which formerly were so many fire-vomiting mouths.

After the basaltic eruption was appeased and set at rest, the volcano, the force of which increased with that of the extinct craters, gave free passage to the fiery overflow of lava, and to the mass of cinders and pumice stone, now scattered over the sides of the mountain, like disheveled hair on the shoulders of a Bacchante.

Here, in a nutshell, I had the whole history of the phenomena from which Iceland arose. All take their rise in the fierce action of interior fires, and to believe that the central mass did not remain in a state of liquid fire, white hot, was simply and purely madness.

This being satisfactorily proved (Q.E.D.), what insensate folly to pretend to penetrate into the interior of the mighty earth!

This mental lecture delivered to myself while proceeding on a journey, did me good. I was quite reassured as to the fate of our enterprise; and therefore went, like a brave soldier mounting a bristling battery, to the assault of old Sneffels.

As we advanced, the road became every moment more difficult. The soil was broken and dangerous. The rocks broke and gave way under our feet, and we had to be scrupulously careful in order to avoid dangerous and constant falls.

Hans advanced as calmly as if he had been walking over Salisbury Plain; sometimes he would disappear behind huge blocks of stone, and we momentarily lost sight of him. There was a little period of anxiety and then there was a shrill whistle, just to tell us where to look for him.

Occasionally he would take it into his head to stop to pick up lumps of rock, and silently pile them up into small heaps, in order that we might not lose our way on our return.

He had no idea of the journey we were about to undertake.

At all events, the precaution was a good one; though how utterly useless and unnecessary—but I must not anticipate.

Three hours of terrible fatigue, walking incessantly, had only brought us to the foot of the great mountain. This will give some notion of what we had still to undergo.

Suddenly, however, Hans cried a halt—that is, he made signs to that effect—and a summary kind of breakfast was laid out on the lava before us. My uncle, who now was simply Professor Hardwigg, was so eager to advance, that he bolted his food like a greedy clown. This halt for refreshment was also a halt for repose. The Professor was therefore compelled to wait the good pleasure of his imperturbable guide, who did not give the signal for departure for a good hour.

The three Icelanders, who were as taciturn as their comrade, did not say a word; but went on eating and drinking very quietly and soberly.

From this, our first real stage, we began to ascend the slopes of the Sneffels volcano. Its magnificent snowy nightcap, as we began to call it, by an optical delusion very common in mountains, appeared to me to be close at hand; and yet how many long weary hours must elapse before we reached its summit. What unheard-of fatigue must we endure!

The stones on the mountain side, held together by no cement of soil, bound together by no roots or creeping herbs, gave way continually under our feet, and went rushing below into the plains, like a series of small avalanches.

In certain places the sides of this stupendous mountain were at an angle so steep that it was impossible to climb upwards, and we were compelled to get round these obstacles as best we might.

Those who understand Alpine climbing will comprehend our difficulties. Often we were obliged to help each other along by means of our climbing poles.

I must say this for my uncle, that he stuck as close to me as possible. He never lost sight of me, and on many occasions his arm supplied me with firm and solid support. He was strong, wiry, and apparently insensible to fatigue. Another great advantage with him was that he had the innate sentiment of equilibrium—for he never slipped or failed in his steps. The Icelanders, though heavily loaded, climbed with the agility of mountaineers.

Looking up, every now and then, at the height of the great volcano of Sneffels, it appeared to me wholly impossible to reach to the summit on that side; at all events, if the angle of inclination did not speedily change.

Fortunately, after an hour of unheard-of fatigues, and of gymnastic exercises that would have been trying to an acrobat, we came to a vast field of ice, which wholly surrounded the bottom of the cone of the volcano. The natives called it the tablecloth, probably from some such reason as the dwellers in the Cape of Good Hope call their mountain Table Mountain, and their roads Table Bay.

Here, to our mutual surprise, we found an actual flight of stone steps, which wonderfully assisted our ascent. This singular flight of stairs was, like everything else, volcanic.

It had been formed by one of those torrents of stones cast up by the eruptions, and of which the Icelandic name is stina. If this singular torrent had not been checked in its descent by the peculiar shape of the flanks of the mountain, it would have swept into the sea, and would have formed new islands.

Such as it was, it served us admirably. The abrupt character of the slopes momentarily increased, but these remarkable stone steps, a little less difficult than those of the Egyptian pyramids, were the one simple natural means by which we were enabled to proceed.

About seven in the evening of that day, after having clambered up two thousand of these rough steps, we found ourselves overlooking a kind of spur or projection of the mountain—a sort of buttress upon which the conelike crater, properly so called, leaned for support.

The ocean lay beneath us at a depth of more than three thousand two hundred feet—a grand and mighty spectacle. We had reached the region of eternal snows.

The cold was keen, searching and intense. The wind blew with extraordinary violence. I was utterly exhausted.

My worthy uncle, the Professor, saw clearly that my legs refused further service, and that, in fact, I was utterly exhausted. Despite his hot and feverish impatience, he decided, with a sigh, upon a halt. He called the eider-duck hunter to his side. That worthy, however, shook his head.

"Ofvanfor," was his sole spoken reply.

"It appears," says my uncle with a woebegone look, "that we must go higher."

He then turned to Hans, and asked him to give some reason for this decisive response.

"Mistour," replied the guide.

"Ja, mistour—yes, the mistour," cried one of the Icelandic guides in a terrified tone.

It was the first time he had spoken.

"What does this mysterious word signify?" I anxiously inquired.

"Look," said my uncle.

I looked down upon the plain below, and I saw a vast, a prodigious volume of pulverized pumice stone, of sand, of dust, rising to the heavens in the form of a mighty waterspout. It resembled the fearful phenomenon of a similar character known to the travelers in the desert of the great Sahara.

The wind was driving it directly towards that side of Sneffels on which we were perched. This opaque veil standing up between us and the sun projected a deep shadow on the flanks of the mountain. If this sand spout broke over us, we must all be infallibly destroyed, crushed in its fearful embraces. This extraordinary phenomenon, very common when the wind shakes the glaciers, and sweeps over the arid plains, is in the Icelandic tongue called "mistour."

"Hastigt, hastigt!" cried our guide.

Now I certainly knew nothing of Danish, but I thoroughly understood that his gestures were meant to quicken us.

The guide turned rapidly in a direction which would take us to the back of the crater, all the while ascending slightly.

We followed rapidly, despite our excessive fatigue.

A quarter of an hour later Hans paused to enable us to look back. The mighty whirlwind of sand was spreading up the slope of the mountain to the very spot where we had proposed to halt. Huge stones were caught up, cast into the air, and thrown about as during an eruption. We were happily a little out of the direction of the wind, and therefore out of reach of danger. But for the precaution and knowledge of our guide, our dislocated bodies, our crushed and broken limbs, would have been cast to the wind, like dust from some unknown meteor.

Hans, however, did not think it prudent to pass the night on the bare side of the cone. We therefore continued our journey in a zigzag direction. The fifteen hundred feet which remained to be accomplished took us at least five hours. The turnings and windings, the no-thoroughfares, the marches and marches, turned that insignificant distance into at least three leagues. I never felt such misery, fatigue and exhaustion in my life. I was ready to faint from hunger and cold. The rarefied air at the same time painfully acted upon my lungs.

At last, when I thought myself at my last gasp, about eleven at night, it being in that region quite dark, we reached the summit of Mount Sneffels! It was in an awful mood of mind, that despite my fatigue, before I descended into the crater which was to shelter us for the night, I paused to behold the sun rise at midnight on the very day of its lowest declension, and enjoyed the spectacle of its ghastly pale rays cast upon the isle which lay sleeping at our feet!

I no longer wondered at people traveling all the way from England to Norway to behold this magical and wondrous spectacle.

Chapter 13

THE SHADOW OF SCARTARIS

Our supper was eaten with ease and rapidity, after which everybody did the best he could for himself within the hollow of the crater. The bed was hard, the shelter unsatisfactory, the situation painful—lying in the open air, five thousand feet above the level of the sea!

Nevertheless, it has seldom happened to me to sleep so well as I did on that particular night. I did not even dream. So much for the effects of what my uncle called "wholesome fatigue."

Next day, when we awoke under the rays of a bright and glorious sun, we were nearly frozen by the keen air. I left my granite couch and made one of the party to enjoy a view of the magnificent spectacle which developed itself, panorama-like, at our feet.

I stood upon the lofty summit of Mount Sneffels' southern peak. Thence I was able to obtain a view of the greater part of the island. The optical delusion, common to all lofty heights, raised the shores of the island, while the central portions appeared depressed. It was by no means too great a flight of fancy to believe that a giant picture was stretched out before me. I could see the deep valleys that crossed each other in every direction. I could see precipices looking like sides of wells, lakes that seemed to be changed into ponds, ponds that looked like puddles, and rivers that were transformed into petty brooks. To my right were glaciers upon glaciers, and multiplied peaks, topped with light clouds of smoke.

The undulation of these infinite numbers of mountains, whose snowy summits make them look as if covered by foam, recalled to my remembrance the surface of a storm-beaten ocean. If I looked towards the west, the ocean lay before me in all its majestic grandeur, a continuation as it were, of these fleecy hilltops.

Where the earth ended and the sea began it was impossible for the eye to distinguish.

I soon felt that strange and mysterious sensation which is awakened in the mind when looking down from lofty hilltops, and now I was able to do so without any feeling of nervousness, having fortunately hardened myself to that kind of sublime contemplation.

I wholly forgot who I was, and where I was. I became intoxicated with a sense of lofty sublimity, without thought of the abysses into which my daring was soon about to plunge me. I was presently, however, brought back to the realities of life by the arrival of the Professor and Hans, who joined me upon the lofty summit of the peak.

My uncle, turning in a westerly direction, pointed out to me a light cloud of vapor, a kind of haze, with a faint outline of land rising out of the waters.

"Greenland!" said he.

"Greenland?" cried I in reply.

"Yes," continued my uncle, who always when explaining anything spoke as if he were in a professor's chair; "we are not more than thirty-five leagues distant from that wonderful land. When the great annual breakup of the ice takes place, white bears come over to Iceland, carried by the floating masses of ice from the north. This, however, is a matter of little consequence.

We are now on the summit of the great, the transcendent Sneffels, and here are its two peaks, north and south. Hans will tell you the name by which the people of Iceland call that on which we stand."

My uncle turned to the imperturbable guide, who nodded, and spoke as usual—one word.

"Scartaris."

My uncle looked at me with a proud and triumphant glance.

"A crater," he said, "you hear?"

I did hear, but I was totally unable to make reply.

The crater of Mount Sneffels represented an inverted cone, the gaping orifice apparently half a mile across; the depth indefinite feet. Conceive what this hole must have been like when full of flame and thunder and lightning. The bottom of the funnel-shaped hollow was about five hundred feet in circumference, by which it will be seen that the slope from the summit to the bottom was very gradual, and we were therefore clearly able to get there without much fatigue or difficulty. Involuntarily, I compared this crater to an enormous loaded cannon; and the comparison completely terrified me.

"To descend into the interior of a cannon," I thought to myself, "when perhaps it is loaded, and will go off at the least shock, is the act of a madman."

But there was no longer any opportunity for me to hesitate. Hans, with a perfectly calm and indifferent air, took his usual post at the head of the adventurous little band. I followed without uttering a syllable.

I felt like the lamb led to the slaughter.

In order to render the descent less difficult, Hans took his way down the interior of the cone in rather a zigzag fashion, making, as the sailors say, long tracks to the eastward, followed by equally long ones to the west. It was necessary to walk through the midst of eruptive rocks, some of which, shaken in their balance, went rolling down with thundering clamor to the bottom of the abyss. These continual falls awoke echoes of singular power and effect.

Many portions of the cone consisted of inferior glaciers. Hans, whenever he met with one of these obstacles, advanced with a great show of precaution, sounding the soil with his long iron pole in order to discover fissures and layers of deep soft snow. In many doubtful or dangerous places, it became necessary for us to be tied together by a long rope in order that should any one of us be unfortunate enough to slip, he would be supported by his companions. This connecting link was doubtless a prudent precaution, but not by any means unattended with danger.

Nevertheless, and despite all the manifold difficulties of the descent, along slopes with which our guide was wholly unacquainted, we made considerable progress without accident. One of our great parcels of rope slipped from one of the Iceland porters, and rushed by a short cut to the bottom of the abyss.

By midday we were at the end of our journey. I looked upwards, and saw only the upper orifice of the cone, which served as a circular frame to a very small portion of the sky—a portion which seemed to me singularly beautiful. Should I ever again gaze on that lovely sunlit sky!

The only exception to this extraordinary landscape, was the Peak of Scartaris, which seemed lost in the great void of the heavens.

The bottom of the crater was composed of three separate shafts, through which, during periods of eruption, when Sneffels was in action, the great central furnace sent forth its burning lava and poisonous vapors. Each of these chimneys or shafts gaped open-mouthed in our path. I kept as far away from them as possible, not even venturing to take the faintest peep downwards.

As for the Professor, after a rapid examination of their disposition and characteristics, he became breathless and panting. He ran from one to the other like a delighted schoolboy, gesticulating wildly, and uttering incomprehensible and disjointed phrases in all sorts of languages.

Hans, the guide, and his humbler companions seated themselves on some piles of lava and looked silently on. They clearly took my uncle for a lunatic; and—waited the result.

Suddenly the Professor uttered a wild, unearthly cry. At first I imagined he had lost his footing, and was falling headlong into one of the yawning gulfs. Nothing of the kind. I saw him, his arms spread out to their widest extent, his legs stretched apart, standing upright before an enormous pedestal, high enough and black enough to bear a gigantic statue of Pluto. His attitude and mien were that of a man utterly stupefied. But his stupefaction was speedily changed to the wildest joy.

"Harry! Harry! come here!" he cried; "make haste—wonderful—wonderful!"

Unable to understand what he meant, I turned to obey his commands. Neither Hans nor the other Icelanders moved a step.

"Look!" said the Professor, in something of the manner of the French general, pointing out the pyramids to his army.

And fully partaking his stupefaction, if not his joy, I read on the eastern side of the huge block of stone, the same characters, half eaten away by the corrosive action of time, the name, to me a thousand times accursed—

"Arne Saknussemm!" cried my uncle, "now, unbeliever, do you begin to have faith?"

It was totally impossible for me to answer a single word. I went back to my pile of lava, in a state of silent awe. The evidence was unanswerable, overwhelming!

In a few moments, however, my thoughts were far away, back in my German home, with Gretchen and the old cook. What would I have given for one of my cousin's smiles, for one of the ancient domestic's omelettes, and for my own feather bed!

How long I remained in this state I know not. All I can say is, that when at last I raised my head from between my hands, there remained at the bottom of the crater only myself, my uncle and Hans. The Icelandic porters had been dismissed and were now descending the exterior slopes of Mount Sneffels, on their way to Stapi. How heartily did I wish myself with them!

Hans slept tranquilly at the foot of a rock in a kind of rill of lava, where he had made himself a rough and ready bed. MY uncle was walking about the bottom of the crater like a wild beast in a cage. I had no desire, neither had I the strength, to move from my recumbent position. Taking example by the guide, I gave way to a kind of painful somnolency, during which I seemed both to hear and feel continued heavings and shudderings in the mountain.

In this way we passed our first night in the interior of a crater.Next morning, a grey, cloudy, heavy sky hung like a funereal pall over the summit of the volcanic cone. I did not notice it so much from the obscurity that reigned around us, as from the rage with which my uncle was devoured.

I fully understood the reason, and again a glimpse of hope made my heart leap with joy. I will briefly explain the cause.

Of the three openings which yawned beneath our steps, only one could have been followed by the adventurous Saknussemm. According to the words of the learned Icelander, it was only to be known by that one particular mentioned in the cryptograph, that the shadow of Scartaris fell upon it, just touching its mouth in the last days of the month of June.

We were, in fact, to consider the pointed peak as the stylus of an immense sun-dial, the shadow of which pointed on one given day, like the inexorable finger of fate, to the yawning chasm which led into the interior of the earth.

Now, as often happens in these regions, should the sun fail to burst through the clouds, no shadow. Consequently, no chance of discovering the right aperture. We had already reached the 25th June. If the kindly heavens would only remain densely clouded for six more days, we should have to put off our voyage of discovery for another year, when certainly there would be one person fewer in the party. I already had sufficient of the mad and monstrous enterprise.

It would be utterly impossible to depict the impotent rage of Professor Hardwigg. The day passed away, and not the faintest outline of a shadow could be seen at the bottom of the crater. Hans the guide never moved from his place. He must have been curious to know what we were about, if indeed he could believe we were about anything. As for my uncle, he never addressed a word to me. He was nursing his wrath to keep it warm! His eyes fixed on the black and foggy atmosphere, his complexion hideous with suppressed passion. Never had his eyes appeared so fierce, his nose so aquiline, his mouth so hard and firm.

On the 26th no change for the better. A mixture of rain and snow fell during the whole day. Hans very quietly built himself a hut of lava into which he retired like Diogenes into his tub. I took a malicious delight in watching the thousand little cascades that flowed down the side of the cone, carrying with them at times a stream of stones into the "vasty deep" below.

My uncle was almost frantic: to be sure, it was enough to make even a patient man angry. He had reached to a certain extent the goal of his desires, and yet he was likely to be wrecked in port.

But if the heavens and the elements are capable of causing us much pain and sorrow, there are two sides to a medal. And there was reserved for Professor Hardwigg a brilliant and sudden surprise which was to compensate him for all his sufferings.

Next day the sky was still overcast, but on Sunday, the 28th, the last day but two of the month, with a sudden change of wind and a new moon there came a change of weather. The sun poured its beaming rays to the very bottom of the crater.

Each hillock, every rock, every stone, every asperity of the soil had its share of the luminous effulgence, and its shadow fell heavily on the soil. Among others, to his insane delight, the shadow of Scartaris was marked and clear, and moved slowly with the radiant start of day.

My uncle moved with it in a state of mental ecstasy.

At twelve o'clock exactly, when the sun had attained its highest altitude for the day, the shadow fell upon the edge of the central pit!

"Here it is," gasped the Professor in an agony of joy, "here it is—we have found it. Forward, my friends, into the Interior of the Earth."

I looked curiously at Hans to see what reply he would make to this terrific announcement.

"Forut," said the guide tranquilly.

"Forward it is," answered my uncle, who was now in the seventh heaven of delight.

When we were quite ready, our watches indicated thirteen minutes past one!

Chapter 14

THE REAL JOURNEY COMMENCES

Our real journey had now commenced. Hitherto our courage and determination had overcome all difficulties. We were fatigued at times; and that was all. Now we were about to encounter unknown and fearful dangers.

I had not as yet ventured to take a glimpse down the horrible abyss into which in a few minutes more I was about to plunge. The fatal moment had, however, at last arrived. I had still the option of refusing or accepting a share in this foolish and audacious enterprise. But I was ashamed to show more fear than the eider-duck hunter. Hans seemed to accept the difficulties of the journey so tranquilly, with such calm indifference, with such perfect recklessness of all danger, that I actually blushed to appear less of a man than he!

Had I been alone with my uncle, I should certainly have sat down and argued the point fully; but in the presence of the guide I held my tongue. I gave one moment to the thought of my charming cousin, and then I advanced to the mouth of the central shaft.

It measured about a hundred feet in diameter, which made about three hundred in circumference. I leaned over a rock which stood on its edge, and looked down. My hair stood on end, my teeth chattered, my limbs trembled. I seemed utterly to lose my centre of gravity, while my head was in a sort of whirl, like that of a drunken man. There is nothing more powerful than this attraction towards an abyss. I was about to fall headlong into the gaping well, when I was drawn back by a firm and powerful hand. It was that of Hans. I had not taken lessons enough at the Frelser's-Kirk of Copenhagen in the art of looking down from lofty eminences without blinking!

However, few as the minutes were during which I gazed down this tremendous and even wondrous shaft, I had a sufficient glimpse of it to give me some idea of its physical conformation. Its sides, which were almost as perpendicular as those of a well, presented numerous projections which doubtless would assist our descent.

It was a sort of wild and savage staircase, without bannister or fence. A rope fastened above, near the surface, would certainly support our weight and enable us to reach the bottom, but how, when we had arrived at its utmost depth, were we to loosen it above? This was, I thought, a question of some importance.

My uncle, however, was one of those men who are nearly always prepared with expedients. He hit upon a very simple method of obviating this difficulty. He unrolled a cord about as thick as my thumb, and at least four hundred feet in length. He allowed about half of it to go down the pit and catch in a hitch over a great block of lava which stood on the edge of the precipice. This done, he threw the second half after the first.

Each of us could now descend by catching the two cords in one hand. When about two hundred feet below, all the explorer had to do was to let go one end and pull away at the other, when the cord would come falling at his feet. In order to go down farther, all that was necessary was to continue the same operation.

This was a very excellent proposition, and no doubt, a correct one. Going down appeared to me easy enough; it was the coming up again that now occupied my thoughts.

"Now," said my uncle, as soon as he had completed this important preparation, "let us see about the baggage. It must be divided into three separate parcels, and each of us must carry one on his back. I allude to the more important and fragile articles."

My worthy and ingenious uncle did not appear to consider that we came under the denomination.

"Hans," he continued, "you will take charge of the tools and some of the provisions; you, Harry, must take possession of another third of the provisions and of the arms. I will load myself with the rest of the eatables, and with the more delicate instruments."

"But," I exclaimed, "our clothes, this mass of cord and ladders—who will undertake to carry them down?"

"They will go down of themselves."

"And how so?" I asked.

"You shall see."

My uncle was not fond of half measures, nor did he like anything in the way of hesitation. Giving his orders to Hans he had the whole of the nonfragile articles made up into one bundle; and the packet, firmly and solidly fastened, was simply pitched over the edge of the gulf.

I heard the moaning of the suddenly displaced air, and the noise of falling stones. My uncle leaning over the abyss followed the descent of his luggage with a perfectly self-satisfied air, and did not rise until it had completely disappeared from sight.

"Now then," he cried, "it is our turn."

I put it in good faith to any man of common sense—was it possible to hear this energetic cry without a shudder?

The Professor fastened his case of instruments on his back.

Hans took charge of the tools, I of the arms. The descent then commenced in the following order: Hans went first, my uncle followed, and I went last. Our progress was made in profound silence—a silence only troubled by the fall of pieces of rock, which breaking from the jagged sides, fell with a roar into the depths below.

I allowed myself to slide, so to speak, holding frantically on the double cord with one hand and with the other keeping myself off the rocks by the assistance of my iron-shod pole. One idea was all the time impressed upon my brain. I feared that the upper support would fail me. The cord appeared to me far too fragile to bear the weight of three such persons as we were, with our luggage. I made as little use of it as possible, trusting to my own agility and doing miracles in the way of feats of dexterity and strength upon the projecting shelves and spurs of lava which my feet seemed to clutch as strongly as my hands.

The guide went first, I have said, and when one of the slippery and frail supports broke from under his feet he had recourse to his usual monosyllabic way of speaking.

"Gif akt—"

"Attention—look out," repeated my uncle.

In about half an hour we reached a kind of small terrace formed by a fragment of rock projecting some distance from the sides of the shaft.

Hans now began to haul upon the cord on one side only, the other going as quietly upward as the other came down. It fell at last, bringing with it a shower of small stones, lava and dust, a disagreeable kind of rain or hail.

While we were seated on this extraordinary bench I ventured once more to look downwards. With a sigh I discovered that the bottom was still wholly invisible. Were we, then, going direct to the interior of the earth?

The performance with the cord recommenced, and a quarter of an hour later we had reached to the depth of another two hundred feet.

I have very strong doubts if the most determined geologist would, during that descent, have studied the nature of the different layers of earth around him. I did not trouble my head much about the matter; whether we were among the combustible carbon, Silurians, or primitive soil, I neither knew nor cared to know.

Not so the inveterate Professor. He must have taken notes all the way down, for, at one of our halts, he began a brief lecture.

"The farther we advance," said he, "the greater is my confidence in the result. The disposition of these volcanic strata absolutely confirms the theories of Sir Humphry Davy. We are still within the region of the primordial soil, the soil in which took place the chemical operation of metals becoming inflamed by coming in contact with the air and water. I at once regret the old and now forever exploded theory of a central fire. At all events, we shall soon know the truth."

Such was the everlasting conclusion to which he came. I, however, was very far from being in humor to discuss the matter. I had something else to think of. My silence was taken for consent; and still we continued to go down.

At the expiration of three hours, we were, to all appearance, as far off as ever from the bottom of the well. When I looked upwards, however, I could see that the upper orifice was every minute decreasing in size. The sides of the shaft were getting closer and closer together, we were approaching the regions of eternal night!

And still we continued to descend!

At length, I noticed that when pieces of stone were detached from the sides of this stupendous precipice, they were swallowed up with less noise than before. The final sound was sooner heard. We were approaching the bottom of the abyss!

As I had been very careful to keep account of an the changes of cord which took place, I was able to tell exactly what was the depth we had reached, as well as the time it had taken.

We had shifted the rope twenty-eight times, each operation taking a quarter of an hour, which in all made seven hours. To this had to be added twenty-eight pauses; in all ten hours and a half. We started at one, it was now, therefore, about eleven o'clock at night.

It does not require great knowledge of arithmetic to know that twenty-eight times two hundred feet makes five thousand six hundred feet in all (more than an English mile).

While I was making this mental calculation a voice broke the silence. It was the voice of Hans.

"Halt!" he cried.

I checked myself very suddenly, just at the moment when I was about to kick my uncle on the head.

"We have reached the end of our journey," said the worthy Professor in a satisfied tone.

"What, the interior of the earth?" said I, slipping down to his side.

"No, you stupid fellow! but we have reached the bottom of the well."

"And I suppose there is no farther progress to be made?" I hopefully exclaimed.

"Oh, yes, I can dimly see a sort of tunnel, which turns off obliquely to the right. At all events, we must see about that tomorrow. Let us sup now, and seek slumber as best we may."

I thought it time, but made no observations on that point. I was fairly launched on a desperate course, and all I had to do was to go forward hopefully and trustingly.

It was not even now quite dark, the light filtering down in a most extraordinary manner.

We opened the provision bag, ate a frugal supper, and each did his best to find a bed amid the pile of stones, dirt, and lava which had accumulated for ages at the bottom of the shaft.

I happened to grope out the pile of ropes, ladders, and clothes which we had thrown down; and upon them I stretched myself. After such a day's labor, my rough bed seemed as soft as down!

For a while I lay in a sort of pleasant trance.

Presently, after lying quietly for some minutes, I opened my eyes and looked upwards. As I did so I made out a brilliant little dot, at the extremity of this long, gigantic telescope.

It was a star without scintillating rays. According to my calculation, it must be Beta in the constellation of the Little Bear.

After this little bit of astronomical recreation, I dropped into a sound sleep.

Chapter 15

WE CONTINUE OUR DESCENT

At eight o'clock the next morning, a faint kind of dawn of day awoke us. The thousand and one prisms of the lava collected the light as it passed and brought it to us like a shower of sparks.

We were able with ease to see objects around us.

"Well, Harry, my boy," cried the delighted Professor, rubbing his hands together, "what say you now? Did you ever pass a more tranquil night in our house in the Konigstrasse? No deafening sounds of cart wheels, no cries of hawkers, no bad language from boatmen or watermen!"

"Well, Uncle, we are quite at the bottom of this well—but to me there is something terrible in this calm."

"Why," said the Professor hotly, "one would say you were already beginning to be afraid. How will you get on presently? Do you know, that as yet, we have not penetrated one inch into the bowels of the earth."

"What can you mean, sir?" was my bewildered and astonished reply.

"I mean to say that we have only just reached the soil of the island itself. This long vertical tube, which ends at the bottom of the crater of Sneffels, ceases here just about on a level with the sea."

"Are you sure, sir?"

"Quite sure. Consult the barometer."

It was quite true that the mercury, after rising gradually in the instrument, as long as our descent was taking place, had stopped precisely at twenty-nine degrees.

"You perceive," said the Professor, "we have as yet only to endure the pressure of air. I am curious to replace the barometer by the manometer."

The barometer, in fact, was about to become useless—as soon as the weight of the air was greater than what was calculated as above the level of the ocean.

"But," said I, "is it not very much to be feared that this ever-increasing pressure may not in the end turn out very painful and inconvenient?"

"No," said he. "We shall descend very slowly, and our lungs will be gradually accustomed to breathe compressed air. It is well known that aeronauts have gone so high as to be nearly without air at all—why, then, should we not accustom ourselves to breathe when we have, say, a little too much of it? For myself, I am certain I shall prefer it. Let us not lose a moment. Where is the packet which preceded us in our descent?"

I smilingly pointed it out to my uncle. Hans had not seen it, and believed it caught somewhere above us: "Huppe" as he phrased it.

"Now," said my uncle, "let us breakfast, and break fast like people who have a long day's work before them."

Biscuit and dried meat, washed down by some mouthfuls of water flavored with Schiedam, was the material of our luxurious meal.

As soon as it was finished, my uncle took from his pocket a notebook destined to be filled by memoranda of our travels. He had already placed his instruments in order, and this is what he wrote:

Monday, June 29th

Chronometer, 8h. 17m. morning.

Barometer, 29.6 inches.

Thermometer, 6 degrees [43 degrees Fahr.]

Direction, E.S.E.

This last observation referred to the obscure gallery, and was indicated to us by the compass.

"Now, Harry," cried the Professor, in an enthusiastic tone of voice, "we are truly about to take our first step into the Interior of the Earth; never before visited by man since the first creation of the world. You may consider, therefore, that at this precise moment our travels really commence."

As my uncle made this remark, he took in one hand the Ruhmkorff coil apparatus, which hung round his neck, and with the other he put the electric current into communication with the worm of the lantern. And a bright light at once illumined that dark and gloomy tunnel!

The effect was magical!

Hans, who carried the second apparatus, had it also put into operation. This ingenious application of electricity to practical purposes enabled us to move along by the light of an artificial day, amid even the flow of the most inflammable and combustible gases.

"Forward!" cried my uncle. Each took up his burden. Hans went first, my uncle followed, and I going third, we entered the somber gallery!

Just as we were about to engulf ourselves in this dismal passage, I lifted up my head, and through the tubelike shaft saw that Iceland sky I was never to see again!

Was it the last I should ever see of any sky?

The stream of lava flowing from the bowels of the earth in 1219 had forced itself a passage through the tunnel. It lined the whole of the inside with its thick and brilliant coating. The electric light added very greatly to the brilliancy of the effect.

The great difficulty of our journey now began. How were we to prevent ourselves from slipping down the steeply inclined plane? Happily some cracks, abrasures of the soil, and other irregularities, served the place of steps; and we descended slowly; allowing our heavy luggage to slip on before, at the end of a long cord.

But that which served as steps under our feet became in other places stalactites. The lava, very porous in certain places, took the form of little round blisters. Crystals of opaque quartz, adorned with limpid drops of natural glass suspended to the roof like lusters, seemed to take fire as we passed beneath them. One would have fancied that the genii of romance were illuminating their underground palaces to receive the sons of men.

"Magnificent, glorious!" I cried in a moment of involuntary enthusiasm, "What a spectacle, Uncle! Do you not admire these variegated shades of lava, which run through a whole series of colors, from reddish brown to pale yellow—by the most insensible degrees? And these crystals, they appear like luminous globes."

"You are beginning to see the charms of travel, Master Harry," cried my uncle. "Wait a bit, until we advance farther. What we have as yet discovered is nothing—onwards, my boy, onwards!It would have been a far more correct and appropriate expression, had he said, "let us slide," for we were going down an inclined plane with perfect ease. The compass indicated that we were moving in a southeasterly direction. The flow of lava had never turned to the right or the left. It had the inflexibility of a straight line.

Nevertheless, to my surprise, we found no perceptible increase in heat. This proved the theories of Humphry Davy to be founded on truth, and more than once I found myself examining the thermometer in silent astonishment.

Two hours after our departure it only marked fifty-four degrees Fahrenheit. I had every reason to believe from this that our descent was far more horizontal than vertical. As for discovering the exact depth to which we had attained, nothing could be easier. The Professor as he advanced measured the angles of deviation and inclination; but he kept the result of his observations to himself.

About eight o'clock in the evening, my uncle gave the signal for halting. Hans seated himself on the ground. The lamps were hung to fissures in the lava rock. We were now in a large cavern where air was not wanting. On the contrary, it abounded. What could be the cause of this—to what atmospheric agitation could be ascribed this draught? But this was a question which I did not care to discuss just then. Fatigue and hunger made me incapable of reasoning. An unceasing march of seven hours had not been kept up without great exhaustion. I was really and truly worn out; and delighted enough I was to hear the word Halt.

Hans laid out some provisions on a lump of lava, and we each supped with keen relish. One thing, however, caused us great uneasiness—our water reserve was already half exhausted. My uncle had full confidence in finding subterranean resources, but hitherto we had completely failed in so doing. I could not help calling my uncle's attention to the circumstance.

"And you are surprised at this total absence of springs?" he said.

"Doubtless—I am very uneasy on the point. We have certainly not enough water to last us five days."

"Be quite easy on that matter," continued my uncle. "I answer for it we shall find plenty of water—in fact, far more than we shall want."

"But when?"

"When we once get through this crust of lava. How can you expect springs to force their way through these solid stone walls?"

"But what is there to prove that this concrete mass of lava does not extend to the centre of the earth? I don't think we have as yet done much in a vertical way."

"What puts that into your head, my boy?" asked my uncle mildly.

"Well, it appears to me that if we had descended very far below the level of the sea—we should find it rather hotter than we have."

"According to your system," said my uncle; "but what does the thermometer say?"

"Scarcely fifteen degrees by Reaumur, which is only an increase of nine since our departure."

"Well, and what conclusion does that bring you to?" inquired the Professor.

"The deduction I draw from this is very simple. According to the most exact observations, the augmentation of the temperature of the interior of the earth is one degree for every hundred feet. But certain local causes may considerably modify this figure. Thus at Yakoust in Siberia, it has been remarked that the heat increases a degree every thirty-six feet. The difference evidently depends on the conductibility of certain rocks. In the neighborhood of an extinct volcano, it has been remarked that the elevation of temperature was only one degree in every five-and-twenty feet. Let us, then, go upon this calculation—which is the most favorable—and calculate."

"Calculate away, my boy."

"Nothing easier," said I, pulling out my notebook and pencil. "Nine times one hundred and twenty-five feet make a depth of eleven hundred and twenty-five feet."

"Archimedes could not have spoken more geometrically."

"Well?"

"Well, according to my observations, we are at least ten thousand feet below the level of the sea."

"Can it be possible?"

"Either my calculation is correct, or there is no truth in figures."

The calculations of the Professor were perfectly correct. We were already six thousand feet deeper down in the bowels of the earth than anyone had ever been before. The lowest known depth to which man had hitherto penetrated was in the mines of Kitzbuhel, in the Tirol, and those of Wurttemberg.

The temperature, which should have been eighty-one, was in this place only fifteen. This was a matter for serious consideration.

Chapter 16

THE EASTERN TUNNEL

The next day was Tuesday, the 30th of June—and at six o'clock in the morning we resumed our journey.

We still continued to follow the gallery of lava, a perfect natural pathway, as easy of descent as some of those inclined planes which, in very old German houses, serve the purpose of staircases. This went on until seventeen minutes past twelve, the precise instant at which we rejoined Hans, who, having been somewhat in advance, had suddenly stopped.

"At last," cried my uncle, "we have reached the end of the shaft."

I looked wonderingly about me. We were in the centre of four cross paths—somber and narrow tunnels. The question now arose as to which it was wise to take; and this of itself was no small difficulty.

My uncle, who did not wish to appear to have any hesitation about the matter before myself or the guide, at once made up his mind. He pointed quietly to the eastern tunnel; and, without delay, we entered within its gloomy recesses.

Besides, had he entertained any feeling of hesitation it might have been prolonged indefinitely, for there was no indication by which to determine on a choice. It was absolutely necessary to trust to chance and good fortune!

The descent of this obscure and narrow gallery was very gradual and winding. Sometimes we gazed through a succession of arches, its course very like the aisles of a Gothic cathedral. The great artistic sculptors and builders of the Middle Ages might have here completed their studies with advantage. Many most beautiful and suggestive ideas of architectural beauty would have been discovered by them. After passing through this phase of the cavernous way, we suddenly came, about a mile farther on, upon a square system of arch, adopted by the early Romans, projecting from the solid rock, and keeping up the weight of the roof.

Suddenly we would come upon a series of low subterranean tunnels which looked like beaver holes, or the work of foxes—through whose narrow and winding ways we had literally to crawl!

The heat still remained at quite a supportable degree. With an involuntary shudder, I reflected on what the heat must have been when the volcano of Sneffels was pouring its smoke, flames, and streams of boiling lava—all of which must have come up by the road we were now following. I could imagine the torrents of hot seething stone darting on, bubbling up with accompaniments of smoke, steam, and sulphurous stench!

"Only to think of the consequences," I mused, "if the old volcano were once more to set to work."

I did not communicate these rather unpleasant reflections to my uncle. He not only would not have understood them, but would have been intensely disgusted. His only idea was to go ahead. He walked, he slid, he clambered over piles of fragments, he rolled down heaps of broken lava, with an earnestness and conviction it was impossible not to admire.

At six o'clock in the evening, after a very wearisome journey, but one not so fatiguing as before, we had made six miles towards the southward, but had not gone more than a mile downwards.

My uncle, as usual, gave the signal to halt. We ate our meal in thoughtful silence, and then retired to sleep.

Our arrangements for the night were very primitive and simple. A traveling rug, in which each rolled himself, was all our bedding. We had no necessity to fear cold or any unpleasant visit. Travelers who bury themselves in the wilds and depths of the African desert, who seek profit and pleasure in the forests of the New World, are compelled to take it in turn to watch during the hours of sleep; but in this region of the earth absolute solitude and complete security reigned supreme.

We had nothing to fear either from savages or from wild beasts.

After a night's sweet repose, we awoke fresh and ready for action. There being nothing to detain us, we started on our journey. We continued to burrow through the lava tunnel as before. It was impossible to make out through what soil we were making way. The tunnel, moreover, instead of going down into the bowels of the earth, became absolutely horizontal.

I even thought, after some examination, that we were actually tending upwards. About ten o'clock in the day this state of things became so clear that, finding the change very fatiguing, I was obliged to slacken my pace and finally come to a halt.

"Well," said the Professor quickly, "what is the matter?"

"The fact is, I am dreadfully tired," was my earnest reply.

"What," cried my uncle, "tired after a three hours' walk, and by so easy a road?"

"Easy enough, I dare say, but very fatiguing."

"But how can that be, when all we have to do is to go downwards."

"I beg your pardon, sir. For some time I have noticed that we are going upwards."

"Upwards," cried my uncle, shrugging his shoulders, "how can that be?"

"There can be no doubt about it. For the last half hour the slopes have been upward—and if we go on in this way much longer we shall find ourselves back in Iceland."

My uncle shook his head with the air of a man who does not want to be convinced. I tried to continue the conversation. He would not answer me, but once more gave the signal for departure. His silence I thought was only caused by concentrated ill-temper.

However this might be, I once more took up my load, and boldly and resolutely followed Hans, who was now in advance of my uncle. I did not like to be beaten or even distanced. I was naturally anxious not to lose sight of my companions. The very idea of being left behind, lost in that terrible labyrinth, made me shiver as with the ague.

Besides, if the ascending path was more arduous and painful to clamber, I had one source of secret consolation and delight. It was to all appearance taking us back to the surface of the earth. That of itself was hopeful. Every step I took confirmed me in my belief, and I began already to build castles in the air in relation to my marriage with my pretty little cousin.

About twelve o'clock there was a great and sudden change in the aspect of the rocky sides of the gallery. I first noticed it from the diminution of the rays of light which cast back the reflection of the lamp. From being coated with shining and resplendent lava, it became living rock. The sides were sloping walls, which sometimes became quite vertical.

We were now in what the geological professors call a state of transition, in the period of Silurian stones, so called because this specimen of early formation is very common in England in the counties formerly inhabited by the Celtic nation known as Silures.

"I can see clearly now," I cried; "the sediment from the waters which once covered the whole earth formed during the second period of its existence these schists and these calcareous rocks. We are turning our backs on the granite rocks, and are like people from Hamburg who would go to Lubeck by way of Hanover."

I might just as well have kept my observations to myself. My geological enthusiasm got the better, however, of my cooler judgment, and Professor Hardwigg heard my observations.

"What is the matter now?" he said, in a tone of great gravity.

"Well," cried I, "do you not see these different layers of calcareous rocks and the first indication of slate strata?"

"Well; what then?"

"We have arrived at that period of the world's existence when the first plants and the first animals made their appearance."

"You think so?"

"Yes, look; examine and judge for yourself."

I induced the Professor with some difficulty to cast the light of his lamp on the sides of the long winding gallery. I expected some exclamation to burst from his lips. I was very much mistaken. The worthy Professor never spoke a word.

It was impossible to say whether he understood me or not. Perhaps it was possible that in his pride—my uncle and a learned professor—he did not like to own that he was wrong in having chosen the eastern tunnel, or was he determined at any price to go to the end of it? It was quite evident we had left the region of lava, and that the road by which we were going could not take us back to the great crater of Mount Sneffels.

As we went along I could not help ruminating on the whole question, and asked myself if I did not lay too great a stress on these sudden and peculiar modifications of the earth's crust.

After all, I was very likely to be mistaken—and it was within the range of probability and possibility that we were not making our way through the strata of rocks which I believed I recognized piled on the lower layer of granitic formation.

"At all events, if I am right," I thought to myself, "I must certainly find some remains of primitive plants, and it will be absolutely necessary to give way to such indubitable evidence. Let us have a good search."

I accordingly lost no opportunity of searching, and had not gone more than about a hundred yards, when the evidence I sought for cropped up in the most incontestable manner before my eyes. It was quite natural that I should expect to find these signs, for during the Silurian period the seas contained no fewer than fifteen hundred different animal and vegetable species. My feet, so long accustomed to the hard and arid lava soil, suddenly found themselves treading on a kind of soft dust, the remains of plants and shells.

Upon the walls themselves I could clearly make out the outline, as plain as a sun picture, of the fucus and the lycopods. The worthy and excellent Professor Hardwigg could not of course make any mistake about the matter; but I believe he deliberately closed his eyes, and continued on his way with a firm and unalterable step.

I began to think that he was carrying his obstinacy a great deal too far. I could no longer act with prudence or composure. I stooped on a sudden and picked up an almost perfect shell, which had undoubtedly belonged to some animal very much resembling some of the present day. Having secured the prize, I followed in the wake of my uncle.

"Do you see this?" I said.

"Well, said the Professor, with the most imperturbable tranquillity, "it is the shell of a crustaceous animal of the extinct order of the trilobites; nothing more, I assure you."

"But," cried I, much troubled at his coolness, "do you draw no conclusion from it?"

"Well, if I may ask, what conclusion do you draw from it yourself?"

"Well, I thought—"

"I know, my boy, what you would say, and you are right, perfectly and incontestably right. We have finally abandoned the crust of lava and the road by which the lava ascended. It is quite possible that I may have been mistaken, but I shall be unable to discover my error until I get to the end of this gallery."

"You are quite right as far as that is concerned," I replied, "and I should highly approve of your decision, if we had not to fear the greatest of all dangers."

"And what is that?"

"Want of water."

"Well, my dear Henry, it can't be helped. We must put ourselves on rations."

And on he went.

Chapter 17

DEEPER AND DEEPER—THE COAL MINE

In truth, we were compelled to put ourselves upon rations. Our supply would certainly last not more than three days. I found this out about supper time. The worst part of the matter was that, in what is called the transition rocks, it was hardly to be expected we should meet with water!

I had read of the horrors of thirst, and I knew that where we were, a brief trial of its sufferings would put an end to our adventures—and our lives! But it was utterly useless to discuss the matter with my uncle. He would have answered by some axiom from Plato.

During the whole of next day we proceeded on our journey through this interminable gallery, arch after arch, tunnel after tunnel. We journeyed without exchanging a word. We had become as mute and reticent as Hans, our guide.

The road had no longer an upward tendency; at all events, if it had, it was not to be made out very clearly. Sometimes there could be no doubt that we were going downwards. But this inclination was scarcely to be distinguished, and was by no means reassuring to the Professor, because the character of the strata was in no wise modified, and the transition character of the rocks became more and more marked.

It was a glorious sight to see how the electric light brought out the sparkles in the walls of the calcareous rocks, and the old red sandstone. One might have fancied oneself in one of those deep cuttings in Devonshire, which have given their name to this kind of soil. Some magnificent specimens of marble projected from the sides of the gallery: some of an agate grey with white veins of variegated character, others of a yellow spotted color, with red veins; farther off might be seen samples of color in which cherry-tinted seams were to be found in all their brightest shades.

The greater number of these marbles were stamped with the marks of primitive animals. Since the previous evening, nature and creation had made considerable progress. Instead of the rudimentary trilobites, I perceived the remains of a more perfect order. Among others, the fish in which the eye of a geologist has been able to discover the first form of the reptile.

The Devonian seas were inhabited by a vast number of animals of this species, which were deposited in tens of thousands in the rocks of new formation.

It was quite evident to me that we were ascending the scale of animal life of which man forms the summit. My excellent uncle, the Professor, appeared not to take notice of these warnings. He was determined at any risk to proceed.

He must have been in expectation of one of two things; either that a vertical well was about to open under his feet, and thus allow him to continue his descent, or that some insurmountable obstacle would compel us to stop and go back by the road we had so long traveled. But evening came again, and, to my horror, neither hope was doomed to be realized!

On Friday, after a night when I began to feel the gnawing agony of thirst, and when in consequence appetite decreased, our little band rose and once more followed the turnings and windings, the ascents and descents, of this interminable gallery.

All were silent and gloomy. I could see that even my uncle had ventured too far.

After about ten hours of further progress—a progress dull and monotonous to the last degree—I remarked that the reverberation, and reflection of our lamps upon the sides of the tunnel, had singularly diminished. The marble, the schist, the calcareous rocks, the red sandstone, had disappeared, leaving in their places a dark and gloomy wall, somber and without brightness. When we reached a remarkably narrow part of the tunnel, I leaned my left hand against the rock.

When I took my hand away, and happened to glance at it, it was quite black. We had reached the coal strata of the Central Earth.

"A coal mine!" I cried.

"A coal mine without miners," responded my uncle, a little severely.

"How can we tell?"

"I can tell," replied my uncle, in a sharp and doctorial tone. "I am perfectly certain that this gallery through successive layers of coal was not cut by the hand of man. But whether it is the work of nature or not is of little concern to us. The hour for our evening meal has come—let us sup."

Hans, the guide, occupied himself in preparing food. I had come to that point when I could no longer eat. All I cared about were the few drops of water which fell to my share. What I suffered it is useless to record. The guide's gourd, not quite half full, was all that was left for us three!

Having finished their repast, my two companions laid themselves down upon their rugs, and found in sleep a remedy for their fatigue and sufferings. As for me, I could not sleep, I lay counting the hours until morning.

The next morning, Saturday, at six o'clock, we started again. Twenty minutes later we suddenly came upon a vast excavation. From its mighty extent I saw at once that the hand of man could have had nothing to do with this coal mine; the vault above would have fallen in; as it was, it was only held together by some miracle of natureThis mighty natural cavern was about a hundred feet wide, by about a hundred and fifty high. The earth had evidently been cast apart by some violent subterranean commotion. The mass, giving way to some prodigious upheaving of nature, had split in two, leaving the vast gap into which we inhabitants of the earth had penetrated for the first time.

The whole singular history of the coal period was written on those dark and gloomy walls. A geologist would have been able easily to follow the different phases of its formation. The seams of coal were separated by strata of sandstone, a compact clay, which appeared to be crushed down by the weight from above.

At that period of the world which preceded the secondary epoch, the earth was covered by a coating of enormous and rich vegetation, due to the double action of tropical heat and perpetual humidity. A vast atmospheric cloud of vapor surrounded the earth on all sides, preventing the rays of the sun from ever reaching it.

Hence the conclusion that these intense heats did not arise from this new source of caloric.

Perhaps even the star of day was not quite ready for its brilliant work—to illumine a universe. Climates did not as yet exist, and a level heat pervaded the whole surface of the globe—the same heat existing at the North Pole as at the equator.

Whence did it come? From the interior of the earth?

In spite of all the learned theories of Professor Hardwigg, a fierce and vehement fire certainly burned within the entrails of the great spheroid. Its action was felt even to the very topmost crust of the earth; the plants then in existence, being deprived of the vivifying rays of the sun, had neither buds, nor flowers, nor odor, but their roots drew a strong and vigorous life from the burning earth of early days.

There were but few of what may be called trees—only herbaceous plants, immense turfs, briers, mosses, rare families, which, however, in those days were counted by tens and tens of thousands.

It is entirely to this exuberant vegetation that coal owes its origin. The crust of the vast globe still yielded under the influence of the seething, boiling mass, which was forever at work beneath. Hence arose numerous fissures, and continual falling in of the upper earth. The dense mass of plants being beneath the waters, soon formed themselves into vast agglomerations.

Then came about the action of natural chemistry; in the depths of the ocean the vegetable mass at first became turf, then, thanks to the influence of gases and subterranean fermentation, they underwent the complete process of mineralization.

In this manner, in early days, were formed those vast and prodigious layers of coal, which an ever—increasing consumption must utterly use up in about three centuries more, if people do not find some more economic light than gas, and some cheaper motive power than steam.

All these reflections, the memories of my school studies, came to my mind while I gazed upon these mighty accumulations of coal, whose riches, however, are scarcely likely to be ever utilized. The working of these mines could only be carried out at an expense that would never yield a profit.

The matter, however, is scarcely worthy consideration, when coal is scattered over the whole surface of the globe, within a few yards of the upper crust. As I looked at these untouched strata, therefore, I knew they would remain as long as the world lasts.

While we still continued our journey, I alone forgot the length of the road, by giving myself up wholly to these geological considerations. The temperature continued to be very much the same as while we were traveling amid the lava and the schists. On the other hand my sense of smell was much affected by a very powerful odor. I immediately knew that the gallery was filled to overflowing with that dangerous gas the miners call fire damp, the explosion of which has caused such fearful and terrible accidents, making a hundred widows and hundreds of orphans in a single hour.

Happily, we were able to illumine our progress by means of the Ruhmkorff apparatus. If we had been so rash and imprudent as to explore this gallery, torch in hand, a terrible explosion would have put an end to our travels, simply because no travelers would be left.

Our excursion through this wondrous coal mine in the very bowels of the earth lasted until evening. My uncle was scarcely able to conceal his impatience and dissatisfaction at the road continuing still to advance in a horizontal direction.

The darkness, dense and opaque a few yards in advance and in the rear, rendered it impossible to make out what was the length of the gallery. For myself, I began to believe that it was simply interminable, and would go on in the same manner for months.

Suddenly, at six o'clock, we stood in front of a wall. To the right, to the left above, below, nowhere was there any passage. We had reached a spot where the rocks said in unmistakable accents—No Thoroughfare.

I stood stupefied. The guide simply folded his arms. My uncle was silent.

"Well, well, so much the better," cried my uncle, at last, "I now know what we are about. We are decidedly not upon the road followed by Saknussemm. All we have to do is to go back.

Let us take one night's good rest, and before three days are over, I promise you we shall have regained the point where the galleries divided."

"Yes, we may, if our strength lasts as long," I cried, in a lamentable voice.

"And why not?"

"Tomorrow, among us three, there will not be a drop of water. It is just gone."

"And your courage with it," said my uncle, speaking in a severe tone.

What could I say? I turned round on my side, and from sheer exhaustion fell into a heavy sleep disturbed by dreams of water! And I awoke unrefreshed.

I would have bartered a diamond mine for a glass of pure spring water!

Chapter 18

THE WRONG ROAD!

Next day, our departure took place at a very early hour. There was no time for the least delay. According to my account, we had five days' hard work to get back to the place where the galleries divided.

I can never tell all the sufferings we endured upon our return. My uncle bore them like a man who has been in the wrong—that is, with concentrated and suppressed anger; Hans, with all the resignation of his pacific character; and I—I confess that I did nothing but complain, and despair. I had no heart for this bad fortune.

But there was one consolation. Defeat at the outset would probably upset the whole journey!

As I had expected from the first, our supply of water gave completely out on our first day's march. Our provision of liquids was reduced to our supply of Schiedam; but this horrible—nay, I will say it—this infernal liquor burnt the throat, and I could not even bear the sight of it. I found the temperature to be stifling. I was paralyzed with fatigue. More than once I was about to fall insensible to the ground. The whole party then halted, and the worthy Icelander and my excellent uncle did their best to console and comfort me. I could, however, plainly see that my uncle was contending painfully against the extreme fatigues of our journey, and the awful torture generated by the absence of water.

At length a time came when I ceased to recollect anything—when all was one awfull hideous, fantastic dream!

At last, on Tuesday, the seventh of the month of July, after crawling on our hands and knees for many hours, more dead than alive, we reached the point of junction between the galleries. I lay like a log, an inert mass of human flesh on the arid lava soil. It was then ten in the morning.

Hans and my uncle, leaning against the wall, tried to nibble away at some pieces of biscuit, while deep groans and sighs escaped from my scorched and swollen lips. Then I fell off into a kind of deep lethargy.

Presently I felt my uncle approach, and lift me up tenderly in his arms.

"Poor boy," I heard him say in a tone of deep commiseration.

I was profoundly touched by these words, being by no means accustomed to signs of womanly weakness in the Professor. I caught his trembling hands in mine and gave them a gentle pressure. He allowed me to do so without resistance, looking at me kindly all the time. His eyes were wet with tears.

I then saw him take the gourd which he wore at his side. To my surprise, or rather to my stupefaction, he placed it to my lips.

"Drink, my boy," he said.

Was it possible my ears had not deceived me? Was my uncle mad? I looked at him, with, I am sure, quite an idiotic expression. I could not believe him. I too much feared the counteraction of disappointment.

"Drink," he said again.

Had I heard aright? Before, however, I could ask myself the question a second time, a mouthful of water cooled my parched lips and throat—one mouthful, but I do believe it brought me back to life.

I thanked my uncle by clasping my hands. My heart was too full to speak.

"Yes," said he, "one mouthful of water, the very last—do you hear, my boy—the very last! I have taken care of it at the bottom of my bottle as the apple of my eye. Twenty times, a hundred times, I have resisted the fearful desire to drink it. But—no—no, Harry, I saved it for you."

"My dear uncle," I exclaimed, and the big tears rolled down my hot and feverish cheeks.

"Yes, my poor boy, I knew that when you reached this place, this crossroad in the earth, you would fall down half dead, and I saved my last drop of water in order to restore you."

"Thanks," I cried; "thanks from my heart."

As little as my thirst was really quenched, I had nevertheless partially recovered my strength. The contracted muscles of my throat relaxed—and the inflammation of my lips in some measure subsided. At all events, I was able to speak.

"Well," I said, "there can be no doubt now as to what we have to do. Water has utterly failed us; our journey is therefore at an end. Let us return."

While I spoke thus, my uncle evidently avoided my face: he held down his head; his eyes were turned in every possible direction but the right one.

"Yes," I continued, getting excited by my own words, "we must go back to Sneffels. May heaven give us strength to enable us once more to revisit the light of day. Would that we now stood on the summit of the crater."

"Go back," said my uncle, speaking to himself, "and must it be so?"

"Go back—yes, and without losing a single moment," I vehemently cried.

For some moments there was silence under that dark and gloomy vault.

"So, my dear Harry," said the Professor in a very singular tone of voice, "those few drops of water have not sufficed to restore your energy and courage."

"Courage!" I cried.

"I see that you are quite as downcast as before—and still give way to discouragement and despair."

What, then, was the man made of, and what other projects were entering his fertile and audacious brain!

"You are not discouraged, sir?"

"What! Give up just as we are on the verge of success?" he cried. "Never, never shall it be said that Professor Hardwigg retreated."

"Then we must make up our minds to perish," I cried with a helpless sigh.

"No, Harry, my boy, certainly not. Go, leave me, I am very far from desiring your death. Take Hans with you. *I will go on alone.*"

"You ask us to leave you?"

"Leave me, I say. I have undertaken this dangerous and perilous adventure. I will carry it to the end—or I will never return to the surface of Mother Earth. Go, Harry—once more I say to you—go!"

My uncle as he spoke was terribly excited. His voice, which before had been tender, almost womanly, became harsh and menacing. He appeared to be struggling with desperate energy against the impossible. I did not wish to abandon him at the bottom of that abyss, while, on the other hand, the instinct of preservation told me to fly.

Meanwhile, our guide was looking on with profound calmness and indifference. He appeared to be an unconcerned party, and yet he perfectly well knew what was going on between us. Our gestures sufficiently indicated the different roads each wished to follow—and which each tried to influence the other to undertake. But Hans appeared not to take the slightest interest in what was really a question of life and death for us all, but waited quite ready to obey the signal which should say go aloft, or to resume his desperate journey into the interior of the earth.

How then I wished with all my heart and soul that I could make him understand my words. My representations, my sighs and groans, the earnest accents in which I should have spoken would have convinced that cold, hard nature. Those fearful dangers and perils of which the stolid guide had no idea, I would have pointed them out to him—I would have, as it were, made him see and feel. Between us, we might have convinced the obstinate Professor. If the worst had come to the worst, we could have compelled him to return to the summit of Sneffels.

I quietly approached Hans. I caught his hand in mine. He never moved a muscle. I indicated to him the road to the top of the crater. He remained motionless. My panting form, my haggard countenance, must have indicated the extent of my sufferings. The Icelander gently shook his head and pointed to my uncle.

"Master," he said.

The word is Icelandic as well as English.

"The master!" I cried, beside myself with fury—"madman! no—I tell you he is not the master of our lives; we must fly! we must drag him with us! do you hear me? Do you understand me, I say?"

I have already explained that I held Hans by the arm. I tried to make him rise from his seat. I struggled with him and tried to force him away. My uncle now interposed.

"My good Henry, be calm," he said. "You will obtain nothing from my devoted follower; therefore, listen to what I have to say."

I folded my arms, as well as I could, and looked my uncle full in the face.

"This wretched want of water," he said, "is the sole obstacle to the success of my project. In the entire gallery, made of lava, schist, and coal, it is true we found not one liquid molecule. It is quite possible that we may be more fortunate in the western tunnel."

My sole reply was to shake my head with an air of deep incredulity.

"Listen to me to the end," said the Professor in his well-known lecturing voice. "While you lay yonder without life or motion, I undertook a reconnoitering journey into the conformation of this other gallery. I have discovered that it goes directly downwards into the bowels of the earth, and in a few hours will take us to the old granitic formation. In this we shall undoubtedly find innumerable springs. The nature of the rock makes this a mathematical certainty, and instinct agrees with logic to say that it is so. Now, this is the serious proposition which I have to make to you. When Christopher Columbus asked of his men three days to discover the land of promise, his men ill, terrified, and hopeless, yet gave him three days—and the New World was discovered. Now I, the Christopher Columbus of this subterranean region, only ask of you one more day. If, when that time is expired, I have not found the water of which we are in search, I swear to you, I will give up my mighty enterprise and return to the earth's surface."

Despite my irritation and despair, I knew how much it cost my uncle to make this proposition, and to hold such conciliatory language. Under the circumstances, what could I do but yield?

"Well," I cried, "let it be as you wish, and may heaven reward your superhuman energy. But as, unless we discover water, our hours are numbered, let us lose no time, but go ahead."

Chapter 19

THE WESTERN GALLERY—A NEW ROUTE

Our descent was now resumed by means of the second gallery. Hans took up his post in front as usual. We had not gone more than a hundred yards when the Professor carefully examined the walls.

"This is the primitive formation—we are on the right road—onwards is our hope!"

When the whole earth got cool in the first hours of the world's morning, the diminution of the volume of the earth produced a state of dislocation in its upper crust, followed by ruptures, crevasses and fissures. The passage was a fissure of this kind, through which, ages ago, had flowed the eruptive granite. The thousand windings and turnings formed an inextricable labyrinth through the ancient soil.

As we descended, successions of layers composing the primitive soil appeared with the utmost fidelity of detail. Geological science considers this primitive soil as the base of the mineral crust, and it has recognized that it is composed of three different strata or layers, all resting on the immovable rock known as granite.

No mineralogists had even found themselves placed in such a marvelous position to study nature in all her real and naked beauty. The sounding rod, a mere machine, could not bring to the surface of the earth the objects of value for the study of its internal structure, which we were about to see with our own eyes, to touch with our own hands.

Remember that I am writing this after the journey.

Across the streak of the rocks, colored by beautiful green tints, wound metallic threads of copper, of manganese, with traces of platinum and gold. I could not help gazing at these riches buried in the entrails of Mother Earth, and of which no man would have the enjoyment to the end of time! These treasures—mighty and inexhaustible, were buried in the morning of the earth's history, at such awful depths, that no crowbar or pickax will ever drag them from their tomb!

The light of our Ruhmkorff's coil, increased tenfold by the myriad of prismatic masses of rock, sent its jets of fire in every direction, and I could fancy myself traveling through a huge hollow diamond, the rays of which produced myriads of extraordinary effects.

Towards six o'clock, this festival of light began sensibly and visibly to decrease, and soon almost ceased. The sides of the gallery assumed a crystallized tint, with a somber hue; white mica began to commingle more freely with feldspar and quartz, to form what may be called the true rock—the stone which is hard above all, that supports, without being crushed, the four stories of the earth's soil.

We were walled by an immense prison of granite!

It was now eight o'clock, and still there was no sign of water. The sufferings I endured were horrible. My uncle now kept at the head of our little column. Nothing could induce him to stop. I, meanwhile, had but one real thought. My ear was keenly on the watch to catch the sound of a spring. But no pleasant sound of falling water fell upon my listening ear.

But at last the time came when my limbs refused to carry me longer. I contended heroically against the terrible tortures

I endured, because I did not wish to compel my uncle to halt. To him I knew this would be the last fatal stroke.

Suddenly I felt a deadly faintness come over me. My eyes could no longer see; my knees shook. I gave one despairing cry—and fell!

"Help, help, I am dying!"

My uncle turned and slowly retraced his steps. He looked at me with folded arms, and then allowed one sentence to escape, in hollow accents, from his lips:

"All is over."

The last thing I saw was a face fearfully distorted with pain and sorrow; and then my eyes closed.

When I again opened them, I saw my companions lying near me, motionless, wrapped in their huge traveling rugs. Were they asleep or dead? For myself, sleep was wholly out of the question. My fainting fit over, I was wakeful as the lark. I suffered too much for sleep to visit my eyelids—the more, that I thought myself sick unto death—dying. The last words spoken by my uncle seemed to be buzzing in my ears—all is over! And it was probable that he was right. In the state of prostration to which I was reduced, it was madness to think of ever again seeing the light of day.

Above were miles upon miles of the earth's crust. As I thought of it, I could fancy the whole weight resting on my shoulders. I was crushed, annihilated! and exhausted myself in vain attempts to turn in my granite bed.

Hours upon hours passed away. A profound and terrible silence reigned around us—a silence of the tomb. Nothing could make itself heard through these gigantic walls of granite. The very thought was stupendous.

Presently, despite my apathy, despite the kind of deadly calm into which I was cast, something aroused me. It was a slight but peculiar noise. While I was watching intently, I observed that the tunnel was becoming dark. Then gazing through the dim light that remained, I thought I saw the Icelander taking his departure, lamp in handWhy had he acted thus? Did Hans the guide mean to abandon us? My uncle lay fast asleep—or dead. I tried to cry out, and arouse him. My voice, feebly issuing from my parched and fevered lips, found no echo in that fearful place. My throat was dry, my tongue stuck to the roof of my mouth. The obscurity had by this time become intense, and at last even the faint sound of the guide's footsteps was lost in the blank distance. My soul seemed filled with anguish, and death appeared welcome, only let it come quickly.

"Hans is leaving us," I cried. "Hans—Hans, if you are a man, come back."

These words were spoken to myself. They could not be heard aloud. Nevertheless, after the first few moments of terror were over, I was ashamed of my suspicions against a man who hitherto had behaved so admirably. Nothing in his conduct or character justified suspicion. Moreover, a moment's reflection reassured me. His departure could not be a flight. Instead of ascending the gallery, he was going deeper down into the gulf. Had he had any bad design, his way would have been upwards.

This reasoning calmed me a little and I began to hope!

The good, and peaceful, and imperturbable Hans would certainly not have arisen from his sleep without some serious and grave motive. Was he bent on a voyage of discovery? During the deep, still silence of the night had he at last heard that sweet murmur about which we were all so anxious?

Chapter 20

WATER, WHERE IS IT? A BITTER DISAPPOINTMENT

During a long, long, weary hour, there crossed my wildly delirious brain all sorts of reasons as to what could have aroused our quiet and faithful guide. The most absurd and ridiculous ideas passed through my head, each more impossible than the other. I believe I was either half or wholly mad.

Suddenly, however, there arose, as it were from the depths of the earth, a voice of comfort. It was the sound of footsteps! Hans was returning.

Presently the uncertain light began to shine upon the walls of the passage, and then it came in view far down the sloping tunnel. At length Hans himself appeared.

He approached my uncle, placed his hand upon his shoulder, and gently awakened him. My uncle, as soon as he saw who it was, instantly arose.

"Well!" exclaimed the Professor.

"Vatten," said the hunter.

I did not know a single word of the Danish language, and yet by a sort of mysterious instinct I understood what the guide had said.

"Water, water!" I cried, in a wild and frantic tone, clapping my hands, and gesticulating like a madman.

"Water!" murmured my uncle, in a voice of deep emotion and gratitude. "Hvar?" ("Where?")

"Nedat." ("Below.")

"Where? below!" I understood every word. I had caught the hunter by the hands, and I shook them heartily, while he looked on with perfect calmness.

The preparations for our departure did not take long, and we were soon making a rapid descent into the tunnel.

An hour later we had advanced a thousand yards, and descended two thousand feet.

At this moment I heard an accustomed and well-known sound running along the floors of the granite rock—a kind of dull and sullen roar, like that of a distant waterfall.

During the first half hour of our advance, not finding the discovered spring, my feelings of intense suffering appeared to return. Once more I began to lose all hope. My uncle, however, observing how downhearted I was again becoming, took up the conversation.

"Hans was right," he exclaimed enthusiastically; "that is the dull roaring of a torrent."

"A torrent," I cried, delighted at even hearing the welcome words.

"There's not the slightest doubt about it," he replied, "a subterranean river is flowing beside us."

I made no reply, but hastened on, once more animated by hope. I began not even to feel the deep fatigue which hitherto had overpowered me. The very sound of this glorious murmuring water already refreshed me. We could hear it increasing in volume every moment. The torrent, which for a long time could be heard flowing over our heads, now ran distinctly along the left wall, roaring, rushing, spluttering, and still falling.

Several times I passed my hand across the rock hoping to

find some trace of humidity—of the slightest percolation. Alas! in vain.

Again a half hour passed in the same weary toil. Again we advanced.

It now became evident that the hunter, during his absence, had not been able to carry his researches any farther. Guided by an instinct peculiar to the dwellers in mountain regions and water finders, he "smelt" the living spring through the rock. Still he had not seen the precious liquid. He had neither quenched his own thirst, nor brought us one drop in his gourd.

Moreover, we soon made the disastrous discovery that, if our progress continued, we should soon be moving away from the torrent, the sound of which gradually diminished. We turned back. Hans halted at the precise spot where the sound of the torrent appeared nearest.

I could bear the suspense and suffering no longer, and seated myself against the wall, behind which I could hear the water seething and effervescing not two feet away. But a solid wall of granite still separated us from it!

Hans looked keenly at me, and, strange enough, for once I thought I saw a smile on his imperturbable face.

He rose from a stone on which he had been seated, and took up the lamp. I could not help rising and following. He moved slowly along the firm and solid granite wall. I watched him with mingled curiosity and eagerness. Presently he halted and placed his ear against the dry stone, moving slowly along and listening with the most extreme care and attention. I understood at once that he was searching for the exact spot where the torrent's roar was most plainly heard. This point he soon found in the lateral wall on the left side, about three feet above the level of the tunnel floor.

I was in a state of intense excitement. I scarcely dared believe what the eider-duck hunter was about to do. It was, however, impossible in a moment more not to both understand and applaud, and even to smother him in my embraces, when I saw him raise the heavy crowbar and commence an attack upon the rock itself.

"Saved!" I cried.

"Yes," cried my uncle, even more excited and delighted than myself; "Hans is quite right. Oh, the worthy, excellent man! We should never have thought of such an idea."

And nobody else, I think, would have done so. Such a process, simple as it seemed, would most certainly not have entered our heads. Nothing could be more dangerous than to begin to work with pickaxes in that particular part of the globe. Supposing while he was at work a break-up were to take place, and supposing the torrent once having gained an inch were to take an ell, and come pouring bodily through the broken rock!

Not one of these dangers was chimerical. They were only too real. But at that moment no fear of falling in of the roof, or even of inundation was capable of stopping us. Our thirst was so intense that to quench it we would have dug below the bed of old Ocean itself.

Hans went quietly to work—a work which neither my uncle nor I would have undertaken at any price. Our impatience was so great that if we had once begun with pickax and crowbar, the rock would soon have split into a hundred fragments. The guide, on the contrary, calm, ready, moderate, wore away the hard rock by little steady blows of his instrument, making no attempt at a larger hole than about six inches. As I stood, I heard, or I thought I heard, the roar of the torrent momentarily increasing in loudness, and at times I almost felt the pleasant sensation of water upon my parched lips.

At the end of what appeared an age, Hans had made a hole which enabled his crowbar to enter two feet into the solid rock. He had been at work exactly an hour. It appeared a dozen. I was getting wild with impatience. My uncle began to think of using more violent measures. I had the greatest difficulty in checking him. He had indeed just got hold of his crowbar when a loud and welcome hiss was heard. Then a stream, or rather jet, of water burst through the wall and came out with such force as to hit the opposite side!

Hans, the guide, who was half upset by the shock, was scarcely able to keep down a cry of pain and grief. I understood his meaning when, plunging my hands into the sparkling jet, I myself gave a wild and frantic cry. The water was scalding hot!

"Boiling," I cried, in bitter disappointment.

"Well, never mind," said my uncle, "it will soon get cool."

The tunnel began to be filled by clouds of vapor, while a small stream ran away into the interior of the earth. In a short time we had some sufficiently cool to drink. We swallowed it in huge mouthfuls.

Oh! what exalted delight—what rich and incomparable luxury! What was this water, whence did it come? To us what was that? The simple fact was—it was water; and, though still with a tingle of warmth about it, it brought back to the heart, that life which, but for it, must surely have faded away. I drank greedily, almost without tasting it.

When, however, I had almost quenched my ravenous thirst, I made a discovery.

"Why, it is chalybeate water!"

"A most excellent stomachic," replied my uncle, "and highly mineralized. Here is a journey worth twenty to Spa."

"It's very good," I replied.

"I should think so. Water found six miles under ground. There is a peculiarly inky flavor about it, which is by no means disagreeable. Hans may congratulate himself on having made a rare discovery. What do you say, nephew, according to the usual custom of travelers, to name the stream after him?"

"Good," said I. And the name of "Hansbach" ("Hans Brook") was at once agreed upon.

Hans was not a bit more proud after hearing our determination than he was before. After having taken a very small modicum of the welcome refreshment, he had seated himself in a corner with his usual imperturbable gravity.

"Now," said I, "it is not worth while letting this water run to waste."

"What is the use," replied my uncle, "the source from which this river rises is inexhaustible."

"Never mind," I continued, "let us fill our goatskin and gourds, and then try to stop the opening up."

My advice, after some hesitation, was followed or attempted to be followed. Hans picked up all the broken pieces of granite he had knocked out, and using some tow he happened to have about him, tried to shut up the fissure he had made in the wall. All he did was to scald his hands. The pressure was too great, and all our attempts were utter failures.

"It is evident," I remarked, "that the upper surface of these springs is situated at a very great height above—as we may fairly infer from the great pressure of the jet."

"That is by no means doubtful," replied my uncle, "if this column of water is about thirty-two thousand feet high, the atmospheric pressure must be something enormous. But a new idea has just struck me."

"And what is that?"

"Why be at so much trouble to close this aperture?"

"Because—"

I hesitated and stammered, having no real reason.

"When our water bottles are empty, we are not at all sure that we shall be able to fill them," observed my uncle.

"I think that is very probable."

"Well, then, let this water run. It will, of course, naturally follow in our track, and will serve to guide and refresh us."

"I think the idea a good one," I cried in reply, "and with this rivulet as a companion, there is no further reason why we should not succeed in our marvelous project."

"Ah, my boy," said the Professor, laughing, "after all, you are coming round."

"More than that, I am now confident of ultimate success."

"One moment, nephew mine. Let us begin by taking some hours of repose."

I had utterly forgotten that it was night. The chronometer, however, informed me of the fact. Soon we were sufficiently restored and refreshed, and had all fallen into a profound sleep.

Chapter 21

UNDER THE OCEAN

By the next day we had nearly forgotten our past sufferings. The first sensation I experienced was surprise at not being thirsty, and I actually asked myself the reason. The running stream, which flowed in rippling wavelets at my feet, was the satisfactory reply.

We breakfasted with a good appetite, and then drank our fill of the excellent water. I felt myself quite a new man, ready to go anywhere my uncle chose to lead. I began to think. Why should not a man as seriously convinced as my uncle, succeed, with so excellent a guide as worthy Hans, and so devoted a nephew as myself? These were the brilliant ideas which now invaded my brain. Had the proposition now been made to go back to the summit of Mount Sneffels, I should have declined the offer in a most indignant manner.

But fortunately there was no question of going up. We were about to descend farther into the interior of the earth.

"Let us be moving," I cried, awakening the echoes of the old world.

We resumed our march on Thursday at eight o'clock in the morning. The great granite tunnel, as it went round by sinuous and winding ways, presented every now and then sharp turns, and in fact all the appearance of a labyrinth. Its direction, however, was in general towards the southwest. My uncle made several pauses in order to consult his compass.

The gallery now began to trend downwards in a horizontal direction, with about two inches of fall in every furlong. The murmuring stream flowed quietly at our feet. I could not but compare it to some familiar spirit, guiding us through the earth, and I dabbled my fingers in its tepid water, which sang like a naiad as we progressed. My good humor began to assume a mythological character.

As for my uncle he began to complain of the horizontal character of the road. His route, he found, began to be indefinitely prolonged, instead of "sliding down the celestial ray," according to his expression.

But we had no choice; and as long as our road led towards the centre—however little progress we made, there was no reason to complain.

Moreover, from time to time the slopes were much greater, the naiad sang more loudly, and we began to dip downwards in earnest.

As yet, however, I felt no painful sensation. I had not got over the excitement of the discovery of water.

That day and the next we did a considerable amount of horizontal, and relatively very little vertical, traveling.

On Friday evening, the tenth of July, according to our estimation, we ought to have been thirty leagues to the southeast of Reykjavik, and about two leagues and a half deep. We now received a rather startling surprise.

Under our feet there opened a horrible well. My uncle was so delighted that he actually clapped his hands—as he saw how steep and sharp was the descent.

"Ah, ah!" he cried, in rapturous delight; "this take us a long way. Look at the projections of the rock. Hah!" he exclaimed, "it's a fearful staircase!"

Hans, however, who in all our troubles had never given up the ropes, took care so to dispose of them as to prevent any accidents. Our descent then began. I dare not call it a perilous descent, for I was already too familiar with that sort of work to look upon it as anything but a very ordinary affair.

This well was a kind of narrow opening in the massive granite of the kind known as a fissure. The contraction of the terrestrial scaffolding, when it suddenly cooled, had been evidently the cause. If it had ever served in former times as a kind of funnel through which passed the eruptive masses vomited by Sneffels, I was at a loss to explain how it had left no mark. We were, in fact, descending a spiral, something like those winding staircases in use in modern houses.

We were compelled every quarter of an hour or thereabouts to sit down in order to rest our legs. Our calves ached. We then seated ourselves on some projecting rock with our legs hanging over, and gossiped while we ate a mouthful—drinking still from the pleasantly warm running stream which had not deserted us.

It is scarcely necessary to say that in this curiously shaped fissure the Hansbach had become a cascade to the detriment of its size. It was still, however, sufficient, and more, for our wants. Besides we knew that, as soon as the declivity ceased to be so abrupt, the stream must resume its peaceful course. At this moment it reminded me of my uncle, his impatience and rage, while when it flowed more peacefully, I pictured to myself the placidity of the Icelandic guide.

During the whole of two days, the sixth and seventh of July, we followed the extraordinary spiral staircase of the fissure, penetrating two leagues farther into the crust of the earth, which put us five leagues below the level of the sea. On the eighth, however, at twelve o'clock in the day, the fissure suddenly assumed a much more gentle slope still trending in a southeast direction.

The road now became comparatively easy, and at the same time dreadfully monotonous. It would have been difficult for matters to have turned out otherwise. Our peculiar journey had no chance of being diversified by landscape and scenery. At all events, such was my idea.

At length, on Wednesday the fifteenth, we were actually seven leagues (twenty-one miles) below the surface of the earth, and fifty leagues distant from the mountain of Sneffels. Though, if the truth be told, we were very tired, our health had resisted all suffering, and was in a most satisfactory state. Our traveler's box of medicaments had not even been opened.

My uncle was careful to note every hour the indications of the compass, of the manometer, and of the thermometer, all which he afterwards published in his elaborate philosophical and scientific account of our remarkable voyage. He was therefore able to give an exact relation of the situation. When, therefore, he informed me that we were fifty leagues in a horizontal direction distant from our starting point, I could not suppress a loud exclamation.

"What is the matter now?" cried my uncle.

"Nothing very important, only an idea has entered my head," was my reply.

"Well, out with it, My boy."

"It is my opinion that if your calculations are correct we are no longer under Iceland."

"Do you think so?"

"We can very easily find out," I replied, pulling out a map and compasses.

"You see," I said, after careful measurement, "that I am not mistaken. We are far beyond Cape Portland; and those fifty leagues to the southeast will take us into the open sea."

"Under the open sea," cried my uncle, rubbing his hands with a delighted air.

"Yes," I cried, "no doubt old Ocean flows over our heads!"

"Well, my dear boy, what can be more natural! Do you not know that in the neighborhood of Newcastle there are coal mines which have been worked far out under the sea?"

Now my worthy uncle, the Professor, no doubt regarded this discovery as a very simple fact, but to me the idea was by no means a pleasant one. And yet when one came to think the matter over seriously, what mattered it whether the plains and mountains of Iceland were suspended over our devoted heads, or the mighty billows of the Atlantic Ocean? The whole question rested on the solidity of the granite roof above us. However, I soon got used to the ideal for the passage now level, now running down, and still always to the southeast, kept going deeper and deeper into the profound abysses of Mother Earth.

Three days later, on the eighteenth day of July, on a Saturday, we reached a kind of vast grotto. My uncle here paid Hans his usual rix-dollars, and it was decided that the next day should be a day of rest.

Chapter 22

SUNDAY BELOW GROUND

I awoke on Sunday morning without any sense of hurry and bustle attendant on an immediate departure. Though the day to be devoted to repose and reflection was spent under such strange circumstances, and in so wonderful a place, the idea was a pleasant one. Besides, we all began to get used to this kind of existence. I had almost ceased to think of the sun, of the moon, of the stars, of the trees, houses, and towns; in fact, about any terrestrial necessities. In our peculiar position we were far above such reflections.

The grotto was a vast and magnificent hall. Along its granitic soil the stream flowed placidly and pleasantly. So great a distance was it now from its fiery source that its water was scarcely lukewarm, and could be drunk without delay or difficulty. After a frugal breakfast, the Professor made up his mind to devote some hours to putting his notes and calculations in order.

"In the first place," he said, "I have a good many to verify and prove, in order that we may know our exact position. I wish to be able on our return to the upper regions to make a map of our journey, a kind of vertical section of the globe, which will be, as it were, the profile of the expedition."

"That would indeed be a curious work, Uncle; but can you make your observations with anything like certainty and precision?"

"I can. I have never on any occasion failed to note with great care the angles and slopes. I am certain as to having made no mistake. Take the compass and examine how she points."

I looked at the instrument with care.

"East one quarter southeast."

"Very good," resumed the Professor, noting the observation, and going through some rapid calculations. "I make out that we have journeyed two hundred and fifty miles from the point of our departure."

"Then the mighty waves of the Atlantic are rolling over our heads?"

"Certainly."

"And at this very moment it is possible that fierce tempests are raging above, and that men and ships are battling against the angry blasts just over our heads?"

"It is quite within the range of possibility," rejoined my uncle, smiling.

"And that whales are playing in shoals, thrashing the bottom of the sea, the roof of our adamantine prison?"

"Be quite at rest on that point; there is no danger of their breaking through. But to return to our calculations. We are to the southeast, two hundred and fifty miles from the base of Sneffels, and, according to my preceding notes, I think we have gone sixteen leagues in a downward direction."

"Sixteen leagues—fifty miles!" I cried.

"I am sure of it."

"But that is the extreme limit allowed by science for the thickness of the earth's crust," I replied, referring to my geological studies.

"I do not contravene that assertion," was his quiet answer.

"And at this stage of our journey, according to all known laws on the increase of heat, there should be here a temperature of *fifteen hundred degrees of Reaumur*."

"There should be—you say, my boy."

"In which case this granite would not exist, but be in a state of fusion."

"But you perceive, my boy, that it is not so, and that facts, as usual, are very stubborn things, overruling all theories."

"I am forced to yield to the evidence of my senses, but I am nevertheless very much surprised."

"What heat does the thermometer really indicate?" continued the philosopher.

"Twenty-seven six-tenths."

"So that science is wrong by fourteen hundred and seventy-four degrees and four-tenths. According to which, it is demonstrated that the proportional increase in temperature is an exploded error. Humphry Davy here shines forth in all his glory. He is right, and I have acted wisely to believe him. Have you any answer to make to this statement?"

Had I chosen to have spoken, I might have said a great deal. I in no way admitted the theory of Humphry Davy—I still held out for the theory of proportional increase of heat, though I did not feel it.

I was far more willing to allow that this chimney of an extinct volcano was covered by lava of a kind refractory to heat—in fact a bad conductor—which did not allow the great increase of temperature to percolate through its sides. The hot water jet supported my view of the matter.

But without entering on a long and useless discussion, or seeking for new arguments to controvert my uncle, I contented myself with taking up facts as they were.

"Well, sir, I take for granted that all your calculations are correct, but allow me to draw from them a rigorous and definite conclusion."

"Go on, my boy—have your say," cried my uncle goodhumoredly.

"At the place where we now are, under the latitude of Iceland, the terrestrial depth is about fifteen hundred and eighty-three leagues."

"Fifteen hundred eighty-three and a quarter."

"Well, suppose we say sixteen hundred in round numbers. Now, out of a voyage of sixteen hundred leagues we have completed sixteen."

"As you say, what then?"

"At the expense of a diagonal journey of no less than eighty-five leagues."

"Exactly."

"We have been twenty days about it."

"Exactly twenty days."

"Now sixteen is the hundredth part of our contemplated expedition. If we go on in this way we shall be two thousand days, that is about five years and a half, going down."

The Professor folded his arms, listened, but did not speak.

"Without counting that if a vertical descent of sixteen leagues costs us a horizontal of eighty-five, we shall have to go about eight thousand leagues to the southeast, and we must therefore come out somewhere in the circumference long before we can hope to reach the centre."

"Bother your calculations," cried my uncle in one of his old rages. "On what basis do they rest? How do you know that this passage does not take us direct to the end we require? Moreover, I have in my favor, fortunately, a precedent. What I have undertaken to do, another has done, and he having succeeded, why should I not be equally successful?"

"I hope, indeed, you will, but still, I suppose I may be allowed to—"

"You are allowed to hold your tongue," cried Professor Hardwigg, "when you talk so unreasonably as this."

I saw at once that the old doctorial Professor was still alive in my uncle—and fearful to rouse his angry passions, I dropped the unpleasant subject.

"Now, then," he explained, "consult the manometer. What does that indicate?"

"A considerable amount of pressure."

"Very good. You see, then, that by descending slowly, and by gradually accustoming ourselves to the density of this lower atmosphere, we shall not suffer."

"Well, I suppose not, except it may be a certain amount of pain in the ears," was my rather grim reply.

"That, my dear boy, is nothing, and you will easily get rid of that source of discomfort by bringing the exterior air in communication with the air contained in your lungs."

"Perfectly," said I, for I had quite made up my mind in no wise to contradict my uncle. "I should fancy almost that I should experience a certain amount of satisfaction in making a plunge into this dense atmosphere. Have you taken note of how wonderfully sound is propagated?"

"Of course I have. There can be no doubt that a journey into the interior of the earth would be an excellent cure for deafness."

"But then, Uncle," I ventured mildly to observe, "this density will continue to increase."

"Yes—according to a law which, however, is scarcely defined. It is true that the intensity of weight will diminish just in proportion to the depth to which we go. You know very well that it is on the surface of the earth that its action is most powerfully felt, while on the contrary, in the very centre of the earth bodies cease to have any weight at all."

"I know that is the case, but as we progress will not the atmosphere finally assume the density of water?"

"I know it; when placed under the pressure of seven hundred

and ten atmospheres," cried my uncle with imperturbable gravity.

"And when we are still lower down?" I asked with natural anxiety.

"Well, lower down, the density will become even greater."

"Then how shall we be able to make our way through this atmospheric fog?"

"Well, my worthy nephew, we must ballast ourselves by filling our pockets with stones," said Professor Hardwigg.

"Faith, Uncle, you have an answer for everything," was my only reply.

I began to feel that it was unwise of me to go any farther into the wide field of hypotheses for I should certainly have revived some difficulty, or rather impossibility, that would have enraged the Professor.

It was evident, nevertheless, that the air under a pressure which might be multiplied by thousands of atmospheres, would end by becoming perfectly solid, and that then admitting our bodies resisted the pressure, we should have to stop, in spite of all the reasonings in the world. Facts overcome all arguments.

But I thought it best not to urge this argument. My uncle would simply have quoted the example of Saknussemm. Supposing the learned Icelander's journey ever really to have taken place—there was one simple answer to be made:

In the sixteenth century neither the barometer nor the manometer had been invented—how, then, could Saknussemm have been able to discover when he did reach the centre of the earth?

This unanswerable and learned objection I, however, kept to myself and, bracing up my courage, awaited the course of events—little aware of how adventurous yet were to be the incidents of our remarkable journey.

The rest of this day of leisure and repose was spent in calculation and conversation. I made it a point to agree with the Professor in everything; but I envied the perfect indifference of Hans, who, without taking any such trouble about the cause and effect, went blindly onwards wherever destiny chose to lead him.

Chapter 23

ALONE

It must in all truth be confessed, things as yet had gone on well, and I should have acted in bad taste to have complained. If the true medium of our difficulties did not increase, it was within the range of possibility that we might ultimately reach the end of our journey. Then what glory would be ours! I began in the newly aroused ardor of my soul to speak enthusiastically to the Professor. Well, was I serious? The whole state in which we existed was a mystery—and it was impossible to know whether or not I was in earnest.

For several days after our memorable halt, the slopes became more rapid—some were even of a most frightful character—almost vertical, so that we were forever going down into the solid interior mass. During some days, we actually descended a league and a half, even two leagues towards the centre of the earth. The descents were sufficiently perilous, and while we were engaged in them we learned fully to appreciate the marvelous coolness of our guide, Hans. Without him we should have been wholly lost. The grave and impassible Icelander devoted himself to us with the most incomprehensible sang-froid and ease; and, thanks to him, many a dangerous pass was got over, where, but for him, we should inevitably have stuck fast.

His silence increased every day. I think that we began to be influenced by this peculiar trait in his character. It is certain that the inanimate objects by which you are surrounded have a direct action on the brain. It must be that a man who shuts himself up between four walls must lose the faculty of associating ideas and words. How many persons condemned to the horrors of solitary confinement have gone mad—simply because the thinking faculties have lain dormant!

During the two weeks that followed our last interesting conversation, there occurred nothing worthy of being especially recorded.

I have, while writing these memoirs, taxed my memory in vain for one incident of travel during this particular period.

But the next event to be related is terrible indeed. Its very memory, even now, makes my soul shudder, and my blood run cold.

It was on the seventh of August. Our constant and successive descents had taken us quite thirty leagues into the interior of the earth, that is to say that there were above us thirty leagues, nearly a hundred miles, of rocks, and oceans, and continents, and towns, to say nothing of living inhabitants. We were in a southeasterly direction, about two hundred leagues from Iceland.

On that memorable day the tunnel had begun to assume an almost horizontal course.

I was on this occasion walking on in front. My uncle had charge of one of the Ruhmkorff coils, I had possession of the other. By means of its light I was busy examining the different layers of granite. I was completely absorbed in my work.

Suddenly halting and turning round, I found that I was alone!

"Well," thought I to myself, "I have certainly been walking too fast—or else Hans and my uncle have stopped to rest. The best thing I can do is to go back and find them. Luckily, there is very little ascent to tire me."

I accordingly retraced my steps and, while doing so, walked for at least a quarter of an hour. Rather uneasy, I paused and looked eagerly around. Not a living soul. I called aloud. No reply. My voice was lost amid the myriad cavernous echoes it aroused!

I began for the first time to feel seriously uneasy. A cold shiver shook my whole body, and perspiration, chill and terrible, burst upon my skin.

"I must be calm," I said, speaking aloud, as boys whistle to drive away fear. "There can be no doubt that I shall find my companions. There cannot be two roads. It is certain that I was considerably ahead; all I have to do is to go back."

Having come to this determination I ascended the tunnel for at least half an hour, unable to decide if I had ever seen certain landmarks before. Every now and then I paused to discover if any loud appeal was made to me, well knowing that in that dense and intensified atmosphere I should hear it a long way off. But no. The most extraordinary silence reigned in this immense gallery. Only the echoes of my own footsteps could be heard.

At last I stopped. I could scarcely realize the fact of my isolation. I was quite willing to think that I had made a mistake, but not that I was lost. If I had made a mistake, I might find my way; if lost—I shuddered to think of it.

"Come, come," said I to myself, "since there is only one road, and they must come by it, we shall at last meet. All I have to do is still to go upwards. Perhaps, however, not seeing me, and forgetting I was ahead, they may have gone back in search of me. Still, even in this case, if I make haste, I shall get up to them. There can be no doubt about the matter."

But as I spoke these last words aloud, it would have been quite clear to any listener—had there been one—that I was by no means convinced of the fact. Moreover in order to associate together these simple ideas and to reunite them under the form of reasoning, required some time. I could not all at once bring my brain to think.

Then another dread doubt fell upon my soul. After all, was I ahead? Of course I was. Hans was no doubt following behind preceded by my uncle. I perfectly recollected his having stopped for a moment to strap his baggage on his shoulder. I now remembered this trifling detail. It was, I believe, just at that very moment that I had determined to continue My route.

"Again," thought I, reasoning as calmly as was possible, "there is another sure means of not losing my way, a thread to guide me through the labyrinthine subterraneous retreat—one which I had forgotten—my faithful river."

This course of reasoning roused my drooping spirits, and I resolved to resume my journey without further delay. No time was to be lost.

It was at this moment that I had reason to bless the thoughtfulness of my uncle, when he refused to allow the eider hunter to close the orifices of the hot spring—that small fissure in the great mass of granite. This beneficent spring after having saved us from thirst during so many days would now enable me to regain the right road.

Having come to this mental decision, I made up my mind, before I started upwards, that ablution would certainly do me a great deal of good.

I stopped to plunge my hands and forehead in the pleasant water of the Hansbach stream, blessing its presence as a certain consolation.

Conceive my horror and stupefaction!—I was treading a hard, dusty, shingly road of granite. The stream on which I reckoned had wholly disappeared!

Chapter 24

LOST!

No words in any human language can depict my utter despair. I was literally buried alive; with no other expectation before me but to die in all the slow horrible torture of hunger and thirst.

Mechanically I crawled about, feeling the dry and arid rock. Never to my fancy had I ever felt anything so dry.

But, I frantically asked myself, how had I lost the course of the flowing stream? There could be no doubt it had ceased to flow in the gallery in which I now was. Now I began to understand the cause of the strange silence which prevailed when last I tried if any appeal from my companions might perchance reach my ear.

It so happened that when I first took an imprudent step in the wrong direction, I did not perceive the absence of the all-important stream.

It was now quite evident that when we halted, another tunnel must have received the waters of the little torrent, and that I had unconsciously entered a different gallery. To what unknown depths had my companions gone? Where was I?

How to get back! Clue or landmark there was absolutely none! My feet left no signs on the granite and shingle. My brain throbbed with agony as I tried to discover the solution of this terrible problem. My situation, after all sophistry and reflection, had finally to be summed up in three awful words—

Lost! Lost!! LOST!!!

Lost at a depth which, to my finite understanding, appeared to be immeasurable.

These thirty leagues of the crust of the earth weighed upon my shoulders like the globe on the shoulders of Atlas. I felt myself crushed by the awful weight. It was indeed a position to drive the sanest man to madness!

I tried to bring my thoughts back to the things of the world so long forgotten. It was with the greatest difficulty that I succeeded in doing so. Hamburg, the house on the Konigstrasse, my dear cousin Gretchen—all that world which had before vanished like a shadow floated before my now vivid imagination.

There they were before me, but how unreal. Under the influence of a terrible hallucination I saw all the incidents of our journey pass before me like the scenes of a panorama. The ship and its inmates, Iceland, M. Fridriksson, and the great summit of Mount Sneffels! I said to myself that, if in my position I retained the most faint and shadowy outline of a hope, it would be a sure sign of approaching delirium. It were better to give way wholly to despair!

In fact, did I but reason with calmness and philosophy, what human power was there in existence able to take me back to the surface of the earth, and ready, too, to split asunder, to rend in twain those huge and mighty vaults which stand above my head? Who could enable me to find my road—and regain my companions?

Insensate folly and madness to entertain even a shadow of hope!

"Oh, Uncle!" was my despairing cry.

This was the only word of reproach which came to my lips; for I thoroughly understood how deeply and sorrowfully the worthy Professor would regret my loss, and how in his turn he would patiently seek for me.

When I at last began to resign myself to the fact that no further aid was to be expected from man, and knowing that I was utterly powerless to do anything for my own salvation, I kneeled with earnest fervor and asked assistance from Heaven. The remembrance of my innocent childhood, the memory of my mother, known only in my infancy, came welling forth from my heart. I had recourse to prayer. And little as I had a right to be remembered by Him whom I had forgotten in the hour of prosperity, and whom I so tardily invoked, I prayed earnestly and sincerely.

This renewal of my youthful faith brought about a much greater amount of calm, and I was enabled to concentrate all my strength and intelligence on the terrible realities of my unprecedented situation.

I had about me that which I had at first wholly forgotten—three days' provisions. Moreover, my water bottle was quite full. Nevertheless, the one thing which it was impossible to do was to remain alone. Try to find my companions I must, at any price. But which course should I take? Should I go upwards, or again descend? Doubtless it was right to retrace my steps in an upward direction.

By doing this with care and coolness, I must reach the point where I had turned away from the rippling stream. I must find the fatal bifurcation or fork. Once at this spot, once the river at my feet, I could, at all events, regain the awful crater of Mount Sneffels. Why had I not thought of this before? This, at last, was a reasonable hope of safety. The most important thing, then, to be done was to discover the bed of the Hansbach.

After a slight meal and a draught of water, I rose like a giant refreshed. Leaning heavily on my pole, I began the ascent of the gallery. The slope was very rapid and rather difficult.

But I advanced hopefully and carefully, like a man who at last is making his way out of a forest, and knows there is only one road to followDuring one whole hour nothing happened to check my progress. As I advanced, I tried to recollect the shape of the tunnel—to recall to my memory certain projections of rocks—to persuade myself that I had followed certain winding routes before. But no one particular sign could I bring to mind, and I was soon forced to allow that this gallery would never take me back to the point at which I had separated myself from my companions. It was absolutely without issue—a mere blind alley in the earth.

The moment at length came when, facing the solid rock, I knew my fate, and fell inanimate on the arid floor!

To describe the horrible state of despair and fear into which I then fell would now be vain and impossible. My last hope, the courage which had sustained me, drooped before the sight of this pitiless granite rock!

Lost in a vast labyrinth, the sinuosities of which spread in every direction, without guide, clue or compass, I knew it was a vain and useless task to attempt flight. All that remained to me was to lie down and die. To lie down and die the most cruel and horrible of deaths!

In my state of mind, the idea came into my head that one day perhaps, when my fossil bones were found, their discovery so far below the level of the earth might give rise to solemn and interesting scientific discussions.

I tried to cry aloud, but hoarse, hollow, and inarticulate sounds alone could make themselves heard through my parched lips. I literally panted for breath.

In the midst of all these horrible sources of anguish and despair, a new horror took possession of my soul. My lamp, by falling down, had got out of order. I had no means of repairing it. Its light was already becoming paler and paler, and soon would expire.

With a strange sense of resignation and despair, I watched the luminous current in the coil getting less and less. A procession of shadows moved flashing along the granite wall. I scarcely dared to lower my eyelids, fearing to lose the last spark of this fugitive light. Every instant it seemed to me that it was about to vanish and to leave me forever—in utter darkness!

At last, one final trembling flame remained in the lamp; I followed it with all my power of vision; I gasped for breath; I concentrated upon it all the power of my soul, as upon the last scintillation of light I was ever destined to see: and then I was to be lost forever in Cimmerian and tenebrous shades.

A wild and plaintive cry escaped my lips. On earth during the most profound and comparatively complete darkness, light never allows a complete destruction and extinction of its power. Light is so diffuse, so subtle, that it permeates everywhere, and whatever little may remain, the retina of the eye will succeed in finding it. In this place nothing—the absolute obscurity made me blind in every sense.

My head was now wholly lost. I raised my arms, trying the effects of the feeling in getting against the cold stone wall. It was painful in the extreme. Madness must have taken possession of me. I knew not what I did. I began to run, to fly, rushing at haphazard in this inextricable labyrinth, always going downwards, running wildly underneath the terrestrial crust, like an inhabitant of the subterranean furnaces, screaming, roaring, howling, until bruised by the pointed rocks, falling and picking myself up all covered with blood, seeking madly to drink the blood which dripped from my torn features, mad because this blood only trickled over my face, and watching always for this horrid wall which ever presented to me the fearful obstacle against which I could not dash my head.

Where was I going? It was impossible to say. I was perfectly ignorant of the matter.

Several hours passed in this way. After a long time, having utterly exhausted my strength, I fell a heavy inert mass along the side of the tunnel, and lost consciousness.

Chapter 25

THE WHISPERING GALLERY

When at last I came back to a sense of life and being, my face was wet, but wet, as I soon knew, with tears. How long this state of insensibility lasted, it is quite impossible for me now to say. I had no means left to me of taking any account of time. Never since the creation of the world had such a solitude as mine existed. I was completely abandoned.

After my fall I lost much blood. I felt myself flooded with the life-giving liquid. My first sensation was perhaps a natural one. Why was I not dead? Because I was alive, there was something left to do. I tried to make up my mind to think no longer. As far as I was able, I drove away all ideas, and utterly overcome by pain and grief, I crouched against the granite wall.

I just commenced to feel the fainting coming on again, and the sensation that this was the last struggle before complete annihilation—when, on a sudden, a violent uproar reached my ears. It had some resemblance to the prolonged rumbling voice of thunder, and I clearly distinguished sonorous voices, lost one after the other, in the distant depths of the gulf.

Whence came this noise? Naturally, it was to be supposed from new phenomena which were taking place in the bosom of the solid mass of Mother Earth! The explosion of some gaseous vapors, or the fall of some solid, of the granitic or other rock.

Again I listened with deep attention. I was extremely anxious to hear if this strange and inexplicable sound was likely to be renewed! A whole quarter of an hour elapsed in painful expectation. Deep and solemn silence reigned in the tunnel. So still that I could hear the beatings of my own heart! I waited, waited with a strange kind of hopefulness.

Suddenly my ear, which leaned accidentally against the wall, appeared to catch, as it were, the faintest echo of a sound. I thought that I heard vague, incoherent and distant voices. I quivered all over with excitement and hope!

"It must be hallucination," I cried. "It cannot be! it is not true!"

But no! By listening more attentively, I really did convince myself that what I heard was truly the sound of human voices. To make any meaning out of the sound, however, was beyond my power. I was too weak even to hear distinctly. Still it was a positive fact that someone was speaking. Of that I was quite certain.

There was a moment of fear. A dread fell upon my soul that it might be my own words brought back to me by a distant echo. Perhaps without knowing it, I might have been crying aloud. I resolutely closed my lips, and once more placed my ear to the huge granite wall.

Yes, for certain. It was in truth the sound of human voices.

I now by the exercise of great determination dragged myself along the sides of the cavern, until I reached a point where I could hear more distinctly. But though I could detect the sound, I could only make out uncertain, strange, and incomprehensible words. They reached my ear as if they had been spoken in a low tone—murmured, as it were, afar off.

At last, I made out the word forlorad repeated several times in a tone betokening great mental anguish and sorrow.

What could this word mean, and who was speaking it? It must be either my uncle or the guide Hans! If, therefore, I could hear them, they must surely be able to hear me.

"Help," I cried at the top of my voice; "help, I am dying!"

I then listened with scarcely a breath; I panted for the slightest sound in the darkness—a cry, a sigh, a question! But silence reigned supreme. No answer came! In this way some minutes passed. A whole flood of ideas flashed through my mind. I began to fear that my voice, weakened by sickness and suffering, could not reach my companions who were in search of me.

"It must be they," I cried; "who else could by any possibility be buried a hundred miles below the level of the earth?" The mere supposition was preposterous.

I began, therefore, to listen again with the most breathless attention. As I moved my ears along the side of the place I was in, I found a mathematical point as it were, where the voices appeared to attain their maximum of intensity. The word forlorad again distinctly reached my ear. Then came again that rolling noise like thunder which had awakened me out of torpor.

"I begin to understand," I said to myself after some little time devoted to reflection; "it is not through the solid mass that the sound reaches my ears. The walls of my cavernous retreat are of solid granite, and the most fearful explosion would not make uproar enough to penetrate them. The sound must come along the gallery itself. The place I was in must possess some peculiar acoustic properties of its own."

Again I listened; and this time—yes, this time—I heard my name distinctly pronounced: cast as it were into space.

It was my uncle, the Professor, who was speaking. He was in conversation with the guide, and the word which had so often reached my ears, forlorad, was a Danish expression.

Then I understood it all. In order to make myself heard, I too must speak as it were along the side of the gallery, which would carry the sound of my voice just as the wire carries the electric fluid from point to point.

But there was no time to lose. If my companions were only to remove a few feet from where they stood, the acoustic effect would be over, my Whispering Gallery would be destroyed. I again therefore crawled towards the wall, and said as clearly and distinctly as I could:

"Uncle Hardwigg."

I then awaited a reply.

Sound does not possess the property of traveling with such extreme rapidity. Besides the density of the air at that depth from light and motion was very far from adding to the rapidity of circulation. Several seconds elapsed, which to my excited imagination, appeared ages; and these words reached my eager ears, and moved my wildly beating heart:

"Harry, my boy, is that you?"

A short delay between question and answer.

"Yes—yes."

....

"Where are you?"

....

"Lost!"

....

"And your lamp?"

....

"Out."

....

"But the guiding stream?"

....

"Is lost!"

....

"Keep your courage, Harry. We will do our best."

....

"One moment, my uncle," I cried; "I have no longer strength to answer your questions. But—for heaven's sake—do you—continue—to speak—to me!" Absolute silence, I felt, would be annihilation.

"Keep up your courage," said my uncle. "As you are so weak, do not speak. We have been searching for you in all directions, both by going upwards and downwards in the gallery. My dear boy, I had begun to give over all hope—and you can never know what bitter tears of sorrow and regret I have shed. At last, supposing you to be still on the road beside the Hansbach, we again descended, firing off guns as signals. Now, however, that we have found you, and that our voices reach each other, it may be a long time before we actually meet. We are conversing by means of some extraordinary acoustic arrangement of the labyrinth. But do not despair, my dear boy. It is something gained even to hear each other."

While he was speaking, my brain was at work reflecting. A certain undefined hope, vague and shapeless as yet, made my heart beat wildly. In the first place, it was absolutely necessary for me to know one thing. I once more, therefore, leaned my head against the wall, which I almost touched with my lips, and again spoke.

"Uncle."

....

"My boy?" was his answer after a few moments.

....

"It is of the utmost consequence that we should know how far we are asunder."

....

"That is not difficult."

....

"You have your chronometer at hand?" I asked.

....

"Certainly."

....

"Well, take it into your hand. Pronounce my name, noting exactly the second at which you speak. I will reply as soon as I hear your words—and you will then note exactly the moment at which my reply reaches you."

....

"Very good; and the mean time between my question and your answer will be the time occupied by my voice in reaching you."

....

"That is exactly what I mean, Uncle," was my eager reply.

....

"Are you ready?"

....

"Yes."

....

"Well, make ready, I am about to pronounce your name," said the Professor.

I applied my ear close to the sides of the cavernous gallery, and as soon as the word "Harry" reached my ear, I turned round and, placing my lips to the wall, repeated the sound.

....

"Forty seconds," said my uncle. "There has elapsed forty seconds between the two words. The sound, therefore, takes twenty seconds to ascend. Now, allowing a thousand and twenty feet for every second—we have twenty thousand four hundred feet—a league and a half and one-eighth."

These words fell on my soul like a kind of death knell.

"A league and a half," I muttered in a low and despairing voice.

....

"It shall be got over, my boy," cried my uncle in a cheery tone; "depend on us."

....

"But do you know whether to ascend or descend?" I asked faintly enough.

....

"We have to descend, and I will tell you why. You have reached a vast open space, a kind of bare crossroad, from which galleries diverge in every direction. That in which you are now lying must necessarily bring you to this point, for it appears that all these mighty fissures, these fractures of the globe's interior, radiate from the vast cavern which we at this moment occupy. Rouse yourself, then, have courage and continue your route. Walk if you can, if not drag yourself along—slide, if nothing else is possible. The slope must be rather rapid—and you will find strong arms to receive you at the end of your journey. Make a start, like a good fellow."

These words served to rouse some kind of courage in my sinking frame.

"Farewell for the present, good uncle, I am about to take my departure. As soon as I start, our voices will cease to commingle. Farewell, then, until we meet again."

....

"Adieu, Harry—until we say Welcome." Such were the last words which reached my anxious ears before I commenced my weary and almost hopeless journey.

This wonderful and surprising conversation which took place through the vast mass of the earth's labyrinth, these words exchanged, the speakers being about five miles apart—ended with hopeful and pleasant expressions. I breathed one more prayer to Heaven, I sent up words of thanksgiving—believing in my inmost heart that He had led me to the only place where the voices of my friends could reach my ears.

This apparently astounding acoustic mystery is easily explainable by simple natural laws; it arose from the conductibility of the rock. There are many instances of this singular propagation of sound which are not perceptible in its less mediate positions. In the interior gallery of St. Paul's, and amid the curious caverns in Sicily, these phenomena are observable. The most marvelous of them all is known as the Ear of Dionysius.

These memories of the past, of my early reading and studies, came fresh to my thoughts. Moreover, I began to reason that if my uncle and I could communicate at so great a distance, no serious obstacle could exist between us. All I had to do was to follow the direction whence the sound had reached me; and logically putting it, I must reach him if my strength did not fail.

I accordingly rose to my feet. I soon found, however, that I could not walk; that I must drag myself along. The slope as I expected was very rapid; but I allowed myself to slip down.

Soon the rapidity of the descent began to assume frightful proportions; and menaced a fearful fall. I clutched at the sides; I grasped at projections of rocks; I threw myself backwards. All in vain. My weakness was so great I could do nothing to save myself.

Suddenly earth failed me.

I was first launched into a dark and gloomy void. I then struck against the projecting asperities of a vertical gallery, a perfect well. My head bounded against a pointed rock, and I lost all knowledge of existence. As far as I was concerned, death had claimed me for his own.

Chapter 26

A RAPID RECOVERY

When I returned to the consciousness of existence, I found myself surrounded by a kind of semiobscurity, lying on some thick and soft coverlets. My uncle was watching—his eyes fixed intently on my countenance, a grave expression on his face, a tear in his eye. At the first sigh which struggled from my bosom, he took hold of my hand. When he saw my eyes open and fix themselves upon his, he uttered a loud cry of joy. "He lives! he lives!"

"Yes, my good uncle," I whispered.

"My dear boy," continued the grim Professor, clasping me to his heart, "you are saved!"

I was deeply and unaffectedly touched by the tone in which these words were uttered, and even more by the kindly care which accompanied them. The Professor, however, was one of those men who must be severely tried in order to induce any display of affection or gentle emotion. At this moment our friend Hans, the guide, joined us. He saw my hand in that of my uncle, and I venture to say that, taciturn as he was, his eyes beamed with lively satisfaction.

"God dag," he said.

"Good day, Hans, good day," I replied, in as hearty a tone as I could assume, "and now, Uncle, that we are together, tell me where we are. I have lost all idea of our position, as of everything else."

"Tomorrow, Harry, tomorrow," he replied. "Today you are far too weak. Your head is surrounded with bandages and poultices that must not be touched. Sleep, my boy, sleep, and tomorrow you will know all that you require."

"But," I cried, "let me know what o'clock it is—what day it is?"

"It is now eleven o'clock at night, and this is once more Sunday. It is now the ninth of the month of August. And I distinctly prohibit you from asking any more questions until the tenth of the same."

I was, if the truth were told, very weak indeed, and my eyes soon closed involuntarily. I did require a good night's rest, and I went off reflecting at the last moment that my perilous adventure in the interior of the earth, in total darkness, had lasted four days!

On the morning of the next day, at my awakening, I began to look around me. My sleeping place, made of all our traveling bedding, was in a charming grotto, adorned with magnificent stalagmites, glittering in all the colors of the rainbow, the floor of soft and silvery sand.

A dim obscurity prevailed. No torch, no lamp was lighted, and yet certain unexplained beams of light penetrated from without, and made their way through the opening of the beautiful grotto.

I, moreover, heard a vague and indefinite murmur, like the ebb and flow of waves upon a strand, and sometimes I verily believed I could hear the sighing of the wind.

I began to believe that, instead of being awake, I must be dreaming. Surely my brain had not been affected by my fall, and all that occurred during the last twenty-four hours was not the frenzied visions of madness? And yet after some reflection, a trial of my faculties, I came to the conclusion that I could not be mistaken. Eyes and ears could not surely both deceive me.

"It is a ray of the blessed daylight," I said to myself, "which has penetrated through some mighty fissure in the rocks. But what is the meaning of this murmur of waves, this unmistakable moaning of the salt-sea billows? I can hear, too, plainly enough, the whistling of the wind. But can I be altogether mistaken? If my uncle, during my illness, has but carried me back to the surface of the earth! Has he, on my account, given up his wondrous expedition, or in some strange manner has it come to an end?"

I was puzzling my brain over these and other questions, when the Professor joined me.

"Good day, Harry," he cried in a joyous tone. "I fancy you are quite well."

"I am very much better," I replied, actually sitting up in my bed.

"I knew that would be the end of it, as you slept both soundly and tranquilly. Hans and I have each taken turn to watch, and every hour we have seen visible signs of amelioration."

"You must be right, Uncle," was my reply, "for I feel as if I could do justice to any meal you could put before me."

"You shall eat, my boy, you shall eat. The fever has left you. Our excellent friend Hans has rubbed your wounds and bruises with I know not what ointment, of which the Icelanders alone possess the secret. And they have healed your bruises in the most marvelous manner. Ah, he's a wise fellow is Master Hans."

While he was speaking, my uncle was placing before me several articles of food, which, despite his earnest injunctions, I readily devoured. As soon as the first rage of hunger was appeased, I overwhelmed him with questions, to which he now no longer hesitated to give answersI then learned, for the first time, that my providential fall had brought me to the bottom of an almost perpendicular gallery. As I came down, amidst a perfect shower of stones, the least of which falling on me would have crushed me to death, they came to the conclusion that I had carried with me an entire dislocated rock. Riding as it were on this terrible chariot, I was cast headlong into my uncle's arms. And into them I fell, insensible and covered with blood.

"It is indeed a miracle," was the Professor's final remark, "that you were not killed a thousand times over. But let us take care never to separate; for surely we should risk never meeting again."

"Let us take care never again to separate."

These words fell with a sort of chill upon my heart. The journey, then, was not over. I looked at my uncle with surprise and astonishment. My uncle, after an instant's examination of my countenance, said: "What is the matter, Harry?"

"I want to ask you a very serious question. You say that I am all right in health?"

"Certainly you are."

"And all my limbs are sound and capable of new exertion?" I asked.

"Most undoubtedly."

"But what about my head?" was my next anxious question.

"Well, your head, except that you have one or two contusions, is exactly where it ought to be—on your shoulders," said my uncle, laughing.

"Well, my own opinion is that my head is not exactly right. In fact, I believe myself slightly delirious."

"What makes you think so?"

"I will explain why I fancy I have lost my senses," I cried. "Have we not returned to the surface of Mother Earth?"

"Certainly not."

"Then truly I must be mad, for do I not see the light of day? do I not hear the whistling of the wind? and can I not distinguish the wash of a great sea?"

"And that is all that makes you uneasy?" said my uncle, with a smile.

"Can you explain?"

"I will not make any attempt to explain; for the whole matter is utterly inexplicable. But you shall see and judge for yourself. You will then find that geological science is as yet in its infancy—and that we are doomed to enlighten the world."

"Let us advance, then," I cried eagerly, no longer able to restrain my curiosity.

"Wait a moment, my dear Harry," he responded; "you must take precautions after your illness before going into the open air."

"The open air?"

"Yes, my boy. I have to warn you that the wind is rather violent—and I have no wish for you to expose yourself without necessary precautions."

"But I beg to assure you that I am perfectly recovered from my illness."

"Have just a little patience, my boy. A relapse would be inconvenient to all parties. We have no time to lose—as our approaching sea voyage may be of long duration."

"Sea voyage?" I cried, more bewildered than ever.

"Yes. You must take another day's rest, and we shall be ready to go on board by tomorrow," replied my uncle, with a peculiar smile.

"Go on board!" The words utterly astonished me.

Go on board—what and how? Had we come upon a river, a lake, had we discovered some inland sea? Was a vessel lying at anchor in some part of the interior of the earth?

My curiosity was worked up to the very highest pitch. My uncle made vain attempts to restrain me. When at last, however, he discovered that my feverish impatience would do more harm than good—and that the satisfaction of my wishes could alone restore me to a calm state of mind—he gave way.

I dressed myself rapidly—and then taking the precaution to please my uncle, of wrapping myself in one of the coverlets, I rushed out of the grotto.

Chapter 27

THE CENTRAL SEA

At first I saw absolutely nothing. My eyes, wholly unused to the effulgence of light, could not bear the sudden brightness; and I was compelled to close them. When I was able to reopen them, I stood still, far more stupefied than astonished. Not all the wildest effects of imagination could have conjured up such a scene! "The sea—the sea," I cried.

"Yes," replied my uncle, in a tone of pardonable pride; "the Central Sea. No future navigator will deny the fact of my having discovered it; and hence of acquiring a right of giving it a name."

It was quite true. A vast, limitless expanse of water, the end of a lake if not of an ocean, spread before us, until it was lost in the distance. The shore, which was very much indented, consisted of a beautiful soft golden sand, mixed with small shells, the long-deserted home of some of the creatures of a past age. The waves broke incessantly—and with a peculiarly sonorous murmur, to be found in underground localities. A slight frothy flake arose as the wind blew along the pellucid waters; and many a dash of spray was blown into my face. The mighty superstructure of rock which rose above to an inconceivable height left only a narrow opening—but where we stood, there was a large margin of strand. On all sides were capes and promontories and enormous cliffs, partially worn by the eternal breaking of the waves, through countless ages! And as I gazed from side to side, the mighty rocks faded away like a fleecy film of cloud.

It was in reality an ocean, with an the usual characteristics of an inland sea, only horribly wild—so rigid, cold and savage.

One thing startled and puzzled me greatly. How was it that I was able to look upon that vast sheet of water instead of being plunged in utter darkness? The vast landscape before me was lit up like day. But there was wanting the dazzling brilliancy, the splendid irradiation of the sun; the pale cold illumination of the moon; the brightness of the stars. The illuminating power in this subterranean region, from its trembling and Rickering character, its clear dry whiteness, the very slight elevation of its temperature, its great superiority to that of the moon, was evidently electric; something in the nature of the aurora borealis, only that its phenomena were constant, and able to light up the whole of the ocean cavern.

The tremendous vault above our heads, the sky, so to speak, appeared to be composed of a conglomeration of nebulous vapors, in constant motion. I should originally have supposed that, under such an atmospheric pressure as must exist in that place, the evaporation of water could not really take place, and yet from the action of some physical law, which escaped my memory, there were heavy and dense clouds rolling along that mighty vault, partially concealing the roof. Electric currents produced astonishing play of light and shade in the distance, especially around the heavier clouds. Deep shadows were cast beneath, and then suddenly, between two clouds, there would come a ray of unusual beauty, and remarkable intensity. And yet it was not like the sun, for it gave no heat.

The effect was sad and excruciatingly melancholy. Instead of a noble firmament of blue, studded with stars, there was above me a heavy roof of granite, which seemed to crush me.

Gazing around, I began to think of the theory of the English captain who compared the earth to a vast hollow sphere in the interior of which the air is retained in a luminous state by means of atmospheric pressure, while two stars, Pluto and Proserpine, circled there in their mysterious orbits. After all, suppose the old fellow was right!

In truth, we were imprisoned—bound as it were, in a vast excavation. Its width it was impossible to make out; the shore, on either hand, widening rapidly until lost to sight; while its length was equally uncertain. A haze on the distant horizon bounded our view. As to its height, we could see that it must be many miles to the roof. Looking upward, it was impossible to discover where the stupendous roof began. The lowest of the clouds must have been floating at an elevation of two thousand yards, a height greater than that of terrestrial vapors, which circumstance was doubtless owing to the extreme density of the air.

I use the word "cavern" in order to give an idea of the place. I cannot describe its awful grandeur; human language fails to convey an idea of its savage sublimity. Whether this singular vacuum had or had not been caused by the sudden cooling of the earth when in a state of fusion, I could not say. I had read of most wonderful and gigantic caverns—but, none in any way like this.

The great grotto of Guachara, in Colombia, visited by the learned Humboldt; the vast and partially explored Mammoth Cave in Kentucky—what were these holes in the earth to that in which I stood in speechless admiration! with its vapory clouds, its electric light, and the mighty ocean slumbering in its bosom! Imagination, not description, can alone give an idea of the splendor and vastness of the cave.

I gazed at these marvels in profound silence. Words were utterly wanting to indicate the sensations of wonder

I experienced. I seemed, as I stood upon that mysterious shore, as if I were some wandering inhabitant of a distant planet, present for the first time at the spectacle of some terrestrial phenomena belonging to another existence. To give body and existence to such new sensations would have required the coinage of new words—and here my feeble brain found itself wholly at fault. I looked on, I thought, I reflected, I admired, in a state of stupefaction not altogether unmingled with fear!

The unexpected spectacle restored some color to my pallid cheeks. I seemed to be actually getting better under the influence of this novelty. Moreover, the vivacity of the dense atmosphere reanimated my body by inflating my lungs with unaccustomed oxygen.

It will be readily conceived that after an imprisonment of forty-seven days, in a dark and miserable tunnel it was with infinite delight that I breathed this saline air. It was like the genial, reviving influence of the salt sea waves.

My uncle had already got over the first surprise.

With the Latin poet Horace his idea was that—

Not to admire is all the art I know,

To make man happy and to keep him so.

"Well," he said, after giving me time thoroughly to appreciate the marvels of this underground sea, "do you feel strong enough to walk up and down?"

"Certainly," was my ready answer, "nothing would give me greater pleasure."

"Well then, my boy," he said, "lean on my arm, and we will stroll along the beach."

I accepted his offer eagerly, and we began to walk along the shores of this extraordinary lake. To our left were abrupt rocks, piled one upon the other—a stupendous titanic pile; down their sides leaped innumerable cascades, which at last, becoming limpid and murmuring streams, were lost in the waters of the lake. Light vapors, which rose here and there, and floated in fleecy clouds from rock to rock, indicated hot springs, which also poured their superfluity into the vast reservoir at our feet.

Among them I recognized our old and faithful stream, the Hansbach, which, lost in that wild basin, seemed as if it had been flowing since the creation of the world.

"We shall miss our excellent friend," I remarked, with a deep sigh.

"Bah!" said my uncle testily, "what matters it? That or another, it is all the same."

I thought the remark ungrateful, and felt almost inclined to say so; but I forbore.

At this moment my attention was attracted by an unexpected spectacle. After we had gone about five hundred yards, we suddenly turned a steep promontory, and found ourselves close to a lofty forest! It consisted of straight trunks with tufted tops, in shape like parasols. The air seemed to have no effect upon these trees—which in spite of a tolerable breeze remained as still and motionless as if they had been petrified.

I hastened forward. I could find no name for these singular formations. Did they not belong to the two thousand and more known trees—or were we to make the discovery of a new growth? By no means. When we at last reached the forest, and stood beneath the trees, my surprise gave way to admiration.

In truth, I was simply in the presence of a very ordinary product of the earth, of singular and gigantic proportions. My uncle unhesitatingly called them by their real names.

"It is only," he said, in his coolest manner, "a forest of mushrooms."

On close examination I found that he was not mistaken. Judge of the development attained by this product of damp hot soils. I had heard that the Lycoperdon giganteum reaches nine feet in circumference, but here were white mushrooms, nearly forty feet high, and with tops of equal dimensions. They grew in countless thousands—the light could not make its way through their massive substance, and beneath them reigned a gloomy and mystic darkness.

Still I wished to go forward. The cold in the shades of this singular forest was intense. For nearly an hour we wandered about in this visible darkness. At length I left the spot, and once more returned to the shores of the lake, to light and comparative warmth.

But the amazing vegetation of subterraneous land was not confined to gigantic mushrooms. New wonders awaited us at every step. We had not gone many hundred yards, when we came upon a mighty group of other trees with discolored leaves—the common humble trees of Mother Earth, of an exorbitant and phenomenal size: lycopods a hundred feet high; flowering ferns as tall as pines; gigantic grasses!

"Astonishing, magnificent, splendid!" cried my uncle; "here we have before us the whole flora of the second period of the world, that of transition. Behold the humble plants of our gardens, which in the first ages of the world were mighty trees. Look around you, my dear Harry. No botanist ever before gazed on such a sight!"

My uncle's enthusiasm, always a little more than was required, was now excusable.

"You are right, Uncle," I remarked. "Providence appears to have designed the preservation in this vast and mysterious hothouse of antediluvian plants, to prove the sagacity of learned men in figuring them so marvelously on paper."

"Well said, my boy—very well said; it is indeed a mighty hothouse. But you would also be within the bounds of reason and common sense, if you added that it is also a vast menagerie."

I looked rather anxiously around. If the animals were as exaggerated as the plants, the matter would certainly be serious.

"A menagerie?"

"Doubtless. Look at the dust we are treading under foot—behold the bones with which the whole soil of the seashore is covered—"

"Bones," I replied, "yes, certainly, the bones of antediluvian animals."

I stooped down as I spoke, and picked up one or two singular remains, relics of a bygone age. It was easy to give a name to these gigantic bones, in some instances as big as trunks of trees.

"Here is, clearly, the lower jawbone of a mastodon," I cried, almost as warmly and enthusiastically as my uncle; "here are the molars of the Dinotherium; here is a leg bone which belonged to the Megatherium. You are right, Uncle, it is indeed a menagerie; for the mighty animals to which these bones once belonged, have lived and died on the shores of this subterranean sea, under the shadow of these plants. Look, yonder are whole skeletons—and yet—"

"And yet, nephew?" said my uncle, noticing that I suddenly came to a full stop.

"I do not understand the presence of such beasts in granite caverns, however vast and prodigious," was my reply.

"Why not?" said my uncle, with very much of his old professional impatience.

"Because it is well known that animal life only existed on earth during the secondary period, when the sedimentary soil was formed by the alluviums, and thus replaced the hot and burning rocks of the primitive age."

"I have listened to you earnestly and with patience, Harry, and I have a simple and clear answer to your objections: and that is, that this itself is a sedimentary soil."

"How can that be at such enormous depth from the surface of the earth?"

"The fact can be explained both simply and geologically. At a certain period, the earth consisted only of an elastic crust, liable to alternative upward and downward movements in virtue of the law of attraction. It is very probable that many a landslip took place in those days, and that large portions of sedimentary soil were cast into huge and mighty chasms."

"Quite possible," I dryly remarked. "But, Uncle, if these antediluvian animals formerly lived in these subterranean regions, what more likely than that one of these monsters may at this moment be concealed behind one of yonder mighty rocks."

As I spoke, I looked keenly around, examining with care every point of the horizon; but nothing alive appeared to exist on these deserted shores.

I now felt rather fatigued, and told my uncle so. The walk and excitement were too much for me in my weak state. I therefore seated myself at the end of a promontory, at the foot of which the waves broke in incessant rolls. I looked round a bay formed by projections of vast granitic rocks. At the extreme end was a little port protected by huge pyramids of stones. A brig and three or four schooners might have lain there with perfect ease. So natural did it seem, that every minute my imagination induced me to expect a vessel coming out under all sail and making for the open sea under the influence of a warm southerly breeze.

But the fantastic illusion never lasted more than a minute. We were the only living creatures in this subterranean world!

During certain periods there was an utter cessation of wind, when a silence deeper, more terrible than the silence of the desert fell upon these solitary and arid rocks—and seemed to hang like a leaden weight upon the waters of this singular ocean. I sought, amid the awful stillness, to penetrate through the distant fog, to tear down the veil which concealed the mysterious distance. What unspoken words were murmured by my trembling lips—what questions did I wish to ask and did not! Where did this sea end—to what did it lead? Should we ever be able to examine its distant shores?

But my uncle had no doubts about the matter. He was convinced that our enterprise would in the end be successful. For my part, I was in a state of painful indecision—I desired to embark on the journey and to succeed, and still I feared the result.

After we had passed an hour or more in silent contemplation of the wondrous spectacle, we rose and went down towards the bank on our way to the grotto, which I was not sorry to gain. After a slight repast, I sought refuge in slumber, and at length, after many and tedious struggles, sleep came over my weary eyes.

Chapter 28

LAUNCHING THE RAFT

On the morning of the next day, to my great surprise, I awoke completely restored. I thought a bath would be delightful after my long illness and sufferings. So, soon after rising, I went and plunged into the waters of this new Mediterranean. The bath was cool, fresh and invigorating.

I came back to breakfast with an excellent appetite. Hans, our worthy guide, thoroughly understood how to cook such eatables as we were able to provide; he had both fire and water at discretion, so that he was enabled slightly to vary the weary monotony of our ordinary repast.

Our morning meal was like a capital English breakfast, with coffee by way of a windup. And never had this delicious beverage been so welcome and refreshing.

My uncle had sufficient regard for my state of health not to interrupt me in the enjoyment of the meal, but he was evidently delighted when I had finished.

"Now then," said he, "come with me. It is the height of the tide, and I am anxious to study its curious phenomena."

"What!'" I cried, rising in astonishment, "did you say the tide, Uncle?"

"Certainly I did."

"You do not mean to say," I replied, in a tone of respectful doubt, "that the influence of the sun and moon is felt here below."

"And pray why not? Are not all bodies influenced by the law of universal attraction? Why should this vast underground sea be exempt from the general law, the rule of the universe? Besides, there is nothing like that which is proved and demonstrated. Despite the great atmospheric pressure down here, you will notice that this inland sea rises and falls with as much regularity as the Atlantic itself."

As my uncle spoke, we reached the sandy shore, and saw and heard the waves breaking monotonously on the beach. They were evidently rising.

"This is truly the flood," I cried, looking at the water at my feet"Yes, my excellent nephew," replied my uncle, rubbing his hands with the gusto of a philosopher, "and you see by these several streaks of foam that the tide rises at least ten or twelve feet."

"It is indeed marvelous."

"By no means," he responded; "on the contrary, it is quite natural."

"It may appear so in your eyes, my dear uncle," was my reply, "but all the phenomena of the place appear to me to partake of the marvelous. It is almost impossible to believe that which I see. Who in his wildest dreams could have imagined that, beneath the crust of our earth, there could exist a real ocean, with ebbing and flowing tides, with its changes of winds, and even its storms! I for one should have laughed the suggestion to scorn."

"But, Harry, my boy, why not?" inquired my uncle, with a pitying smile; "is there any physical reason in opposition to it?"

"Well, if we give up the great theory of the central heat of the earth, I certainly can offer no reasons why anything should be looked upon as impossible."

"Then you will own," he added, "that the system of Sir Humphry Davy is wholly justified by what we have seen?"

"I allow that it is—and that point once granted, I certainly can see no reason for doubting the existence of seas and other wonders, even countries, in the interior of the globe."

"That is so—but of course these varied countries are uninhabited?"

"Well, I grant that it is more likely than not: still, I do not see why this sea should not have given shelter to some species of unknown fish."

"Hitherto we have not discovered any, and the probabilities are rather against our ever doing so," observed the Professor.

I was losing my skepticism in the presence of these wonders.

"Well, I am determined to solve the question. It is my intention to try my luck with my fishing line and hook."

"Certainly; make the experiment," said my uncle, pleased with my enthusiasm. "While we are about it, it will certainly be only proper to discover all the secrets of this extraordinary region."

"But, after all, where are we now?" I asked; "all this time I have quite forgotten to ask you a question, which, doubtless, your philosophical instruments have long since answered."

"Well," replied the Professor, "examining the situation from only one point of view, we are now distant three hundred and fifty leagues from Iceland."

"So much?" was my exclamation.

"I have gone over the matter several times, and am sure not to have made a mistake of five hundred yards," replied my uncle positively.

"And as to the direction—are we still going to the southeast?"

"Yes, with a western declination of nineteen degrees, forty-two minutes, just as it is above. As for the inclination I have discovered a very curious fact."

"What may that be, Uncle? Your information interests me."

"Why, that the needle instead of dipping towards the pole

as it does on earth, in the northern hemisphere, has an upward tendency."

"This proves," I cried, "that the great point of magnetic attraction lies somewhere between the surface of the earth and the spot we have succeeded in reaching."

"Exactly, my observant nephew," exclaimed my uncle, elated and delighted, "and it is quite probable that if we succeed in getting toward the polar regions—somewhere near the seventy-third degree of latitude, where Sir James Ross discovered the magnetic pole, we shall behold the needle point directly upward. We have therefore discovered by analogy, that this great centre of attraction is not situated at a very great depth."

"Well," said I, rather surprised, "this discovery will astonish experimental philosophers. It was never suspected."

"Science, great, mighty and in the end unerring," replied my uncle dogmatically, "science has fallen into many errors—errors which have been fortunate and useful rather than otherwise, for they have been the steppingstones to truth."

After some further discussion, I turned to another matter.

"Have you any idea of the depth we have reached?"

"We are now," continued the Professor, "exactly thirty-five leagues—above a hundred miles—down into the interior of the earth."

"So," said I, after measuring the distance on the map, "we are now beneath the Scottish Highlands, and have over our heads the lofty Grampian Hills."

"You are quite right," said the Professor, laughing; "it sounds very alarming, the weight being heavy—but the vault which supports this vast mass of earth and rock is solid and safe; the mighty Architect of the Universe has constructed it of solid materials. Man, even in his highest flights of vivid and poetic imagination, never thought of such things! What are the finest arches of our bridges, what the vaulted roofs of our cathedrals, to that mighty dome above us, and beneath which floats an ocean with its storms and calms and tides!"

"I admire it all as much as you can, Uncle, and have no fear that our granite sky will fall upon our heads. But now that we have discussed matters of science and discovery, what are your future intentions? Are you not thinking of getting back to the surface of our beautiful earth?"

This was said more as a feeler than with any hope of success.

"Go back, nephew," cried my uncle in a tone of alarm, "you are not surely thinking of anything so absurd or cowardly. No, my intention is to advance and continue our journey. We have as yet been singularly fortunate, and henceforth I hope we shall be more so."

"But," said I, "how are we to cross yonder liquid plain?"

"It is not my intention to leap into it head foremost, or even to swim across it, like Leander over the Hellespont. But as oceans are, after all, only great lakes, inasmuch as they are surrounded by land, so does it stand to reason, that this central sea is circumscribed by granite surroundings."

"Doubtless," was my natural reply.

"Well, then, do you not think that when once we reach the other end, we shall find some means of continuing our journey?"

"Probably, but what extent do you allow to this internal ocean?"

"Well, I should fancy it to extend about forty or fifty leagues—more or less."

"But even supposing this approximation to be a correct one—what then?" I asked.

"My dear boy, we have no time for further discussion. We shall embark tomorrow."

I looked around with surprise and incredulity. I could see

nothing in the shape of boat or vessel.

"What!" I cried, "we are about to launch out upon an unknown sea; and where, if I may ask, is the vessel to carry us?"

"Well, my dear boy, it will not be exactly what you would call a vessel. For the present we must be content with a good and solid raft."

"A raft," I cried, incredulously, "but down here a raft is as impossible of construction as a vessel—and I am at a loss to imagine—"

"My good Harry—if you were to listen instead of talking so much, you would hear," said my uncle, waxing a little impatient.

"I should hear?"

"Yes—certain knocks with the hammer, which Hans is now employing to make the raft. He has been at work for many hours."

"Making a raft?"

"Yes."

"But where has he found trees suitable for such a construction?"

"He found the trees all ready to his hand. Come, and you shall see our excellent guide at work."

More and more amazed at what I heard and saw, I followed my uncle like one in a dream.

After a walk of about a quarter of an hour, I saw Hans at work on the other side of the promontory which formed our natural port. A few minutes more and I was beside him. To my great surprise, on the sandy shore lay a half-finished raft. It was made from beams of a very peculiar wood, and a great number of limbs, joints, boughs, and pieces lay about, sufficient to have constructed a fleet of ships and boats.

I turned to my uncle, silent with astonishment and awe.

"Where did all this wood come from?" I cried; "what wood is it?"

"Well, there is pinewood, fir, and the palms of the northern regions, mineralized by the action of the sea," he replied, sententiously.

"Can it be possible?"

"Yes," said the learned Professor, "what you see is called fossil wood."

"But then," cried I, after reflecting for a moment, "like the lignites, it must be as hard and as heavy as iron, and therefore will certainly not float."

"Sometimes that is the case. Many of these woods have become true anthracites, but others again, like those you see before you, have only undergone one phase of fossil transformation. But there is no proof like demonstration," added my uncle, picking one or two of these precious waifs and casting them into the sea.

The piece of wood, after having disappeared for a moment, came to the surface, and floated about with the oscillation produced by wind and tide.

"Are you convinced?" said my uncle, with a self-satisfied smile.

"I am convinced," I cried, "that what I see is incredible."

The fact was that my journey into the interior of the earth was rapidly changing all preconceived notions, and day by day preparing me for the marvelous.

I should not have been surprised to have seen a fleet of native canoes afloat upon that silent sea.

The very next evening, thanks to the industry and ability of Hans, the raft was finished. It was about ten feet long and five feet wide. The beams bound together with stout ropes, were solid and firm, and once launched by our united efforts, the improvised vessel floated tranquilly upon the waters of what the Professor had well named the Central Sea.

Chapter 29

ON THE WATERS— A RAFT VOYAGE

On the thirteenth of August we were up betimes. There was no time to be lost. We now had to inaugurate a new kind of locomotion, which would have the advantage of being rapid and not fatiguing.

A mast, made of two pieces of wood fastened together, to give additional strength, a yard made from another one, the sail a linen sheet from our bed. We were fortunately in no want of cordage, and the whole on trial appeared solid and seaworthy.

At six o'clock in the morning, when the eager and enthusiastic Professor gave the signal to embark, the victuals, the luggage, all our instruments, our weapons, and a goodly supply of sweet water, which we had collected from springs in the rocks, were placed on the raft.

Hans had, with considerable ingenuity, contrived a rudder, which enabled him to guide the floating apparatus with ease. He took the tiller, as a matter of course. The worthy man was as good a sailor as he was a guide and duck hunter. I then let go the painter which held us to the shore, the sail was brought to the wind, and we made a rapid offing.

Our sea voyage had at length commenced; and once more we were making for distant and unknown regions.

Just as we were about to leave the little port where the raft had been constructed, my uncle, who was very strong as to geographic nomenclature, wanted to give it a name, and among others, suggested mine.

"Well," said I, "before you decide I have another to propose."

"Well; out with it."

"I should like to call it Gretchen. Port Gretchen will sound very well on our future map."

"Well then, Port Gretchen let it be," said the Professor.

And thus it was that the memory of my dear girl was attached to our adventurous and memorable expedition.

When we left the shore the wind was blowing from the northward and eastward. We went directly before the wind at a much greater speed than might have been expected from a raft. The dense layers of atmosphere at that depth had great propelling power and acted upon the sail with considerable force.

At the end of an hour, my uncle, who had been taking careful observations, was enabled to judge of the rapidity with which we moved. It was far beyond anything seen in the upper world.

"If," he said, "we continue to advance at our present rate, we shall have traveled at least thirty leagues in twenty-four hours. With a mere raft this is an almost incredible velocity."

I certainly was surprised, and without making any reply went forward upon the raft. Already the northern shore was fading away on the edge of the horizon. The two shores appeared to separate more and more, leaving a wide and open space for our departure. Before me I could see nothing but the vast and apparently limitless sea—upon which we floated—the only living objects in sight.

Huge and dark clouds cast their grey shadows below—shadows which seemed to crush that colorless and sullen water by their weight. Anything more suggestive of gloom and of regions of nether darkness I never beheld. Silvery rays of electric light, reflected here and there upon some small spots of water, brought up luminous sparkles in the long wake of our cumbrous bark. Presently we were wholly out of sight of land; not a vestige could be seen, nor any indication of where we were going. So still and motionless did we seem without any distant point to fix our eyes on that but for the phosphoric light at the wake of the raft I should have fancied that we were still and motionless.

But I knew that we were advancing at a very rapid rate.

About twelve o'clock in the day, vast collections of seaweed were discovered surrounding us on all sides. I was aware of the extraordinary vegetative power of these plants, which have been known to creep along the bottom of the great ocean, and stop the advance of large ships. But never were seaweeds ever seen, so gigantic and wonderful as those of the Central Sea. I could well imagine how, seen at a distance, tossing and heaving on the summit of the billows, the long lines of algae have been taken for living things, and thus have been fertile sources of the belief in sea serpents.

Our raft swept past great specimens of fucus or seawrack, from three to four thousand feet in length, immense, incredibly long, looking like snakes that stretched out far beyond our horizon. It afforded me great amusement to gaze on their variegated ribbon-like endless lengths. Hour after hour passed without our coming to the termination of these floating weeds. If my astonishment increased, my patience was well-nigh exhausted.

What natural force could possibly have produced such abnormal and extraordinary plants? What must have been the aspect of the globe, during the first centuries of its formation, when under the combined action of heat and humidity, the vegetable kingdom occupied its vast surface to the exclusion of everything else?

These were considerations of never-ending interest for the geologist and the philosopher.

All this while we were advancing on our journey; and at length night came; but as I had remarked the evening before, the luminous state of the atmosphere was in nothing diminished. Whatever was the cause, it was a phenomenon upon the duration of which we could calculate with certainty.

As soon as our supper had been disposed of, and some little speculative conversation indulged in, I stretched myself at the foot of the mast, and presently went to sleep.

Hans remained motionless at the tiller, allowing the raft to rise and fall on the waves. The wind being aft, and the sail square, all he had to do was to keep his oar in the centre.

Ever since we had taken our departure from the newly named Port Gretchen, my worthy uncle had directed me to keep a regular log of our day's navigation, with instructions to put down even the most minute particulars, every interesting and curious phenomenon, the direction of the wind, our rate of sailing, the distance we went; in a word, every incident of our extraordinary voyage.

From our log, therefore, I tell the story of our voyage on the Central Sea.

Friday, August 14th. A steady breeze from the northwest. Raft progressing with extreme rapidity, and going perfectly straight. Coast still dimly visible about thirty leagues to leeward. Nothing to be seen beyond the horizon in front. The extraordinary intensity of the light neither increases nor diminishes. It is singularly stationary. The weather remarkably fine; that is to say, the clouds have ascended very high, and are light and fleecy, and surrounded by an atmosphere resembling silver in fusion.

Thermometer, +32 degrees centigrade.

About twelve o'clock in the day our guide Hans having prepared and baited a hook, cast his line into the subterranean waters. The bait he used was a small piece of meat, by means of which he concealed his hook. Anxious as I was, I was for a long time doomed to disappointment. Were these waters supplied with fish or not? That was the important question. No—was my decided answer. Then there came a sudden and rather hard tug. Hans coolly drew it in, and with it a fish, which struggled violently to escape.

"A fish!" cried my uncle.

"It is a sturgeon!" I cried, "certainly a small sturgeon."

The Professor examined the fish carefully, noting every characteristic; and he did not coincide in my opinion. The fish had a flat head, round body, and the lower extremities covered with bony scales; its mouth was wholly without teeth, the pectoral fins, which were highly developed, sprouted direct from the body, which properly speaking had no tail. The animal certainly belonged to the order in which naturalists class the sturgeon, but it differed from that fish in many essential particulars.

My uncle, after all, was not mistaken. After a long and patient examination, he said:

"This fish, my dear boy, belongs to a family which has been extinct for ages, and of which no trace has ever been found on earth, except fossil remains in the Devonian strata."

"You do not mean to say," I cried, "that we have captured a live specimen of a fish belonging to the primitive stock that existed before the deluge?"

"We have," said the Professor, who all this time was continuing his observations, "and you may see by careful examination that these fossil fish have no identity with existing species. To hold in one's hand, therefore, a living specimen of the order, is enough to make a naturalist happy for life."

"But," cried I, "to what family does it belong?"

"To the order of Ganoides—an order of fish having angular scales, covered with bright enamel—forming one of the family of the Cephalaspides, of the genus—"

"Well, sir," I remarked, as I noticed my uncle hesitated to conclude.

"To the genus Pterychtis—yes, I am certain of it. Still, though I am confident of the correctness of my surmise, this fish offers to our notice a remarkable peculiarity, never known to exist in any other fish but those which are the natives of subterranean waters, wells, lakes, in caverns, and suchlike hidden pools."

"And what may that be?"

"It is blind."

"Blind!" I cried, much surprised.

"Not only blind," continued the Professor, "but absolutely without organs of sight."

I now examined our discovery for myself. It was singular, to be sure, but it was really a fact. This, however, might be a solitary instance, I suggested. The hook was baited again and once more thrown into the water. This subterranean ocean must have been tolerably well supplied with fish, for in two hours we took a large number of Pterychtis, as well as other fish belonging to another supposed extinct family—the Dipterides (a genus of fish, furnished with two fins only, whence the name), though my uncle could not class it exactly. All, without exception, however, were blind. This unexpected capture enabled us to renew our stock of provisions in a very satisfactory way.

We were now convinced that this subterranean sea contained only fish known to us as fossil specimens—and fish and reptiles alike were all the more perfect the farther back they dated their origin.

We began to hope that we should find some of those saurians which science has succeeded in reconstructing from bits of bone or cartilage.

I took up the telescope and carefully examined the horizon—looked over the whole sea; it was utterly and entirely deserted. Doubtless we were still too near the coast.After an examination of the ocean, I looked upward, towards the strange and mysterious sky. Why should not one of the birds reconstructed by the immortal Cuvier flap his stupendous wings aloft in the dull strata of subterranean air? It would, of course, find quite sufficient food from the fish in the sea. I gazed for some time upon the void above. It was as silent and as deserted as the shores we had but lately left.

Nevertheless, though I could neither see nor discover anything, my imagination carried me away into wild hypotheses. I was in a kind of waking dream. I thought I saw on the surface of the water those enormous antediluvian turtles as big as floating islands. Upon those dull and somber shores passed a spectral row of the mammifers of early days, the great Liptotherium found in the cavernous hollow of the Brazilian hills, the Mesicotherium, a native of the glacial regions of Siberia.

Farther on, the pachydermatous Lophrodon, that gigantic tapir, which concealed itself behind rocks, ready to do battle for its prey with the Anoplotherium, a singular animal partaking of the nature of the rhinoceros, the horse, the hippopotamus and the camel.

There was the giant Mastodon, twisting and turning his horrid trunk, with which he crushed the rocks of the shore to powder, while the Megatherium—his back raised like a cat in a passion, his enormous claws stretched out, dug into the earth for food, at the same time that he awoke the sonorous echoes of the whole place with his terrible roar.

Higher up still, the first monkey ever seen on the face of the globe clambered, gamboling and playing up the granite hills. Still farther away, ran the Pterodactyl, with the winged hand, gliding or rather sailing through the dense and compressed air like a huge bat.

Above all, near the leaden granitic sky, were immense birds, more powerful than the cassowary and the ostrich, which spread their mighty wings and fluttered against the huge stone vault of the inland sea.

I thought, such was the effect of my imagination, that I saw this whole tribe of antediluvian creatures. I carried myself back to far ages, long before man existed—when, in fact, the earth was in too imperfect a state for him to live upon it.

My dream was of countless ages before the existence of man. The mammifers first disappeared, then the mighty birds, then the reptiles of the secondary period, presently the fish, the crustacea, the mollusks, and finally the vertebrata. The zoophytes of the period of transition in their turn sank into annihilation.

The whole panorama of the world's life before the historic period, seemed to be born over again, and mine was the only human heart that beat in this unpeopled world! There were no more seasons; there were no more climates; the natural heat of the world increased unceasingly, and neutralized that of the great radiant Sun.

Vegetation was exaggerated in an extraordinary manner. I passed like a shadow in the midst of brushwood as lofty as the giant trees of California, and trod underfoot the moist and humid soil, reeking with a rank and varied vegetation.

I leaned against the huge column-like trunks of giant trees, to which those of Canada were as ferns. Whole ages passed, hundreds upon hundreds of years were concentrated into a single day.

Next, unrolled before me like a panorama, came the great and wondrous series of terrestrial transformations. Plants disappeared; the granitic rocks lost all trace of solidity; the liquid state was suddenly substituted for that which had before existed. This was caused by intense heat acting on the organic matter of the earth. The waters flowed over the whole surface of the globe; they boiled; they were volatilized, or turned into vapor; a kind of steam cloud wrapped the whole earth, the globe itself becoming at last nothing but one huge sphere of gas, indescribable in color, between white heat and red, as big and as brilliant as the sun.

In the very centre of this prodigious mass, fourteen hundred thousand times as large as our globe, I was whirled round in space, and brought into close conjunction with the planets. My body was subtilized, or rather became volatile, and commingled in a state of atomic vapor, with the prodigious clouds, which rushed forward like a mighty comet into infinite space!

What an extraordinary dream! Where would it finally take me? My feverish hand began to write down the marvelous details—details more like the imaginings of a lunatic than anything sober and real. I had during this period of hallucination forgotten everything—the Professor, the guide, and the raft on which we were floating. My mind was in a state of semioblivion.

"What is the matter, Harry?" said my uncle suddenly.

My eyes, which were wide opened like those of a somnambulist, were fixed upon him, but I did not see him, nor could I clearly make out anything around me.

"Take care, my boy," again cried my uncle, "you will fall into the sea."

As he uttered these words, I felt myself seized on the other side by the firm hand of our devoted guide. Had it not been for the presence of mind of Hans, I must infallibly have fallen into the waves and been drowned.

"Have you gone mad?" cried my uncle, shaking me on the other side.

"What—what is the matter?" I said at last, coming to myself.

"Are you ill, Henry?" continued the Professor in an anxious tone.

"No—no; but I have had an extraordinary dream. It, however, has passed away. All now seems well," I added, looking around me with strangely puzzled eyes.

"All right," said my uncle; "a beautiful breeze, a splendid sea. We are going along at a rapid rate, and if I am not out in my calculations we shall soon see land. I shall not be sorry to exchange the narrow limits of our raft for the mysterious strand of the subterranean ocean."

As my uncle uttered these words, I rose and carefully scanned the horizon. But the line of water was still confounded with the lowering clouds that hung aloft, and in the distance appeared to touch the edge of the water.

Chapter 30

TERRIFIC SAURIAN COMBAT

Saturday, August 15th. The sea still retains its uniform monotony. The same leaden hue, the same eternal glare from above. No indication of land being in sight. The horizon appears to retreat before us, more and more as we advance.

My head, still dull and heavy from the effects of my extraordinary dream, which I cannot as yet banish from my mind.

The Professor, who has not dreamed, is, however, in one of his morose and unaccountable humors. Spends his time in scanning the horizon, at every point of the compass. His telescope is raised every moment to his eyes, and when he finds nothing to give any clue to our whereabouts, he assumes a Napoleonic attitude and walks anxiously.

I remarked that my uncle, the Professor, had a strong tendency to resume his old impatient character, and I could not but make a note of this disagreeable circumstance in my journal. I saw clearly that it had required all the influence of my danger and suffering, to extract from him one scintillation of humane feeling. Now that I was quite recovered, his original nature had conquered and obtained the upper hand.

And, after all, what had he to be angry and annoyed about, now more than at any other time? Was not the journey being accomplished under the most favorable circumstances? Was not the raft progressing with the most marvelous rapidity?

What, then, could be the matter? After one or two preliminary hems, I determined to inquire.

"You seem uneasy, Uncle," said I, when for about the hundredth time he put down his telescope and walked up and down, muttering to himself.

"No, I am not uneasy," he replied in a dry harsh tone, "by no means."

"Perhaps I should have said impatient," I replied, softening the force of my remark.

"Enough to make me so, I think."

"And yet we are advancing at a rate seldom attained by a raft," I remarked.

"What matters that?" cried my uncle. "I am not vexed at the rate we go at, but I am annoyed to find the sea so much vaster than I expected."

I then recollected that the Professor, before our departure, had estimated the length of this subterranean ocean as at most about thirty leagues. Now we had traveled at least over thrice that distance without discovering any trace of the distant shore. I began to understand my uncle's anger.

"We are not going down," suddenly exclaimed the Professor. "We are not progressing with our great discoveries. All this is utter loss of time. After all, I did not come from home to undertake a party of pleasure. This voyage on a raft over a pond annoys and wearies me."

He called this adventurous journey a party of pleasure, and this great inland sea a pond!

"But," argued I, "if we have followed the route indicated by the great Saknussemm, we cannot be going far wrong."

"'That is the question,' as the great, the immortal Shakespeare, has it. Are we following the route indicated by that wondrous sage? Did Saknussemm ever fall in with this great sheet of water? If he did, did he cross it? I begin to fear that the rivulet we adopted for a guide has led us wrong."

"In any case, we can never regret having come thus far. It is worth the whole journey to have enjoyed this magnificent spectacle—it is something to have seen."

"I care nothing about seeing, nor about magnificent spectacles. I came down into the interior of the earth with an object, and that object I mean to attain. Don't talk to me about admiring scenery, or any other sentimental trash."

After this I thought it well to hold my tongue, and allow the Professor to bite his lips until the blood came, without further remark.

At six o'clock in the evening, our matter-of-fact guide, Hans, asked for his week's salary, and receiving his three rix-dollars, put them carefully in his pocket. He was perfectly contented and satisfied.

Sunday, August 16th. Nothing new to record. The same weather as before. The wind has a slight tendency to freshen up, with signs of an approaching gale. When I awoke, My first observation was in regard to the intensity of the light. I keep on fearing, day after day, that the extraordinary electric phenomenon should become first obscured, and then go wholly out, leaving us in total darkness. Nothing, however, of the kind occurs. The shadow of the raft, its mast and sails, is clearly distinguished on the surface of the water.

This wondrous sea is, after all, infinite in its extent. It must be quite as wide as the Mediterranean—or perhaps even as the great Atlantic Ocean. Why, after all, should it not be so?

My uncle has on more than one occasion, tried deep-sea soundings. He tied the cross of one of our heaviest crowbars to the extremity of a cord, which he allowed to run out to the extent of two hundred fathoms. We had the greatest difficulty in hoisting in our novel kind of lead.

When the crowbar was finally dragged on board, Hans called my attention to some singular marks upon its surface. The piece of iron looked as if it had been crushed between two very hard substances.

I looked at our worthy guide with an inquiring glance.

"Tander," said he.

Of course I was at a loss to understand. I turned round towards my uncle, absorbed in gloomy reflections. I had little wish to disturb him from his reverie. I accordingly turned once more towards our worthy Icelander.

Hans very quietly and significantly opened his mouth once or twice, as if in the act of biting, and in this way made me understand his meaning.

"Teeth!" cried I, with stupefaction, as I examined the bar of iron with more attention.

Yes. There can be no doubt about the matter. The indentations on the bar of iron are the marks of teeth! What jaws must the owner of such molars be possessed of! Have well then, come upon a monster of unknown species, which still exists within the vast waste of waters—a monster more voracious than a shark, more terrible and bulky than the whale? I am unable to withdraw my eyes from the bar of iron, actually half crushed!

Is, then, my dream about to come true—a dread and terrible reality?

All day my thoughts were bent upon these speculations, and my imagination scarcely regained a degree of calmness and power of reflection until after a sleep of many hours.

This day, as on other Sundays, we observed as a day of rest and pious meditation.

Monday, August 17th. I have been trying to realize from memory the particular instincts of those antediluvian animals of the secondary period, which succeeding to the mollusca, to the crustacea, and to the fish, preceded the appearance of the race of mammifers. The generation of reptiles then reigned supreme upon the earth. These hideous monsters ruled everything in the seas of the secondary period, which formed the strata of which the Jura mountains are composed. Nature had endowed them with perfect organization. What a gigantic structure was theirs; what vast and prodigious strength they possessed!

The existing saurians, which include all such reptiles as lizards, crocodiles, and alligators, even the largest and most formidable of their class, are but feeble imitations of their mighty sires, the animals of ages long ago. If there were giants in the days of old, there were also gigantic animals.

I shuddered as I evolved from my mind the idea and recollection of these awful monsters. No eye of man had seen them in the flesh. They took their walks abroad upon the face of the earth thousands of ages before man came into existence, and their fossil bones, discovered in the limestone, have allowed us to reconstruct them anatomically, and thus to get some faint idea of their colossal formation.

I recollect once seeing in the great Museum of Hamburg the skeleton of one of these wonderful saurians. It measured no less than thirty feet from the nose to the tail. Am I, then, an inhabitant of the earth of the present day, destined to find myself face to face with a representative of this antediluvian family? I can scarcely believe it possible; I can hardly believe it true. And yet these marks of powerful teeth upon the bar of iron! Can there be a doubt from their shape that the bite is the bite of a crocodile?

My eyes stare wildly and with terror upon the subterranean sea. Every moment I expect one of these monsters to rise from its vast cavernous depths.

I fancy that the worthy Professor in some measure shares

my notions, if not my fears, for, after an attentive examination of the crowbar, he cast his eyes rapidly over the mighty and mysterious ocean.

"What could possess him to leave the land," I thought, "as if the depth of this water was of any importance to us. No doubt he has disturbed some terrible monster in his watery home, and perhaps we may pay dearly for our temerity."

Anxious to be prepared for the worst, I examined our weapons, and saw that they were in a fit state for use. My uncle looked on at me and nodded his head approvingly. He, too, has noticed what we have to fear.

Already the uplifting of the waters on the surface indicates that something is in motion below. The danger approaches. It comes nearer and nearer. It behooves us to be on the watch.

Tuesday, August 18th. Evening came at last, the hour when the desire for sleep caused our eyelids to be heavy. Night there is not, properly speaking, in this place, any more than there is in summer in the arctic regions. Hans, however, is immovable at the rudder. When he snatches a moment of rest I really cannot say. I take advantage of his vigilance to take some little repose.

But two hours after I was awakened from a heavy sleep by an awful shock. The raft appeared to have struck upon a sunken rock. It was lifted right out of the water by some wondrous and mysterious power, and then started off twenty fathoms distant.

"Eh, what is it?" cried my uncle starting up. "Are we shipwrecked, or what?"

Hans raised his hand and pointed to where, about two hundred yards off, a large black mass was moving up and down.

I looked with awe. My worst fears were realized.

"It is a colossal monster!" I cried, clasping my hands.

"Yes," cried the agitated Professor, "and there yonder is a huge sea lizard of terrible size and shape."

"And farther on behold a prodigious crocodile. Look at his hideous jaws, and that row of monstrous teeth. Ha! he has gone."

"A whale! a whale!" shouted the Professor, "I can see her enormous fins. See, see, how she blows air and water!"

Two liquid columns rose to a vast height above the level of the sea, into which they fell with a terrific crash, waking up the echoes of that awful place. We stood still—surprised, stupefied, terror-stricken at the sight of this group of fearful marine monsters, more hideous in the reality than in my dream. They were of supernatural dimensions; the very smallest of the whole party could with ease have crushed our raft and ourselves with a single bite.

Hans, seizing the rudder which had flown out of his hand, puts it hard aweather in order to escape from such dangerous vicinity; but no sooner does he do so, than he finds he is flying from Scylla to Charybdis. To leeward is a turtle about forty feet wide, and a serpent quite as long, with an enormous and hideous head peering from out the waters.

Look which way we will, it is impossible for us to fly. The fearful reptiles advanced upon us; they turned and twisted about the raft with awful rapidity. They formed around our devoted vessel a series of concentric circles. I took up my rifle in desperation. But what effect can a rifle ball produce upon the armor scales with which the bodies of these horrid monsters are covered?

We remain still and dumb from utter horror. They advance upon us, nearer and nearer. Our fate appears certain, fearful and terrible. On one side the mighty crocodile, on the other the great sea serpent. The rest of the fearful crowd of marine prodigies have plunged beneath the briny waves and disappeared!

I am about to fire at any risk and try the effect of a shot. Hans, the guide, however, interfered by a sign to check me. The two hideous and ravenous monsters passed within fifty fathoms of the raft, and then made a rush at one another—their fury and rage preventing them from seeing us.

The combat commenced. We distinctly made out every action of the two hideous monsters.

But to my excited imagination the other animals appeared about to take part in the fierce and deadly struggle—the monster, the whale, the lizard, and the turtle. I distinctly saw them every moment. I pointed them out to the Icelander. But he only shook his head.

"Tva," he said.

"What—two only does he say. Surely he is mistaken," I cried in a tone of wonder.

"He is quite right," replied my uncle coolly and philosophically, examining the terrible duel with his telescope and speaking as if he were in a lecture room.

"How can that be?"

"Yes, it is so. The first of these hideous monsters has the snout of a porpoise, the head of a lizard, the teeth of a crocodile; and it is this that has deceived us. It is the most fearful of all antediluvian reptiles, the world—renowned Ichthyosaurus or great fish lizard."

"And the other?"

"The other is a monstrous serpent, concealed under the hard vaulted shell of the turtle, the terrible enemy of its fearful rival, the Plesiosaurus, or sea crocodile."

Hans was quite right. The two monsters only, disturbed the surface of the sea!

At last have mortal eyes gazed upon two reptiles of the great primitive ocean! I see the flaming red eyes of the Ichthyosaurus, each as big, or bigger than a man's head. Nature in its infinite wisdom had gifted this wondrous marine animal with an optical apparatus of extreme power, capable of resisting the pressure of the heavy layers of water which rolled over him in the depths of the ocean where he usually fed. It has by some authors truly been called the whale of the saurian race, for it is as big and quick in its motions as our king of the seas. This one measures not less than a hundred feet in length, and I can form some idea of his girth when I see him lift his prodigious tail out of the waters. His jaw is of awful size and strength, and according to the best-informed naturalists, it does not contain less than a hundred and eighty-two teeth.

The other was the mighty Plesiosaurus, a serpent with a cylindrical trunk, with a short stumpy tail, with fins like a bank of oars in a Roman galley.Its whole body covered by a carapace or shell, and its neck, as flexible as that of a swan, rose more than thirty feet above the waves, a tower of animated flesh!

These animals attacked one another with inconceivable fury. Such a combat was never seen before by mortal eyes, and to us who did see it, it appeared more like the phantasmagoric creation of a dream than anything else. They raised mountains of water, which dashed in spray over the raft, already tossed to and fro by the waves. Twenty times we seemed on the point of being upset and hurled headlong into the waves. Hideous hisses appeared to shake the gloomy granite roof of that mighty cavern—hisses which carried terror to our hearts. The awful combatants held each other in a tight embrace. I could not make out one from the other. Still the combat could not last forever; and woe unto us, whichsoever became the victor.

One hour, two hours, three hours passed away, without any decisive result. The struggle continued with the same deadly tenacity, but without apparent result. The deadly opponents now approached, now drew away from the raft. Once or twice we fancied they were about to leave us altogether, but instead of that, they came nearer and nearer.

We crouched on the raft ready to fire at them at a moment's notice, poor as the prospect of hurting or terrifying them was. Still we were determined not to perish without a struggle.

Suddenly the Ichthyosaurus and the Plesiosaurus disappeared beneath the waves, leaving behind them a maelstrom in the midst of the sea. We were nearly drawn down by the indraft of the water!

Several minutes elapsed before anything was again seen. Was this wonderful combat to end in the depths of the ocean? Was the last act of this terrible drama to take place without spectators?

It was impossible for us to say.

Suddenly, at no great distance from us, an enormous mass rises out of the waters—the head of the great Plesiosaurus. The terrible monster is now wounded unto death. I can see nothing now of his enormous body. All that could be distinguished was his serpent-like neck, which he twisted and curled in all the agonies of death. Now he struck the waters with it as if it had been a gigantic whip, and then again wriggled like a worm cut in two. The water was spurted up to a great distance in all directions. A great portion of it swept over our raft and nearly blinded us. But soon the end of the beast approached nearer and nearer; his movements slackened visibly; his contortions almost ceased; and at last the body of the mighty snake lay an inert, dead mass on the surface of the now calm and placid waters.

As for the Ichthyosaurus, has he gone down to his mighty cavern under the sea to rest, or will he reappear to destroy us?

This question remained unanswered. And we had breathing time.

Chapter 31

THE SEA MONSTER

Wednesday, August 19th. Fortunately the wind, which for the present blows with some violence, has allowed us to escape from the scene of the unparalleled and extraordinary struggle. Hans with his usual imperturbable calm remained at the helm. My uncle, who for a short time had been withdrawn from his absorbing reveries by the novel incidents of this sea fight, fell back again apparently into a brown study. His eyes were fixed impatiently on the widespread ocean.

Our voyage now became monotonous and uniform. Dull as it has become, I have no desire to have it broken by any repetition of the perils and adventures of yesterday.

Thursday, August 20th. The wind is now N. N. E., and blows very irregularly. It has changed to fitful gusts. The temperature is exceedingly high. We are now progressing at the average rate of about ten miles and a half per hour.

About twelve o'clock a distant sound as of thunder fell upon our ears. I make a note of the fact without even venturing a suggestion as to its cause. It was one continued roar as of a sea falling over mighty rocks.

"Far off in the distance," said the Professor dogmatically, "there is some rock or some island against which the seal lashed to fury by the wind, is breaking violently."

Hans, without saying a word, clambered to the top of the mast, but could make out nothing. The ocean was level in every direction as far as the eye could reach.

Three hours passed away without any sign to indicate what might be before us. The sound began to assume that of a mighty cataract.

I expressed my opinion on this point strongly to my uncle. He merely shook his head. I, however, am strongly impressed by a conviction that I am not wrong. Are we advancing towards some mighty waterfall which shall cast us into the abyss? Probably this mode of descending into the abyss may be agreeable to the Professor, because it would be something like the vertical descent he is so eager to make. I entertain a very different opinion.

Whatever be the truth, it is certain that not many leagues distant there must be some very extraordinary phenomenon, for as we advance the roar becomes something mighty and stupendous. Is it in the water, or in the air?

I cast hasty glances aloft at the suspended vapors, and I seek to penetrate their mighty depths. But the vault above is tranquil. The clouds, which are now elevated to the very summit, appear utterly still and motionless, and completely lost in the irradiation of electric light. It is necessary, therefore, to seek for the cause of this phenomenon elsewhere.

I examine the horizon, now perfectly calm, pure, and free from all haze. Its aspect still remains unchanged. But if this awful noise proceeds from a cataract—if, so to speak in plain English, this vast interior ocean is precipitated into a lower basin—if these tremendous roars are produced by the noise of falling waters, the current would increase in activity, and its increasing swiftness would give me some idea of the extent of the peril with which we are menaced. I consult the current. It simply does not exist: there is no such thing. An empty bottle cast into the water lies to leeward without motion.

About four o'clock Hans rises, clambers up the mast, and

reaches the truck itself. From this elevated position his looks are cast around. They take in a vast circumference of the ocean. At last, his eyes remain fixed. His face expresses no astonishment, but his eyes slightly dilate.

"He has seen something at last," cried my uncle.

"I think so," I replied.

Hans came down, stood beside us, and pointed with his right hand to the south.

"Der nere," he said.

"There," replied my uncle.

And seizing his telescope, he looked at it with great attention for about a minute, which to me appeared an age. I knew not what to think or expect.

"Yes, yes," he cried in a tone of considerable surprise, "there it is."

"What?" I asked.

"A tremendous spurt of water rising out of the waves."

"Some other marine monster," I cried, already alarmed.

"Perhaps."

"Then let us steer more to the westward, for we know what we have to expect from antediluvian animals," was my eager reply.

"Go ahead," said my uncle.

I turned towards Hans. Hans was at the tiller steering with his usual imperturbable calm.

Nevertheless, if from the distance which separated us from this creature, a distance which must be estimated at not less than a dozen leagues, one could see the column of water spurting from the blow-hole of the great animal, his dimensions must be something preternatural. To fly is, therefore, the course to be suggested by ordinary prudence. But we have not come into that part of the world to be prudent. Such is my uncle's determination.

We, accordingly, continued to advance. The nearer we come, the loftier is the spouting water. What monster can fill himself with such huge volumes of water, and then unceasingly spout them out in such lofty jets?

At eight o'clock in the evening, reckoning as above ground, where there is day and night, we are not more than two leagues from the mighty beast. Its long, black, enormous, mountainous body, lies on the top of the water like an island. But then sailors have been said to have gone ashore on sleeping whales, mistaking them for land. Is it illusion, or is it fear? Its length cannot be less than a thousand fathoms. What, then, is this cetaceous monster of which no Cuvier ever thought?

It is quite motionless and presents the appearance of sleep. The sea seems unable to lift him upwards; it is rather the waves which break on his huge and gigantic frame. The waterspout, rising to a height of five hundred feet, breaks in spray with a dull, sullen roar.

We advance, like senseless lunatics, towards this mighty mass.

I honestly confess that I was abjectly afraid. I declared that I would go no farther. I threatened in my terror to cut the sheet of the sail. I attacked the Professor with considerable acrimony, calling him foolhardy, mad, I know not what. He made no answer.

Suddenly the imperturbable Hans once more pointed his finger to the menacing object:

"*Holme*!"

"An island!" cried my uncle.

"An island?" I replied, shrugging my shoulders at this poor attempt at deception.

"Of course it is," cried my uncle, bursting into a loud and joyous laugh.

"But the waterspout?"

"Geyser," said Hans.

"Yes, of course—a geyser," replied my uncle, still laughing, "a geyser like those common in Iceland. Jets like this are the great wonders of the country."

At first I would not allow that I had been so grossly deceived. What could be more ridiculous than to have taken an island for a marine monster? But kick as one may, one must yield to evidence, and I was finally convinced of my error. It was nothing, after all, but a natural phenomenon.

As we approached nearer and nearer, the dimensions of the liquid sheaf of waters became truly grand and stupendous. The island had, at a distance, presented the appearance of an enormous whale, whose head rose high above the waters. The geyser, a word the Icelanders pronounce geysir, and which signifies fury, rose majestically from its summit. Dull detonations are heard every now and then, and the enormous jet, taken as it were with sudden fury, shakes its plume of vapor, and bounds into the first layer of the clouds. It is alone. Neither spurts of vapor nor hot springs surround it, and the whole volcanic power of that region is concentrated in one sublime column. The rays of electric light mix with this dazzling sheaf, every drop as it falls assuming the prismatic colors of the rainbow.

"Let us go on shore," said the Professor, after some minutes of silence.

It is necessary, however, to take great precaution, in order to avoid the weight of falling waters, which would cause the raft to founder in an instant. Hans, however, steers admirably, and brings us to the other extremity of the island.

I was the first to leap on the rock. My uncle followed, while the eider-duck hunter remained still, like a man above any childish sources of astonishment. We were now walking on granite mixed with siliceous sandstone; the soil shivered under our feet like the sides of boilers in which over-heated steam is forcibly confined. It is burning. We soon came in sight of the little central basin from which rose the geyser. I plunged a thermometer into the water which ran bubbling from the centre, and it marked a heat of a hundred and sixty-three degrees!

This water, therefore, came from some place where the heat was intense. This was singularly in contradiction with the theories of Professor Hardwigg. I could not help telling him my opinion on the subject.

"Well," said he sharply, "and what does this prove against my doctrine?"

"Nothing," replied I dryly, seeing that I was running my head against a foregone conclusion.

Nevertheless, I am compelled to confess that until now we have been most remarkably fortunate, and that this voyage is being accomplished in most favorable conditions of temperature; but it appears evident, in fact, certain, that we shall sooner or later arrive at one of those regions where the central heat will reach its utmost limits, and will go far beyond all the possible gradations of thermometers.

Visions of the Hades of the ancients, believed to be in the centre of the earth, floated through my imagination.

We shall, however, see what we shall see. That is the Professor's favorite phrase now. Having christened the volcanic island by the name of his nephew, the leader of the expedition turned away and gave the signal for embarkation.

I stood still, however, for some minutes, gazing upon the magnificent geyser. I soon was able to perceive that the upward tendency of the water was irregular; now it diminished in intensity, and then, suddenly, it regained new vigor, which I attributed to the variation of the pressure of the accumulated vapors in its reservoir.

At last we took our departure, going carefully round the projecting, and rather dangerous, rocks of the southern side. Hans had taken advantage of this brief halt to repair the raft.

Before we took our final departure from the island, however, I made some observations to calculate the distance we had gone over, and I put them down in my journal. Since we left Port Gretchen, we had traveled two hundred and seventy leagues—more than eight hundred miles—on this great inland sea; we were, therefore, six hundred and twenty leagues from Iceland, and exactly under England.

Chapter 32

THE BATTLE OF THE ELEMENTS

Friday, August 21st. This morning the magnificent geyser had wholly disappeared. The wind had freshened up, and we were fast leaving the neighborhood of Henry's Island. Even the roaring sound of the mighty column was lost to the ear.

The weather, if, under the circumstances, we may use such an expression, is about to change very suddenly. The atmosphere is being gradually loaded with vapors, which carry with them the electricity formed by the constant evaporation of the saline waters; the clouds are slowly but sensibly falling towards the sea, and are assuming a dark-olive texture; the electric rays can scarcely pierce through the opaque curtain which has fallen like a drop scene before this wondrous theater, on the stage of which another and terrible drama is soon to be enacted. This time it is no fight of animals; it is the fearful battle of the elements.

I feel that I am very peculiarly influenced, as all creatures are on land when a deluge is about to take place.

The cumuli, a perfectly oval kind of cloud, piled upon the south, presented a most awful and sinister appearance, with the pitiless aspect often seen before a storm. The air is extremely heavy; the sea is comparatively calm.

In the distance, the clouds have assumed the appearance of enormous balls of cotton, or rather pods, piled one above the other in picturesque confusion. By degrees, they appear to swell out, break, and gain in number what they lose in grandeur; their heaviness is so great that they are unable to lift themselves from the horizon; but under the influence of the upper currents of air, they are gradually broken up, become much darker, and then present the appearance of one single layer of a formidable character; now and then a lighter cloud, still lit up from above, rebounds upon this grey carpet, and is lost in the opaque mass.

There can be no doubt that the entire atmosphere is saturated with electric fluid; I am myself wholly impregnated; my hairs literally stand on end as if under the influence of a galvanic battery. If one of my companions ventured to touch me, I think he would receive rather a violent and unpleasant shock.

About ten o'clock in the morning, the symptoms of the storm became more thorough and decisive; the wind appeared to soften down as if to take breath for a renewed attack; the vast funereal pall above us looked like a huge bag—like the cave of AEolus, in which the storm was collecting its forces for the attack.

I tried all I could not to believe in the menacing signs of the sky, and yet I could not avoid saying, as it were involuntarily:

"I believe we are going to have bad weather."

The Professor made me no answer. He was in a horrible, in a detestable humor—to see the ocean stretching interminably before his eyes. On hearing my words he simply shrugged his shoulders.

"We shall have a tremendous storm," I said again, pointing to the horizon. "These clouds are falling lower and lower upon the sea, as if to crush it."

A great silence prevailed. The wind wholly ceased. Nature assumed a dead calm, and ceased to breathe. Upon the mast, where I noticed a sort of slight ignis fatuus, the sail hangs in loose heavy folds. The raft is motionless in the midst of a dark heavy sea—without undulation, without motion. It is as still as glass. But as we are making no progress, what is the use of keeping up the sail, which may be the cause of our perdition if the tempest should suddenly strike us without warning.

"Let us lower the sail," I said, "it is only an act of common prudence."

"No—no," cried my uncle, in an exasperated tone, "a hundred times, no. Let the wind strike us and do its worst, let the storm sweep us away where it will—only let me see the glimmer of some coast—of some rocky cliffs, even if they dash our raft into a thousand pieces. No! keep up the sail—no matter what happens."

These words were scarcely uttered when the southern horizon underwent a sudden and violent change. The long accumulated vapors were resolved into water, and the air required to fill up the void produced became a wild and raging tempest.

It came from the most distant corners of the mighty cavern. It raged from every point of the compass. It roared; it yelled; it shrieked with glee as of demons let loose. The darkness increased and became indeed darkness visible.

The raft rose and fell with the storm, and bounded over the waves. My uncle was cast headlong upon the deck. I with great difficulty dragged myself towards him. He was holding on with might and main to the end of a cable, and appeared to gaze with pleasure and delight at the spectacle of the unchained elements.

Hans never moved a muscle. His long hair driven hither and thither by the tempest and scattered wildly over his motionless face, gave him a most extraordinary appearance—for every single hair was illuminated by little sparkling sprigs.

His countenance presents the extraordinary appearance of an antediluvian man, a true contemporary of the Megatherium.

Still the mast holds good against the storm. The sail spreads out and fills like a soap bubble about to burst. The raft rushes on at a pace impossible to estimate, but still less swiftly than the body of water displaced beneath it, the rapidity of which may be seen by the lines which fly right and left in the wake.

"The sail, the sail!" I cried, making a trumpet of my hands, and then endeavoring to lower it.

"Let it alone!" said my uncle, more exasperated than ever.

"*Nej*," said Hans, gently shaking his head.

Nevertheless, the rain formed a roaring cataract before this horizon of which we were in search, and to which we were rushing like madmen.

But before this wilderness of waters reached us, the mighty veil of cloud was torn in twain; the sea began to foam wildly; and the electricity, produced by some vast and extraordinary chemical action in the upper layer of cloud, is brought into play. To the fearful claps of thunder are added dazzling flashes of lightning, such as I had never seen. The flashes crossed one another, hurled from every side; while the thunder came pealing like an echo. The mass of vapor becomes incandescent; the hailstones which strike the metal of our boots and our weapons are actually luminous; the waves as they rise appear to be fire-eating monsters, beneath which seethes an intense fire, their crests surmounted by combs of flame.

My eyes are dazzled, blinded by the intensity of light, my ears are deafened by the awful roar of the elements. I am compelled to hold onto the mast, which bends like a reed beneath the violence of the storm, to which none ever before seen by mariners bore any resemblance.

Here my traveling notes become very incomplete, loose and vague. I have only been able to make out one or two fugitive observations, jotted down in a mere mechanical way. But even their brevity, even their obscurity, show the emotions which overcame me.Sunday, August 23rd. Where have we got to? In what region are we wandering? We are still carried forward with inconceivable rapidity.

The night has been fearful, something not to be described. The storm shows no signs of cessation. We exist in the midst of an uproar which has no name. The detonations as of artillery are incessant. Our ears literally bleed. We are unable to exchange a word, or hear each other speak.

The lightning never ceases to flash for a single instant. I can see the zigzags after a rapid dart strike the arched roof of this mightiest of mighty vaults. If it were to give way and fall upon us! Other lightnings plunge their forked streaks in every direction, and take the form of globes of fire, which explode like bombshells over a beleaguered city. The general crash and roar do not apparently increase; it has already gone far beyond what human ear can appreciate. If all the powder magazines in the world were to explode together, it would be impossible for us to hear worse noise.

There is a constant emission of light from the storm clouds; the electric matter is incessantly released; evidently the gaseous principles of the air are out of order; innumerable columns of water rush up like waterspouts, and fall back upon the surface of the ocean in foam.

Whither are we going? My uncle still lies at full length upon the raft, without speaking—without taking any note of time.

The heat increases. I look at the thermometer, to my surprise it indicates—*The exact figure is here rubbed out in my manuscript.*

Monday, August 24th. This terrible storm will never end. Why should not this state of the atmosphere, so dense and murky, once modified, again remain definitive?

We are utterly broken and harassed by fatigue. Hans remains just as usual. The raft runs to the southeast invariably. We have now already run two hundred leagues from the newly discovered island.

About twelve o'clock the storm became worse than ever. We are obliged now to fasten every bit of cargo tightly on the deck of the raft, or everything would be swept away. We make ourselves fast, too, each man lashing the other. The waves drive over us, so that several times we are actually under water.

We had been under the painful necessity of abstaining from speech for three days and three nights. We opened our mouths, we moved our lips, but no sound came. Even when we placed our mouths to each other's ears it was the same.

The wind carried the voice away.

My uncle once contrived to get his head close to mine after several almost vain endeavors. He appeared to my nearly exhausted senses to articulate some word. I had a notion, more from intuition than anything else, that he said to me, "We are lost."

I took out my notebook, from which under the most desperate circumstances I never parted, and wrote a few words as legibly as I could:

"Take in sail."

With a deep sigh he nodded his head and acquiesced.

His head had scarcely time to fall back in the position from which he had momentarily raised it than a disk or ball of fire appeared on the very edge of the raft—our devoted, our doomed craft. The mast and sail are carried away bodily, and I see them swept away to a prodigious height like a kite.

We were frozen, actually shivered with terror. The ball of fire, half white, half azure-colored, about the size of a ten-inch bombshell, moved along, turning with prodigious rapidity to leeward of the storm. It ran about here, there, and everywhere, it clambered up one of the bulwarks of the raft, it leaped upon the sack of provisions, and then finally descended lightly, fell like a football and landed on our powder barrel.

Horrible situation. An explosion of course was now inevitable.

By heaven's mercy, it was not so.

The dazzling disk moved on one side, it approached Hans, who looked at it with singular fixity; then it approached my uncle, who cast himself on his knees to avoid it; it came towards me, as I stood pale and shuddering in the dazzling light and heat; it pirouetted round my feet, which I endeavored to withdraw.

An odor of nitrous gas filled the whole air; it penetrated to the throat, to the lungs. I felt ready to choke.

Why is it that I cannot withdraw my feet? Are they riveted to the flooring of the raft?

No.

The fall of the electric globe has turned all the iron on board into loadstones—the instruments, the tools, the arms are clanging together with awful and horrible noise; the nails of my heavy boots adhere closely to the plate of iron incrustated in the wood. I cannot withdraw my foot.

It is the old story again of the mountain of adamant.

At last, by a violent and almost superhuman effort, I tear it away just as the ball which is still executing its gyratory motions is about to run round it and drag me with it—if—

Oh, what intense stupendous light! The globe of fire bursts—we are enveloped in cascades of living fire, which flood the space around with luminous matter.

Then all went out and darkness once more fell upon the deep! I had just time to see my uncle once more cast apparently senseless on the flooring of the raft, Hans at the helm, "spitting fire" under the influence of the electricity which seemed to have gone through him.

Whither are we going, I ask? and echo answers, Whither?

....

Tuesday, August 25th. I have just come out of a long fainting fit. The awful and hideous storm still continues; the lightning has increased in vividness, and pours out its fiery wrath like a brood of serpents let loose in the atmosphere.

Are we still upon the sea? Yes, and being carried along with incredible velocity.

We have passed under England, under the Channel, under France, probably under the whole extent of Europe.

Another awful clamor in the distance. This time it is certain that the sea is breaking upon the rocks at no great distance. Then—

....

....

Chapter 33

OUR ROUTE REVERSED

Here ends what I call "My Journal" of our voyage on board the raft, which journal was happily saved from the wreck. I proceed with my narrative as I did before I commenced my daily notes.

What happened when the terrible shock took place, when the raft was cast upon the rocky shore, it would be impossible for me now to say. I felt myself precipitated violently into the boiling waves, and if I escaped from a certain and cruel death, it was wholly owing to the determination of the faithful Hans, who, clutching me by the arm, saved me from the yawning abyss.

The courageous Icelander then carried me in his powerful arms, far out of the reach of the waves, and laid me down upon a burning expanse of sand, where I found myself some time afterwards in the company of my uncle, the Professor.

Then he quietly returned towards the fatal rocks, against which the furious waves were beating, in order to save any stray waifs from the wreck. This man was always practical and thoughtful. I could not utter a word; I was quite overcome with emotion; my whole body was broken and bruised with fatigue; it took hours before I was anything like myself.

Meanwhile, there fell a fearful deluge of rain, drenching us to the skin. Its very violence, however, proclaimed the approaching end of the storm. Some overhanging rocks afforded us a slight protection from the torrents.

Under this shelter, Hans prepared some food, which, however, I was unable to touch; and, exhausted by the three weary days and nights of watching, we fell into a deep and painful sleep. My dreams were fearful, but at last exhausted nature asserted her supremacy, and I slumbered.

Next day when I awoke the change was magical. The weather was magnificent. Air and sea, as if by mutual consent, had regained their serenity. Every trace of the storm, even the faintest, had disappeared. I was saluted on my awakening by the first joyous tones I had heard from the Professor for many a day. His gaiety, indeed, was something terrible.

"Well, my lad," he cried, rubbing his hands together, "have you slept soundly?"

Might it not have been supposed that we were in the old house on the Konigstrasse; that I had just come down quietly to my breakfast; and that my marriage with Gretchen was to take place that very day? My uncle's coolness was exasperating.

Alas, considering how the tempest had driven us in an easterly direction, we had passed under the whole of Germany, under the city of Hamburg where I had been so happy, under the very street which contained all I loved and cared for in the world.

It was a positive fact that I was only separated from her by a distance of forty leagues. But these forty leagues were of hard, impenetrable granite!

All these dreary and miserable reflections passed through my mind, before I attempted to answer my uncle's question.

"Why, what is the matter?" he cried. "Cannot you say whether you have slept well or not?"

"I have slept very well," was my reply, "but every bone in my body aches. I suppose that will lead to nothing."

"Nothing at all, my boy. It is only the result of the fatigue of the last few days—that is all."

"You appear—if I may be allowed to say so—to be very jolly this morning," I said.

"Delighted, my dear boy, delighted. Was never happier in my life. We have at last reached the wished-for port."

"The end of our expedition?" cried I, in a tone of considerable surprise.

"No; but to the confines of that sea which I began to fear would never end, but go round the whole world. We will now tranquilly resume our journey by land, and once again endeavor to dive into the centre of the earth."

"My dear uncle," I began, in a hesitating kind of way, "allow me to ask you one question."

"Certainly, Harry; a dozen if you think proper."

"One will suffice. How about getting back?" I asked.

"How about getting back? What a question to ask. We have not as yet reached the end of our journey."

"I know that. All I want to know is how you propose we shall manage the return voyage?"

"In the most simple manner in the world," said the imperturbable Professor. "Once we reach the exact centre of this sphere, either we shall find a new road by which to ascend to the surface, or we shall simply turn round and go back by the way we came. I have every reason to believe that while we are traveling forward, it will not close behind us."

"Then one of the first matters to see to will be to repair the raft," was my rather melancholy response.

"Of course. We must attend to that above all things," continued the Professor.

"Then comes the all-important question of provisions," I urged. "Have we anything like enough left to enable us to accomplish such great, such amazing, designs as you contemplate carrying out?"

"I have seen into the matter, and my answer is in the affirmative. Hans is a very clever fellow, and I have reason to believe that he has saved the greater part of the cargo. But the best way to satisfy your scruples is to come and judge for yourself."

Saying which, he led the way out of the kind of open grotto in which we had taken shelter. I had almost begun to hope that which I should rather have feared, and this was the impossibility of such a shipwreck leaving even the slightest signs of what it had carried as freight. I was, however, thoroughly mistaken.

As soon as I reached the shores of this inland sea, I found Hans standing gravely in the midst of a large number of things laid out in complete order. My uncle wrung his hands with deep and silent gratitude. His heart was too full for speech.

This man, whose superhuman devotion to his employers I not only never saw surpassed, nor even equaled, had been hard at work all the time we slept, and at the risk of his life had succeeded in saving the most precious articles of our cargo.

Of course, under the circumstances, we necessarily experienced several severe losses. Our weapons had wholly vanished. But experience had taught us to do without them. The provision of powder had, however, remained intact, after having narrowly escaped blowing us all to atoms in the storm.

"Well," said the Professor, who was now ready to make the best of everything, "as we have no guns, all we have to do is to give up all idea of hunting."

"Yes, my dear sir, we can do without them, but what about all our instruments?"

"Here is the manometer, the most useful of all, and which I gladly accept in lieu of the rest. With it alone I can calculate the depth as we proceed; by its means alone I shall be able to decide when we have reached the centre of the earth. Ha, ha! but for this little instrument we might make a mistake, and run the risk of coming out at the antipodes!"

All this was said amid bursts of unnatural laughter.

"But the compass," I cried, "without that what can we do?"

"Here it is, safe and sound!" he cried, with real joy, "ah, ah, and here we have the chronometer and the thermometers. Hans the hunter is indeed an invaluable man!"

It was impossible to deny this fact. As far as the nautical and other instruments were concerned, nothing was wanting. Then on further examination, I found ladders, cords, pickaxes, crowbars, and shovels, all scattered about on the shore.

There was, however, finally the most important question of all, and that was, provisions.

"But what are we to do for food?" I asked.

"Let us see to the commissariat department", replied my uncle gravely.

The boxes which contained our supply of food for the voyage were placed in a row along the strand, and were in a capital state of preservation; the sea had in every case respected their contents, and to sum up in one sentence, taking into consideration, biscuits, salt meat, Schiedam and dried fish, we could still calculate on having about four months' supply, if used with prudence and caution.

"Four months," cried the sanguine Professor in high glee. "Then we shall have plenty of time both to go and to come, and with what remains I undertake to give a grand dinner to my colleagues of the Johanneum."

I sighed. I should by this time have become used to the temperament of my uncle, and yet this man astonished me more and more every day. He was the greatest human enigma I ever had known.

"Now," he, "before we do anything else, we must lay in a

stock of fresh water. The rain has fallen in abundance, and filled the hollows of the granite. There is a rich supply of water, and we have no fear of suffering from thirst, which in our circumstances is of the last importance. As for the raft, I shall recommend Hans to repair it to the best of his abilities; though I have every reason to believe we shall not require it again."

"How is that?" I cried, more amazed than ever at my uncle's style of reasoning.

"I have an idea, my dear boy; it is none other than this simple fact; we shall not come out by the same opening as that by which we entered."

I began to look at my uncle with vague suspicion. An idea had more than once taken possession of me; and this was, that he was going mad. And yet, little did I think how true and prophetic his words were doomed to be.

"And now," he said, "having seen to all these matters of detail, to breakfast."

I followed him to a sort of projecting cape, after he had given his last instructions to our guide. In this original position, with dried meat, biscuit, and a delicious cup of tea, we made a satisfactory meal—I may say one of the most welcome and pleasant I ever remember. Exhaustion, the keen atmosphere, the state of calm after so much agitation, all contributed to give me an excellent appetite. Indeed, it contributed very much to producing a pleasant and cheerful state of mind.

While breakfast was in hand, and between the sips of warm tea, I asked my uncle if he had any idea of how we now stood in relation to the world above.

"For my part," I added, "I think it will be rather difficult to determine."

"Well, if we were compelled to fix the exact spot," said my uncle, "it might be difficult, since during the three days of that awful tempest I could keep no account either of the quickness of our pace, or of the direction in which the raft was going. Still, we will endeavor to approximate to the truth. We shall not, I believe, be so very far out."

"Well, if I recollect rightly," I replied, "our last observation was made at the geyser island."

"Harry's Island, my boy! Harry's Island. Do not decline the honor of having named it; given your name to an island discovered by us, the first human beings who trod it since the creation of the world!"

"Let it be so, then. At Harry's Island we had already gone over two hundred and seventy leagues of sea, and we were, I believe, about six hundred leagues, more or less, from Iceland."

"Good. I am glad to see that you remember so well. Let us start from that point, and let us count four days of storm, during which our rate of traveling must have been very great. I should say that our velocity must have been about eighty leagues to the twenty-four hours."

I agreed that I thought this a fair calculation. There were then three hundred leagues to be added to the grand total.

"Yes, and the Central Sea must extend at least six hundred leagues from side to side. Do you know, my boy, Harry, that we have discovered an inland lake larger than the Mediterranean?"

"Certainly, and we only know of its extent in one way. It may be hundreds of miles in length."

"Very likely."

"Then," said I, after calculating for some for some minutes, "if your previsions are right, we are at this moment exactly under the Mediterranean itself."

"Do you think so?"

"Yes, I am almost certain of it. Are we not nine hundred leagues distant from Reykjavik?"

"That is perfectly true, and a famous bit of road we have traveled, my boy. But why we should be under the

Mediterranean more than under Turkey or the Atlantic Ocean can only be known when we are sure of not having deviated from our course; and of this we know nothing."

"I do not think we were driven very far from our course; the wind appears to me to have been always about the same. My opinion is that this shore must be situated to the southeast of Port Gretchen."

"Good—I hope so. It will, however, be easy to decide the matter by taking the bearings from our departure by means of the compass. Come along, and we will consult that invaluable invention."

The Professor now walked eagerly in the direction of the rock where the indefatigable Hans had placed the instruments in safety. My uncle was gay and lighthearted; he rubbed his hands, and assumed all sorts of attitudes. He was to all appearance once more a young man. Since I had known him, never had he been so amiable and pleasant. I followed him, rather curious to know whether I had made any mistake in my estimation of our position.

As soon as we had reached the rock, my uncle took the compass, placed it horizontally before him, and looked keenly at the needle.

As he had at first shaken it to give it vivacity, it oscillated considerably, and then slowly assumed its right position under the influence of the magnetic power.

The Professor bent his eyes curiously over the wondrous instrument. A violent start immediately showed the extent of his emotion.

He closed his eyes, rubbed them, and took another and a keener survey.

Then he turned slowly round to me, stupefaction depicted on his countenance.

"What is the matter?" said I, beginning to be alarmed.

He could not speak. He was too overwhelmed for words. He simply pointed to the instrument.

I examined it eagerly according to his mute directions, and a loud cry of surprise escaped my lips. The needle of the compass pointed due north—in the direction we expected was the south!

It pointed to the shore instead of to the high seas.

I shook the compass; I examined it with a curious and anxious eye. It was in a state of perfection. No blemish in any way explained the phenomenon. Whatever position we forced the needle into, it returned invariably to the same unexpected point.

It was useless attempting to conceal from ourselves the fatal truth.

There could be no doubt about it, unwelcome as was the fact, that during the tempest, there had been a sudden slant of wind, of which we had been unable to take any account, and thus the raft had carried us back to the shores we had left, apparently forever, so many days before!

Chapter 34

A VOYAGE OF DISCOVERY

It would be altogether impossible for me to give any idea of the utter astonishment which overcame the Professor on making this extraordinary discovery. Amazement, incredulity, and rage were blended in such a way as to alarm me.

During the whole course of my Life I had never seen a man at first so chapfallen; and then so furiously indignant.

The terrible fatigues of our sea voyage, the fearful dangers we had passed through, had all, all, gone for nothing. We had to begin them all over again.

Instead of progressing, as we fondly expected, during a voyage of so many days, we had retreated. Every hour of our expedition on the raft had been so much lost time!

Presently, however, the indomitable energy of my uncle overcame every other consideration.

"So," he said, between his set teeth, "fatality will play me these terrible tricks. The elements themselves conspire to overwhelm me with mortification. Air, fire, and water combine their united efforts to oppose my passage. Well, they shall see what the earnest will of a determined man can do. I will not yield, I will not retreat even one inch; and we shall see who shall triumph in this great contest—man or nature."

Standing upright on a rock, irritated and menacing, Professor Hardwigg, like the ferocious Ajax, seemed to defy the fates. I, however, took upon myself to interfere, and to impose some sort of check upon such insensate enthusiasm.

"Listen to me, Uncle," I said, in a firm but temperate tone of voice, "there must be some limit to ambition here below. It is utterly useless to struggle against the impossible. Pray listen to reason. We are utterly unprepared for a sea voyage; it is simply madness to think of performing a journey of five hundred leagues upon a wretched pile of beams, with a counterpane for a sail, a paltry stick for a mast, and a tempest to contend with. As we are totally incapable of steering our frail craft, we shall become the mere plaything of the storm, and it is acting the part of madmen if we, a second time, run any risk upon this dangerous and treacherous Central Sea."

These are only a few of the reasons and arguments I put together—reasons and arguments which to me appeared unanswerable. I was allowed to go on without interruption for about ten minutes. The explanation to this I soon discovered. The Professor was not even listening, and did not hear a word of all my eloquence.

"To the raft!" he cried in a hoarse voice, when I paused for a reply.

Such was the result of my strenuous effort to resist his iron will. I tried again; I begged and implored him; I got into a passion; but I had to deal with a will more determined than my own. I seemed to feel like the waves which fought and battled against the huge mass of granite at our feet, which had smiled grimly for so many ages at their puny efforts.

Hans, meanwhile, without taking part in our discussion, had been repairing the raft. One would have supposed that he instinctively guessed at the further projects of my uncle.

By means of some fragments of cordage, he had again made the raft seaworthy.

While I had been speaking, he had hoisted a new mast and sail, the latter already fluttering and waving in the breeze.

The worthy Professor spoke a few words to our imperturbable guide, who immediately began to put our baggage on board and to prepare for our departure. The atmosphere was now tolerably clear and pure, and the northeast wind blew steadily and serenely. It appeared likely to last for some time.

What, then, could I do? Could I undertake to resist the iron will of two men? It was simply impossible if even I could have hoped for the support of Hans. This, however, was out of the question. It appeared to me that the Icelander had set aside all personal will and identity. He was a picture of abnegation.

I could hope for nothing from one so infatuated with and devoted to his master. All I could do, therefore, was to swim with the stream.

In a mood of stolid and sullen resignation, I was about to take my accustomed place on the raft when my uncle placed his hand upon my shoulder.

"There is no hurry, my boy," he said, "we shall not start until tomorrow."

I looked the picture of resignation to the dire will of fate.

"Under the circumstances," he said, "I ought to neglect no precautions. As fate has cast me upon these shores, I shall not leave without having completely examined them."

In order to understand this remark, I must explain that though we had been driven back to the northern shore, we had landed at a very different spot from that which had been our starting point.

Port Gretchen must, we calculated, be very much to the westward. Nothing, therefore, was more natural and reasonable than that we should reconnoiter this new shore upon which we had so unexpectedly landed.

"Let us go on a journey of discovery," I cried.

And leaving Hans to his important operation, we started on our expedition. The distance between the foreshore at high water and the foot of the rocks was considerable. It would take about half an hour's walking to get from one to the other.

As we trudged along, our feet crushed innumerable shells of every shape and size—once the dwelling place of animals of every period of creation.

I particularly noticed some enormous shells—carapaces (turtle and tortoise species) the diameter of which exceeded fifteen feet.

They had in past ages belonged to those gigantic Glyptodons of the Pliocene period, of which the modern turtle is but a minute specimen. In addition, the whole soil was covered by a vast quantity of stony relics, having the appearance of flints worn by the action of the waves, and lying in successive layers one above the other. I came to the conclusion that in past ages the sea must have covered the whole district. Upon the scattered rocks, now lying far beyond its reach, the mighty waves of ages had left evident marks of their passage.

On reflection, this appeared to me partially to explain the existence of this remarkable ocean, forty leagues below the surface of the earth's crust. According to my new, and perhaps fanciful, theory, this liquid mass must be gradually lost in the deep bowels of the earth. I had also no doubt that this mysterious sea was fed by infiltration of the ocean above, through imperceptible fissures.

Nevertheless, it was impossible not to admit that these fissures must now be nearly choked up, for if not, the cavern, or rather the immense and stupendous reservoir, would have been completely filled in a short space of time. Perhaps even this water, having to contend against the accumulated subterraneous fires of the interior of the earth, had become partially vaporized. Hence the explanation of those heavy clouds suspended over our heads, and the superabundant display of that electricity which occasioned such terrible storms in this deep and cavernous sea.

This lucid explanation of the phenomena we had witnessed appeared to me quite satisfactory. However great and mighty the marvels of nature may seem to us, they are always to be explained by physical reasons. Everything is subordinate to some great law of nature.

It now appeared clear that we were walking upon a kind of sedimentary soil, formed like all the soils of that period, so frequent on the surface of the globe, by the subsidence of the waters. The Professor, who was now in his element, carefully examined every rocky fissure. Let him only find an opening and it directly became important to him to examine its depth.

For a whole mile we followed the windings of the Central Sea, when suddenly an important change took place in the aspect of the soil. It seemed to have been rudely cast up, convulsionized, as it were, by a violent upheaving of the lower strata. In many places, hollows here and hillocks there attested great dislocations at some other period of the terrestrial mass.

We advanced with great difficulty over the broken masses of granite mixed with flint, quartz, and alluvial deposits, when a large field, more even than a field, a plain of bones, appeared suddenly before our eyes! It looked like an immense cemetery, where generation after generation had mingled their mortal dust.

Lofty barrows of early remains rose at intervals. They undulated away to the limits of the distant horizon and were lost in a thick and brown fog.

On that spot, some three square miles in extent, was accumulated the whole history of animal life—scarcely one creature upon the comparatively modern soil of the upper and inhabited world had not there existed.

Nevertheless, we were drawn forward by an all-absorbing and impatient curiosity. Our feet crushed with a dry and crackling sound the remains of those prehistoric fossils, for which the museums of great cities quarrel, even when they obtain only rare and curious morsels. A thousand such naturalists as Cuvier would not have sufficed to recompose the skeletons of the organic beings which lay in this magnificent osseous collection.

I was utterly confounded. My uncle stood for some minutes with his arms raised on high towards the thick granite vault which served us for a sky. His mouth was wide open; his eyes sparkled wildly behind his spectacles (which he had fortunately saved), his head bobbed up and down and from side to side, while his whole attitude and mien expressed unbounded astonishment.

He stood in the presence of an endless, wondrous, and inexhaustibly rich collection of antediluvian monsters, piled up for his own private and peculiar satisfaction.

Fancy an enthusiastic lover of books carried suddenly into the very midst of the famous library of Alexandria burned by the sacrilegious Omar, and which some miracle had restored to its pristine splendor! Such was something of the state of mind in which Uncle Hardwigg was now placed.

For some time he stood thus, literally aghast at the magnitude of his discovery.

But it was even a greater excitement when, darting wildly over this mass of organic dust, he caught up a naked skull and addressed me in a quivering voice:

"Harry, my boy—Harry—this is a human head!"

"A human head, Uncle!" I said, no less amazed and stupefied than himself.

"Yes, nephew. Ah! Mr. Milne-Edwards—ah! Mr. De Quatrefages—why are you not here where I am—I, Professor Hardwigg!"

Chapter 35

DISCOVERY UPON DISCOVERY

In order fully to understand the exclamation made by my uncle, and his allusions to these illustrious and learned men, it will be necessary to enter into certain explanations in regard to a circumstance of the highest importance to paleontology, or the science of fossil life, which had taken place a short time before our departure from the upper regions of the earth.

On the 28th of March, 1863, some navigators under the direction of M. Boucher de Perthes, were at work in the great quarries of Moulin-Quignon, near Abbeville, in the department of the Somme, in France. While at work, they unexpectedly came upon a human jawbone buried fourteen feet below the surface of the soil. It was the first fossil of the kind that had ever been brought to the light of day. Near this unexpected human relic were found stone hatchets and carved flints, colored and clothed by time in one uniform brilliant tint of verdigris.

The report of this extraordinary and unexpected discovery spread not only all over France, but over England and Germany. Many learned men belonging to various scientific bodies, and noteworthy among others, Messrs. Milne-Edwards and De Quatrefages, took the affair very much to heart, demonstrated the incontestable authenticity of the bone in question, and became—to use the phrase then recognized in England—the most ardent supporters of the "jawbone question."

To the eminent geologists of the United Kingdom who looked upon the fact as certain—Messrs. Falconer, Buck, Carpenter, and others—were soon united the learned men of Germany, and among those in the first rank, the most eager, the most enthusiastic, was my worthy uncle, Professor Hardwigg.

The authenticity of a human fossil of the Quaternary period seemed then to be incontestably demonstrated, and even to be admitted by the most skeptical.

This system or theory, call it what you will, had, it is true, a bitter adversary in M. Elie de Beaumont. This learned man, who holds such a high place in the scientific world, holds that the soil of Moulin-Quignon does not belong to the diluvium but to a much less ancient stratum, and, in accordance with Cuvier in this respect, he would by no means admit that the human species was contemporary with the animals of the Quaternary epoch. My worthy uncle, Professor Hardwigg, in concert with the great majority of geologists, had held firm, had disputed, discussed, and finally, after considerable talking and writing, M. Elie de Beaumont had been pretty well left alone in his opinions.

We were familiar with all the details of this discussion, but were far from being aware then that since our departure the matter had entered upon a new phase. Other similar jawbones, though belonging to individuals of varied types and very different natures, had been found in the movable grey sands of certain grottoes in France, Switzerland, and Belgium; together with arms, utensils, tools, bones of children, of men in the prime of life, and of old men. The existence of men in the Quaternary period became, therefore, more positive every day.

But this was far from being all. New remains, dug up from the Pliocene or Tertiary deposits, had enabled the more far-seeing or audacious among learned men to assign even a far greater degree of antiquity to the human race. These remains, it is true, were not those of men; that is, were not the bones of men, but objects decidedly having served the human race: shinbones, thighbones of fossil animals, regularly scooped out, and in fact sculptured—bearing the unmistakable signs of human handiwork.

By means of these wondrous and unexpected discoveries, man ascended endless centuries in the scale of time; he, in fact, preceded the mastodon; became the contemporary of the *Elephas meridionalis*—the southern elephant; acquired an antiquity of over a hundred thousand years, since that is the date given by the most eminent geologists to the Pliocene period of the earth. Such was then the state of paleontologic science, and what we moreover knew sufficed to explain our attitude before this great cemetery of the plains of the Hardwigg Ocean.

It will now be easy to understand the Professor's mingled astonishment and joy when, on advancing about twenty yards, he found himself in the presence of, I may say face to face with, a specimen of the human race actually belonging to the Quaternary period!

It was indeed a human skull, perfectly recognizable. Had a soil of very peculiar nature, like that of the cemetery of St. Michel at Bordeaux, preserved it during countless ages? This was the question I asked myself, but which I was wholly unable to answer. But this head with stretched and parchmenty skin, with the teeth whole, the hair abundant, was before our eyes as in life!

I stood mute, almost paralyzed with wonder and awe before this dread apparition of another age. My uncle, who on almost every occasion was a great talker, remained for a time completely dumfounded. He was too full of emotion for speech to be possible. After a while, however, we raised up the body to which the skull belonged. We stood it on end. It seemed, to our excited imaginations, to look at us with its terrible hollow eyes.

After some minutes of silence, the man was vanquished by the Professor. Human instincts succumbed to scientific pride and exultation. Professor Hardwigg, carried away by his enthusiasm, forgot all the circumstances of our journey, the extraordinary position in which we were placed, the immense cavern which stretched far away over our heads. There can be no doubt that he thought himself at the Institution addressing his attentive pupils, for he put on his most doctorial style, waved his hand, and began:

"Gentlemen, I have the honor on this auspicious occasion to present to you a man of the Quaternary period of our globe. Many learned men have denied his very existence, while other able persons, perhaps of even higher authority, have affirmed their belief in the reality of his life. If the St. Thomases of paleontology were present, they would reverentially touch him with their fingers and believe in his existence, thus acknowledging their obstinate heresy. I know that science should be careful in relation to all discoveries of this nature. I am not without having heard of the many Barnums and other quacks who have made a trade of suchlike pretended discoveries. I have, of course, heard of the discovery of the kneebones of Ajax, of the pretended finding of the body of Orestes by the Spartiates, and of the body of Asterius, ten spans long, fifteen feet—of which we read in Pausanias.

"I have read everything in relation to the skeleton of Trapani, discovered in the fourteenth century, and which many persons chose to regard as that of Polyphemus, and the history of the giant dug up during the sixteenth century in the environs of Palmyra. You are well aware as I am, gentlemen, of the existence of the celebrated analysis made near Lucerne, in 1577, of the great bones which the celebrated Doctor Felix Plater declared belonged to a giant about nineteen feet high. I have devoured all the treatises of Cassanion, and all those memoirs, pamphlets, speeches, and replies published in reference to the skeleton of Teutobochus, king of the Cimbri, the invader of Gaul, dug out of a gravel pit in Dauphine, in 1613. In the eighteenth century I should have denied, with Peter Campet, the existence of the preadamites of Scheuchzer. I have had in my hands the writing called Gigans—"

Here my uncle was afflicted by the natural infirmity which prevented him from pronouncing difficult words in public. It was not exactly stuttering, but a strange sort of constitutional hesitation.

"The writing named Gigans—" he repeated.

He, however, could get no further.

"Giganteo—"

Impossible! The unfortunate word would not come out. There would have been great laughter at the Institution, had the mistake happened there.

"Gigantosteology!" at last exclaimed Professor Hardwigg between two savage growls.

Having got over our difficulty, and getting more and more excited—

"Yes, gentlemen, I am well acquainted with all these matters, and know, also, that Cuvier and Blumenbach fully recognized in these bones the undeniable remains of mammoths of the Quaternary period. But after what we now see, to allow a doubt is to insult scientific inquiry. There is the body; you can see it; you can touch it. It is not a skeleton, it is a complete and uninjured body, preserved with an anthropological object."

I did not attempt to controvert this singular and astounding assertion.

"If I could but wash this corpse in a solution of sulphuric acid," continued my uncle, "I would undertake to remove all the earthy particles, and these resplendent shells, which are incrusted all over this body. But I am without this precious dissolving medium. Nevertheless, such as it is, this body will tell its own history."

Here the Professor held up the fossil body, and exhibited it with rare dexterity. No professional showman could have shown more activity.

"As on examination you will see," my uncle continued, "it is only about six feet in length, which is a long way from the pretended giants of early days. As to the particular race to which it belonged, it is incontestably Caucasian. It is of the white race, that is, of our own. The skull of this fossil being is a perfect ovoid without any remarkable or prominent development of the cheekbones, and without any projection of the jaw. It presents no indication of the prognathism which modifies the facial angle. Measure the angle for yourselves, and you will find that it is just ninety degrees. But I will advance still farther on the road of inquiry and deduction, and I dare venture to say that this human sample or specimen belongs to the Japhetic family, which spread over the world from India to the uttermost limits of western Europe. There is no occasion, gentlemen, to smile at my remarks."

Of course nobody smiled. But the excellent Professor was so accustomed to beaming countenances at his lectures, that he believed he saw all his audience laughing during the delivery of his learned dissertation.

"Yes," he continued, with renewed animation, "this is a fossil man, a contemporary of the mastodons, with the bones of which this whole amphitheater is covered. But if I am called on to explain how he came to this place, how these various strata by which he is covered have fallen into this vast cavity, I can undertake to give you no explanation. Doubtless, if we carry ourselves back to the Quaternary epoch, we shall find that great and mighty convulsions took place in the crust of the earth; the continually cooling operation, through which the earth had to pass, produced fissures, landslips, and chasms, through which a large portion of the earth made its way. I come to no absolute conclusion, but there is the man, surrounded by the works of his hands, his hatchets and his carved flints, which belong to the stony period; and the only rational supposition is, that, like myself, he visited the centre of the earth as a traveling tourist, a pioneer of science. At all events, there can be no doubt of his great age, and of his being one of the oldest race of human beings."

The Professor with these words ceased his oration, and I burst forth into loud and "unanimous" applause. Besides, after all, my uncle was right. Much more learned men than his nephew would have found it rather hard to refute his facts and arguments.

Another circumstance soon presented itself. This fossilized body was not the only one in this vast plain of bones—the cemetery of an extinct world. Other bodies were found, as we trod the dusty plain, and my uncle was able to choose the most marvelous of these specimens in order to convince the most incredulous.

In truth, it was a surprising spectacle, the successive remains of generations and generations of men and animals confounded together in one vast cemetery. But a great question now presented itself to our notice, and one we were actually afraid to contemplate in all its bearings.

Had these once animated beings been buried so far beneath the soil by some tremendous convulsion of nature, after they had been earth to earth and ashes to ashes, or had they lived here below, in this subterranean world, under this factitious sky, borne, married, and given in marriage, and died at last, just like ordinary inhabitants of the earth?

Up to the present moment, marine monsters, fish, and suchlike animals had alone been seen alive!

The question which rendered us rather uneasy, was a pertinent one. Were any of these men of the abyss wandering about the deserted shores of this wondrous sea of the centre of the earth?

This was a question which rendered me very uneasy and uncomfortable. How, should they really be in existence, would they receive us men from above?

Chapter 36

WHAT IS IT?

For a long and weary hour we tramped over this great bed of bones. We advanced regardless of everything, drawn on by ardent curiosity. What other marvels did this great cavern contain—what other wondrous treasures for the scientific man? My eyes were quite prepared for any number of surprises, my imagination lived in expectation of something new and wonderful.

The borders of the great Central Ocean had for some time disappeared behind the hills that were scattered over the ground occupied by the plain of bones. The imprudent and enthusiastic Professor, who did not care whether he lost himself or not, hurried me forward. We advanced silently, bathed in waves of electric fluid.

By reason of a phenomenon which I cannot explain, and thanks to its extreme diffusion, now complete, the light illumined equally the sides of every hill and rock. Its seat appeared to be nowhere, in no determined force, and produced no shade whatever.

The appearance presented was that of a tropical country at midday in summer—in the midst of the equatorial regions and under the vertical rays of the sun.

All signs of vapor had disappeared. The rocks, the distant mountains, some confused masses of far-off forests, assumed a weird and mysterious aspect under this equal distribution of the luminous fluid!

We resembled, to a certain extent, the mysterious personage in one of Hoffmann's fantastic tales—the man who lost his shadow.

After we had walked about a mile farther, we came to the edge of a vast forest not, however, one of the vast mushroom forests we had discovered near Port Gretchen.

It was the glorious and wild vegetation of the Tertiary period, in all its superb magnificence. Huge palms, of a species now unknown, superb palmacites—a genus of fossil palms from the coal formation—pines, yews, cypress, and conifers or cone-bearing trees, the whole bound together by an inextricable and complicated mass of creeping plants.

A beautiful carpet of mosses and ferns grew beneath the trees. Pleasant brooks murmured beneath umbrageous boughs, little worthy of this name, for no shade did they give. Upon their borders grew small treelike shrubs, such as are seen in the hot countries on our own inhabited globe.

The one thing wanting in these plants, these shrubs, these trees—was color! Forever deprived of the vivifying warmth of the sun, they were vapid and colorless. All shade was lost in one uniform tint, of a brown and faded character. The leaves were wholly devoid of verdure, and the flowers, so numerous during the Tertiary period which gave them birth, were without color and without perfume, something like paper discolored by long exposure to the atmosphere.

My uncle ventured beneath the gigantic groves. I followed him, though not without a certain amount of apprehension. Since nature had shown herself capable of producing such stupendous vegetable supplies, why might we not meet with mammals just as large, and therefore dangerous?

I particularly remarked, in the clearings left by trees that had fallen and been partially consumed by time, many leguminous (beanlike) shrubs, such as the maple and other eatable trees, dear to ruminating animals. Then there appeared confounded together and intermixed, the trees of such varied lands, specimens of the vegetation of every part of the globe; there was the oak near the palm tree, the Australian eucalyptus, an interesting class of the order Myrtaceae—leaning against the tall Norwegian pine, the poplar of the north, mixing its branches with those of the New Zealand kauris. It was enough to drive the most ingenious classifier of the upper regions out of his mind, and to upset all his received ideas about botany.

Suddenly I stopped short and restrained my uncle.

The extreme diffuseness of the light enabled me to see the smallest objects in the distant copses. I thought I saw—no, I really did see with my own eyes—immense, gigantic animals moving about under the mighty trees. Yes, they were truly gigantic animals, a whole herd of mastodons, not fossils, but living, and exactly like those discovered in 1801, on the marshy banks of the great Ohio, in North America.

Yes, I could see these enormous elephants, whose trunks were tearing down large boughs, and working in and out the trees like a legion of serpents. I could hear the sounds of the mighty tusks uprooting huge trees!

The boughs crackled, and the whole masses of leaves and green branches went down the capacious throats of these terrible monsters!

That wondrous dream, when I saw the antehistorical times revivified, when the Tertiary and Quaternary periods passed before me, was now realized!

And there we were alone, far down in the bowels of the earth, at the mercy of its ferocious inhabitants!

My uncle paused, full of wonder and astonishment.

"Come!" he said at last, when his first surprise was over, "Come along, my boy, and let us see them nearer."

"No," replied I, restraining his efforts to drag me forward, "we are wholly without arms. What should we do in the midst of that flock of gigantic quadrupeds? Come away, Uncle, I implore you. No human creature can with impunity brave the ferocious anger of these monsters."

"No human creature," said my uncle, suddenly lowering his voice to a mysterious whisper, "you are mistaken, my dear Henry. Look! look yonder! It seems to me that I behold a human being—a being like ourselves—a man!"

I looked, shrugging my shoulders, decided to push incredulity to its very last limits. But whatever might have been my wish, I was compelled to yield to the weight of ocular demonstration.

Yes—not more than a quarter of a mile off, leaning against the trunk of an enormous tree, was a human being—a Proteus of these subterranean regions, a new son of Neptune keeping this innumerable herd of mastodons.

Immanis pecoris custos, immanior ipse!
The keeper of gigantic cattle, himself still more gigantic!

Yes—it was no longer a fossil whose corpse we had raised from the ground in the great cemetery, but a giant capable of guiding and driving these prodigious monsters. His height was above twelve feet. His head, as big as the head of a buffalo, was lost in a mane of matted hair. It was indeed a huge mane, like those which belonged to the elephants of the earlier ages of the world.

In his hand was a branch of a tree, which served as a crook for this antediluvian shepherd.

We remained profoundly still, speechless with surprise.

But we might at any moment be seen by him. Nothing remained for us but instant flight.

"Come, come!" I cried, dragging my uncle along; and, for the first time, he made no resistance to my wishes.

A quarter of an hour later we were far away from that terrible monster!

Now that I think of the matter calmly, and that I reflect upon it dispassionately; now that months, years, have passed since this strange and unnatural adventure befell us—what am I to think, what am I to believe?

No, it is utterly impossible! Our ears must have deceived us, and our eyes have cheated us! we have not seen what we believed we had seen. No human being could by any possibility have existed in that subterranean world! No generation of men could inhabit the lower caverns of the globe without taking note of those who peopled the surface, without communication with them. It was folly, folly, folly! nothing else!

I am rather inclined to admit the existence of some animal resembling in structure the human race—of some monkey of the first geological epochs, like that discovered by M. Lartet in the ossiferous deposit of Sansan.

But this animal, or being, whichsoever it was, surpassed in height all things known to modern science. Never mind. However unlikely it may be, it might have been a monkey—but a man, a living man, and with him a whole generation of gigantic animals, buried in the entrails of the earth—it was too monstrous to be believed!

Chapter 37

THE MYSTERIOUS DAGGER

During this time, we had left the bright and transparent forest far behind us. We were mute with astonishment, overcome by a kind of feeling which was next door to apathy. We kept running in spite of ourselves. It was a perfect Right, which resembled one of those horrible sensations we sometimes meet with in our dreams.

Instinctively we made our way towards the Central Sea, and I cannot now tell what wild thoughts passed through my mind, nor of what follies I might have been guilty, but for a very serious preoccupation which brought me back to practical life.

Though I was aware that we were treading on a soil quite new to us, I, however, every now and then noticed certain aggregations of rock, the shape of which forcibly reminded me of those near Port Gretchen.

This confirmed, moreover, the indications of the compass and our extraordinary and unlooked-for, as well as involuntary, return to the north of this great Central Sea. It was so like our starting point, that I could scarcely doubt the reality of our position. Streams and cascades fell in hundreds over the numerous projections of the rocks.

I actually thought I could see our faithful and monotonous Hans and the wonderful grotto in which I had come back to life after my tremendous fall.

Then, as we advanced still farther, the position of the

cliffs, the appearance of a stream, the unexpected profile of a rock, threw me again into a state of bewildering doubt.

After some time, I explained my state of mental indecision to my uncle. He confessed to a similar feeling of hesitation. He was totally unable to make up his mind in the midst of this extraordinary but uniform panorama.

"There can be no doubt," I insisted, "that we have not landed exactly at the place whence we first took our departure; but the tempest has brought us above our starting point. I think, therefore, that if we follow the coast we shall once more find Port Gretchen."

"In that case," cried my uncle, "it is useless to continue our exploration. The very best thing we can do is to make our way back to the raft. Are you quite sure, Harry, that you are not mistaken?"

"It is difficult," was my reply, "to come to any decision, for all these rocks are exactly alike. There is no marked difference between them. At the same time, the impression on my mind is that I recognize the promontory at the foot of which our worthy Hans constructed the raft. We are, I am nearly convinced, near the little port: if this be not it," I added, carefully examining a creek which appeared singularly familiar to my mind.

"My dear Harry—if this were the case, we should find traces of our own footsteps, some signs of our passage; and I can really see nothing to indicate our having passed this way."

"But I see something," I cried, in an impetuous tone of voice, as I rushed forward and eagerly picked up something which shone in the sand under my feet.

"What is it?" cried the astonished and bewildered Professor.

"This," was my reply.

And I handed to my startled relative a rusty dagger, of singular shape.

"What made you bring with you so useless a weapon?" he exclaimed. "It was needlessly hampering yourself."

"I bring it? It is quite new to me. I never saw it before—are you sure it is not out of your collection?"

"Not that I know of," said the Professor, puzzled. "I have no recollection of the circumstance. It was never my property."

"This is very extraordinary," I said, musing over the novel and singular incident.

"Not at all. There is a very simple explanation, Harry. The Icelanders are known to keep up the use of these antiquated weapons, and this must have belonged to Hans, who has let it fall without knowing it."

I shook my head. That dagger had never been in the possession of the pacific and taciturn Hans. I knew him and his habits too well.

"Then what can it be—unless it be the weapon of some antediluvian warrior," I continued, "of some living man, a contemporary of that mighty shepherd from whom we have just escaped? But no—mystery upon mystery—this is no weapon of the stony epoch, nor even of the bronze period. It is made of excellent steel—"

Ere I could finish my sentence, my uncle stopped me short from entering upon a whole train of theories, and spoke in his most cold and decided tone of voice.

"Calm yourself, my dear boy, and endeavor to use your reason. This weapon, upon which we have fallen so unexpectedly, is a true *dague*, one of those worn by gentlemen in their belts during the sixteenth century. Its use was to give the *coup de grace*, the final blow, to the foe who would not surrender. It is clearly of Spanish workmanship. It belongs neither to you, nor to me, nor the eider-down hunter, nor to any of the living beings who may still exist so marvelously in the interior of the earth."

"What can you mean, Uncle?" I said, now lost in a host of surmises.

"Look closely at it," he continued; "these jagged edges were never made by the resistance of human blood and bone. The blade is covered with a regular coating of iron mold and rust, which is not a day old, not a year old, not a century old, but much more—"

The Professor began to get quite excited, according to custom, and was allowing himself to be carried away by his fertile imagination. I could have said something. He stopped me.

"Harry," he cried, "we are now on the verge of a great discovery. This blade of a dagger you have so marvelously discovered, after being abandoned upon the sand for more than a hundred, two hundred, even three hundred years, has been indented by someone endeavoring to carve an inscription on these rocks."

"But this poniard never got here of itself," I exclaimed, "it could not have twisted itself. Someone, therefore, must have preceded us upon the shores of this extraordinary sea."

"Yes, a man."

"But what man has been sufficiently desperate to do such a thing?"

"A man who has somewhere written his name with this very dagger—a man who has endeavored once more to indicate the right road to the interior of the earth. Let us look around, my boy. You know not the importance of your singular and happy discovery."

Prodigiously interested, we walked along the wall of rock, examining the smallest fissures, which might finally expand into the much wished—for gully or shaft.

We at last reached a spot where the shore became extremely narrow. The sea almost bathed the foot of the rocks, which were here very lofty and steep. There was scarcely a path wider than two yards at any point. At last, under a huge over-hanging rock, we discovered the entrance of a dark and gloomy tunnel.

There, on a square tablet of granite, which had been smoothed by rubbing it with another stone, we could see two mysterious, and much worn letters, the two initials of the bold and extraordinary traveler who had preceded us on our adventurous journey.

"A. S.!" cried my uncle. "You see, I was right. Arne Saknussemm, always Arne Saknussemm!"

Chapter 38

NO OUTLET—BLASTING THE ROCK

Ever since the commencement of our marvelous journey, I had experienced many surprises, had suffered from many illusions. I thought that I was case-hardened against all surprises and could neither see nor hear anything to amaze me again.

I was like a many who, having been round the world, finds himself wholly blase and proof against the marvelous.

When, however, I saw these two letters, which had been engraven three hundred years before, I stood fixed in an attitude of mute surprise.

Not only was there the signature of the learned and enterprising alchemist written in the rock, but I held in my hand the very identical instrument with which he had laboriously engraved it.

It was impossible, without showing an amount of incredulity scarcely becoming a sane man, to deny the existence of the traveler, and the reality of that voyage which I believed all along to have been a myth—the mystification of some fertile brain.

While these reflections were passing through my mind, my uncle, the Professor, gave way to an access of feverish and poetical excitement.

"Wonderful and glorious genius, great Saknussemm," he cried, "you have left no stone unturned, no resource omitted, to show to other mortals the way into the interior of our mighty globe, and your fellow creatures can find the trail left by your illustrious footsteps, three hundred years ago, at the bottom of these obscure subterranean abodes. You have been careful to secure for others the contemplation of these wonders and marvels of creation. Your name engraved at every important stage of your glorious journey leads the hopeful traveler direct to the great and mighty discovery to which you devoted such energy and courage. The audacious traveler, who shall follow your footsteps to the last, will doubtless find your initials engraved with your own hand upon the centre of the earth. I will be that audacious traveler—I, too, will sign my name upon the very same spot, upon the central granite stone of this wondrous work of the Creator. But in justice to your devotion, to your courage, and to your being the first to indicate the road, let this cape, seen by you upon the shores of this sea discovered by you, be called, of all time, Cape Saknussemm."

This is what I heard, and I began to be roused to the pitch of enthusiasm indicated by those words. A fierce excitement roused me. I forgot everything. The dangers of the voyage and the perils of the return journey were now as nothinWhat another man had done in ages past could, I felt, be done again; I was determined to do it myself, and now nothing that man had accomplished appeared to me impossible.

"Forward—forward," I cried in a burst of genuine and hearty enthusiasm.

I had already started in the direction of the somber and gloomy gallery when the Professor stopped me; he, the man so rash and hasty, he, the man so easily roused to the highest pitch of enthusiasm, checked me, and asked me to be patient and show more calm.

"Let us return to our good friend, Hans," he said; "we will then bring the raft down to this place."

I must say that though I at once yielded to my uncle's request, it was not without dissatisfaction, and I hastened along the rocks of that wonderful coast.

"Do you know, my dear uncle," I said, as we walked along, "that we have been singularly helped by a concurrence of circumstances, right up to this very moment."

"So you begin to see it, do you, Harry?" said the Professor with a smile.

"Doubtless," I responded, "and strangely enough, even the tempest has been the means of putting us on the right road. Blessings on the tempest! It brought us safely back to the very spot from which fine weather would have driven us forever. Supposing we had succeeded in reaching the southern and distant shores of this extraordinary sea, what would have become of us? The name of Saknussemm would never have appeared to us, and at this moment we should have been cast away upon an inhospitable coast, probably without an outlet."

"Yes, Harry, my boy, there is certainly something providential in that wandering at the mercy of wind and waves towards the south: we have come back exactly north; and what is better still, we fall upon this great discovery of Cape Saknussemm. I mean to say, that it is more than surprising; there is something in it which is far beyond my comprehension. The coincidence is unheard of, marvelous!"

"What matter! It is not our duty to explain facts, but to make the best possible use of them."

"Doubtless, my boy; but if you will allow me—" said the really delighted Professor.

"Excuse me, sir, but I see exactly how it will be; we shall take the northern route; we shall pass under the northern regions of Europe, under Sweden, under Russia, under Siberia, and who knows where—instead of burying ourselves under the burning plains and deserts of Africa, or beneath the mighty waves of the ocean; and that is all, at this stage of our journey, that I care to know. Let us advance, and Heaven will be our guide!"

"Yes, Harry, you are right, quite right; all is for the best. Let us abandon this horizontal sea, which could never have led to anything satisfactory. We shall descend, descend, and everlastingly descend. Do you know, my dear boy, that to reach the interior of the earth we have only five thousand miles to travel!"

"Bah!" I cried, carried away by a burst of enthusiasm, "the distance is scarcely worth speaking about. The thing is to make a start."

My wild, mad, and incoherent speeches continued until we rejoined our patient and phlegmatic guide. All was, we found, prepared for an immediate departure. There was not a single parcel but what was in its proper place. We all took up our posts on the raft, and the sail being hoisted, Hans received his directions, and guided the frail bark towards Cape Saknussemm, as we had definitely named it.

The wind was very unfavorable to a craft that was unable to sail close to the wind. It was constructed to go before the blast. We were continually reduced to pushing ourselves forward by means of poles. On several occasions the rocks ran far out into deep water and we were compelled to make a long round. At last, after three long and weary hours of navigation, that is to say, about six o'clock in the evening, we found a place at which we could land.

I jumped on shore first. In my present state of excitement and enthusiasm, I was always first. My uncle and the Icelander followed. The voyage from the port to this point of the sea had by no means calmed me. It had rather produced the opposite effect. I even proposed to burn our vessel, that is, to destroy our raft, in order to completely cut off our retreat. But my uncle sternly opposed this wild project. I began to think him particularly lukewarm and unenthusiastic.

"At any rate, my dear uncle," I said, "let us start without delay."

"Yes, my boy, I am quite as eager to do so as you can be. But, in the first place, let us examine this mysterious gallery, in order to find if we shall need to prepare and mend our ladders."

My uncle now began to see to the efficiency of our Ruhmkorff coil, which would doubtless soon be needed; the raft, securely fastened to a rock, was left alone. Moreover, the opening into the new gallery was not twenty paces distant from the spot. Our little troop, with myself at the head, advanced.

The orifice, which was almost circular, presented a diameter of about five feet; the somber tunnel was cut in the living rock, and coated on the inside by the different material which had once passed through it in a state of fusion. The lower part was about level with the water, so that we were able to penetrate to the interior without difficulty.

We followed an almost horizontal direction; when, at the end of about a dozen paces, our further advance was checked by the interposition of an enormous block of granite rock.

"Accursed stone!" I cried furiously, on perceiving that we were stopped by what seemed an insurmountable obstacle.

In vain we looked to the right, in vain we looked to the left; in vain examined it above and below. There existed no passage, no sign of any other tunnel. I experienced the most bitter and painful disappointment. So enraged was I that I would not admit the reality of any obstacle. I stooped to my knees; I looked under the mass of stone. No hole, no interstice. I then looked above. The same barrier of granite! Hans, with the lamp, examined the sides of the tunnel in every direction.

But all in vain! It was necessary to renounce all hope of passing through.

I had seated myself upon the ground. My uncle walked angrily and hopelessly up and down. He was evidently desperate.

"But," I cried, after some moments' thought, "what about Arne Saknussemm?"

"You are right," replied my uncle, "he can never have been checked by a lump of rock."

"No—ten thousand times no," I cried, with extreme vivacity. "This huge lump of rock, in consequence of some singular concussion, or process, one of those magnetic phenomena which have so often shaken the terrestrial crust, has in some unexpected way closed up the passage. Many and many years have passed away since the return of Saknussemm, and the fall of this huge block of granite. Is it not quite evident that this gallery was formerly the outlet for the pent-up lava in the interior of the earth, and that these eruptive matters then circulated freely? Look at these recent fissures in the granite roof; it is evidently formed of pieces of enormous stone, placed here as if by the hand of a giant, who had worked to make a strong and substantial arch. One day, after an unusually strong shock, the vast rock which stands in our way, and which was doubtless the key of a kind of arch, fell through to a level with the soil and has barred our further progress. We are right, then, in thinking that this is an unexpected obstacle, with which Saknussemm did not meet; and if we do not upset it in some way, we are unworthy of following in the footsteps of the great discoverer; and incapable of finding our way to the centre of the earth!"

In this wild way I addressed my uncle. The zeal of the Professor, his earnest longing for success, had become part and parcel of my being. I wholly forgot the past; I utterly despised the future. Nothing existed for me upon the surface of this spheroid in the bosom of which I was engulfed, no towns, no country, no Hamburg, no Koenigstrasse, not even my poor Gretchen, who by this time would believe me utterly lost in the interior of the earth!

"Well," cried my uncle, roused to enthusiasm by my words, "Let us go to work with pickaxes, with crowbars, with anything that comes to hand—but down with these terrible walls."

"It is far too tough and too big to be destroyed by a pickax or crowbar," I replied.

"What then?"

"As I said, it is useless to think of overcoming such a difficulty by means of ordinary tools."

"What then?"

"What else but gunpowder, a subterranean mine? Let us blow up the obstacle that stands in our way."

"Gunpowder!"

"Yes; all we have to do is to get rid of this paltry obstacle."

"To work, Hans, to work!" cried the Professor.

The Icelander went back to the raft, and soon returned with a huge crowbar, with which he began to dig a hole in the rock, which was to serve as a mine. It was by no means a slight task. It was necessary for our purpose to make a cavity large enough to hold fifty pounds of fulminating gun cotton, the expansive power of which is four times as great as that of ordinary gunpowder.

I had now roused myself to an almost miraculous state of excitement. While Hans was at work, I actively assisted my uncle to prepare a long wick, made from damp gunpowder, the mass of which we finally enclosed in a bag of linen.

"We are bound to go through," I cried, enthusiastically.

"We are bound to go through," responded the Professor, tapping me on the back.

At midnight, our work as miners was completely finished; the charge of fulminating cotton was thrust into the hollow, and the match, which we had made of considerable length, was ready.

A spark was now sufficient to ignite this formidable engine, and to blow the rock to atoms!

"We will now rest until tomorrow."

It was absolutely necessary to resign myself to my fate, and to consent to wait for the explosion for six weary hours!

Chapter 39

THE EXPLOSION AND ITS RESULTS

The next day, which was the twenty-seventh of August, was a date celebrated in our wondrous subterranean journey. I never think of it even now, but I shudder with horror. My heart beats wildly at the very memory of that awful day.

From this time forward, our reason, our judgment, our human ingenuity, have nothing to do with the course of events. We are about to become the plaything of the great phenomena of the earth!

At six o'clock we were all up and ready. The dreaded moment was arriving when we were about to seek an opening into the interior of the earth by means of gunpowder. What would be the consequences of breaking through the crust of the earth?

I begged that it might be my duty to set fire to the mine. I looked upon it as an honor. This task once performed, I could rejoin my friends upon the raft, which had not been unloaded. As soon as we were all ready, we were to sail away to some distance to avoid the consequences of the explosion, the effects of which would certainly not be concentrated in the interior of the earth.

The slow match we calculated to burn for about ten minutes, more or less, before it reached the chamber in which the great body of powder was confined. I should therefore have plenty of time to reach the raft and put off to a safe distance.

I prepared to execute my self-allotted task—not, it must be confessed, without considerable emotion.

After a hearty repast, my uncle and the hunter-guide embarked on board the raft, while I remained alone upon the desolate shore.

I was provided with a lantern which was to enable me to set fire to the wick of the infernal machine.

"Go, my boy," said my uncle, "and Heaven be with you. But come back as soon as you can. I shall be all impatience."

"Be easy on that matter," I replied, "there is no fear of my delaying on the road."

Having said this, I advanced toward the opening of the somber gallery. My heart beat wildly. I opened my lantern and seized the extremity of the wick.

The Professor, who was looking on, held his chronometer in his hand.

"Are you ready?" cried he.

"Quite ready."

"Well, then, fire away!"

I hastened to put the light to the wick, which crackled and sparkled, hissing and spitting like a serpent; then, running as fast as I could, I returned to the shore.

"Get on board, my lad, and you, Hans, shove off," cried my uncle.

By a vigorous application of his pole Hans sent us flying over the water. The raft was quite twenty fathoms distant.

It was a moment of palpitating interest, of deep anxiety. My uncle, the Professor, never took his eyes off the chronometer.

"Only five minutes more," he said in a low tone, "only four, only three."

My pulse went a hundred to the minute. I could hear my heart beating.

"Only two, one! Now, then, mountains of granite, crumble beneath the power of man!"

What happened after that? As to the terrific roar of the explosion, I do not think I heard it. But the form of the rocks completely changed in my eyes—they seemed to be drawn aside like a curtain. I saw a fathomless, a bottomless abyss, which yawned beneath the turgid waves. The sea, which seemed suddenly to have gone mad, then became one great mountainous mass, upon the top of which the raft rose perpendicularly.

We were all thrown down. In less than a second the light gave place to the most profound obscurity. Then I felt all solid support give way not to my feet, but to the raft itself. I thought it was going bodily down a tremendous well. I tried to speak, to question my uncle. Nothing could be heard but the roaring of the mighty waves. We clung together in utter silence.

Despite the awful darkness, despite the noise, the surprise, the emotion, I thoroughly understood what had happened.

Beyond the rock which had been blown up, there existed a mighty abyss. The explosion had caused a kind of earthquake in this soil, broken by fissures and rents. The gulf, thus suddenly thrown open, was about to swallow the inland seal which, transformed into a mighty torrent, was dragging us with it.

Only one idea filled my mind. We were utterly and completely lost!

One hour, two hours—what more I cannot say, passed in this manner. We sat close together, elbow touching elbow, knee touching knee! We held one another's hands not to be thrown off the raft. We were subjected to the most violent shocks, whenever our sole dependence, a frail wooden raft, struck against the rocky sides of the channel. Fortunately for us, these concussions became less and less frequent, which made me fancy that the gallery was getting wider and wider. There could be now no doubt that we had chanced upon the road once followed by Saknussemm, but instead of going down in a proper manner, we had, through our own imprudence, drawn a whole sea with us!

These ideas presented themselves to my mind in a very vague and obscure manner. I felt rather than reasoned. I put my ideas together only confusedly, while spinning along like a man going down a waterfall. To judge by the air which, as it were, whipped my face, we must have been rushing at a perfectly lightning rate.

To attempt under these circumstances to light a torch was simply impossible, and the last remains of our electric machine, of our Ruhmkorff coil, had been destroyed during the fearful explosion.

I was therefore very much confused to see at last a bright light shining close to me. The calm countenance of the guide seemed to gleam upon me. The clever and patient hunter had succeeded in lighting the lantern; and though, in the keen and thorough draft, the flame Flickered and vacillated and was nearly put out, it served partially to dissipate the awful obscurity.

The gallery into which we had entered was very wide. I was, therefore, quite right in that part of my conjecture. The insufficient light did not allow us to see both of the walls at the same time. The slope of waters, which was carrying us away, was far greater than that of the most rapid river of America. The whole surface of the stream seemed to be composed of liquid arrows, darted forward with extreme violence and power. I can give no idea of the impression it made upon me.

The raft, at times, caught in certain whirlpools, and rushed forward, yet turned on itself all the time. How it did not upset I shall never be able to understand. When it approached the sides of the gallery, I took care to throw upon them the light of the lantern, and I was able to judge of the rapidity of motion by looking at the projecting masses of rock, which as soon as seen were again invisible. So rapid was our progress that points of rock at a considerable distance one from the other appeared like portions of transverse lines, which enclosed us in a kind of net, like that of a line of telegraphic wires.

I believe we were now going at a rate of not less than a hundred miles an hour.

My uncle and I looked at one another with wild and haggard eyes; we clung convulsively to the stump of the mast, which, at the moment when the catastrophe took place, had snapped short off. We turned our backs as much as possible to the wind, in order not to be stifled by a rapidity of motion which nothing human could face and live.

And still the long monotonous hours went on. The situation did not change in the least, though a discovery I suddenly made seemed to complicate it very much.

When we had slightly recovered our equilibrium, I proceeded to examine our cargo. I then made the unsatisfactory discovery that the greater part of it had utterly disappeared.

I became alarmed, and determined to discover what were our resources. My heart beat at the idea, but it was absolutely necessary to know on what we had to depend. With this view, I took the lantern and looked around.

Of all our former collection of nautical and philosophical instruments, there remained only the chronometer and the compass. The ladders and ropes were reduced to a small piece of rope fastened to the stump of the mast. Not a pickax, not a crowbar, not a hammer, and, far worse than all, no food—not enough for one day!

This discovery was a prelude to a certain and horrible death.

Seated gloomily on the raft, clasping the stump of the mast mechanically, I thought of all I had read as to sufferings from starvation.

I remembered everything that history had taught me on the subject, and I shuddered at the remembrance of the agonies to be endured.

Maddened at the prospects of enduring the miseries of starvation, I persuaded myself that I must be mistaken. I examined the cracks in the raft; I poked between the joints and beams; I examined every possible hole and corner. The result was—simply nothing!

Our stock of provisions consisted of nothing but a piece of dry meat and some soaked and half-moldy biscuits.

I gazed around me scared and frightened. I could not understand the awful truth. And yet of what consequence was it in regard to any new danger? Supposing that we had had provisions for months, and even for years, how could we ever get out of the awful abyss into which we were being hurled by the irresistible torrent we had let loose?

Why should we trouble ourselves about the sufferings and tortures to be endured from hunger when death stared us in the face under so many other swifter and perhaps even more horrid forms?

It was very doubtful, under the circumstances in which we were placed, if we should have time to die of inanition.

But the human frame is singularly constituted.

I know not how it was; but, from some singular hallucination of the mind, I forgot the real, serious, and immediate danger to which we were exposed, to think of the menaces of the future, which appeared before us in all their naked terror. Besides, after all, suggested Hope, perhaps we might finally escape the fury of the raging torrent, and once more revisit the glimpses of the moon, on the surface of our beautiful Mother Earth.

How was it to be done? I had not the remotest idea. Where were we to come out? No matter, so that we did.

One chance in a thousand is always a chance, while death from hunger gave us not even the faintest glimpse of hope. It left to the imagination nothing but blank horror, without the faintest chance of escape!

I had the greatest mind to reveal all to my uncle, to explain to him the extraordinary and wretched position to which we were reduced, in order that, between the two, we might make a calculation as to the exact space of time which remained for us to live.It was, it appeared to me, the only thing to be done. But I had the courage to hold my tongue, to gnaw at my entrails like the Spartan boy. I wished to leave him all his coolness.

At this moment, the light of the lantern slowly fell, and at last went out!

The wick had wholly burnt to an end. The obscurity became absolute. It was no longer possible to see through the impenetrable darkness! There was one torch left, but it was impossible to keep it alight. Then, like a child, I shut my eyes, that I might not see the darkness.

After a great lapse of time, the rapidity of our journey increased. I could feel it by the rush of air upon my face. The slope of the waters was excessive. I began to feel that we were no longer going down a slope; we were falling. I felt as one does in a dream, going down bodily—falling; falling; falling!

I felt that the hands of my uncle and Hans were vigorously clasping my arms.

Suddenly, after a lapse of time scarcely appreciable, I felt something like a shock. The raft had not struck a hard body, but had suddenly been checked in its course. A waterspout, a liquid column of water, fell upon us. I felt suffocating. I was being drowned.

Still the sudden inundation did not last. In a few seconds I felt myself once more able to breathe. My uncle and Hans pressed my arms, and the raft carried us all three away.

Chapter 40

THE APE GIGANS

It is difficult for me to determine what was the real time, but I should suppose, by after calculation, that it must have been ten at night.

I lay in a stupor, a half dream, during which I saw visions of astounding character. Monsters of the deep were side by side with the mighty elephantine shepherd. Gigantic fish and animals seemed to form strange conjunctions.

The raft took a sudden turn, whirled round, entered another tunnel—this time illumined in a most singular manner. The roof was formed of porous stalactite, through which a moonlit vapor appeared to pass, casting its brilliant light upon our gaunt and haggard figures. The light increased as we advanced, while the roof ascended; until at last, we were once more in a kind of water cavern, the lofty dome of which disappeared in a luminous cloud!

A rugged cavern of small extent appeared to offer a halting place to our weary bodies.

My uncle and the guide moved as men in a dream. I was afraid to waken them, knowing the danger of such a sudden start. I seated myself beside them to watch.

As I did so, I became aware of something moving in the distance, which at once fascinated my eyes. It was floating, apparently, upon the surface of the water, advancing by means of what at first appeared paddles. I looked with glaring eyes.

One glance told me that it was something monstrous.

But what?

It was the great "shark-crocodile" of the early writers on geology. About the size of an ordinary whale, with hideous jaws and two gigantic eyes, it advanced. Its eyes fixed on me with terrible sternness. Some indefinite warning told me that it had marked me for its own.

I attempted to rise—to escape, no matter where, but my knees shook under me; my limbs trembled violently; I almost lost my senses. And still the mighty monster advanced. My uncle and the guide made no effort to save themselves.

With a strange noise, like none other I had ever heard, the beast came on. His jaws were at least seven feet apart, and his distended mouth looked large enough to have swallowed a boatful of men.

We were about ten feet distant when I discovered that much as his body resembled that of a crocodile, his mouth was wholly that of a shark.

His twofold nature now became apparent. To snatch us up at a mouthful it was necessary for him to turn on his back, which motion necessarily caused his legs to kick up helplessly in the air.

I actually laughed even in the very jaws of death!

But next minute, with a wild cry, I darted away into the interior of the cave, leaving my unhappy comrades to their fate! This cavern was deep and dreary. After about a hundred yards, I paused and looked around.

The whole floor, composed of sand and malachite, was strewn with bones, freshly gnawed bones of reptiles and fish, with a mixture of mammalia. My very soul grew sick as my body shuddered with horror. I had truly, according to the old proverb, fallen out of the frying pan into the fire. Some beast larger and more ferocious even than the shark-crocodile inhabited this den.

What could I do? The mouth of the cave was guarded by one ferocious monster, the interior was inhabited by something too hideous to contemplate. Flight was impossible!

Only one resource remained, and that was to find some small hiding place to which the fearful denizens of the cavern could not penetrate. I gazed wildly around, and at last discovered a fissure in the rock, to which I rushed in the hope of recovering my scattered senses.

Crouching down, I waited shivering as in an ague fit. No man is brave in presence of an earthquake, or a bursting boiler, or an exploding torpedo. I could not be expected to feel much courage in presence of the fearful fate that appeared to await me.

An hour passed. I heard all the time a strange rumbling outside the cave.

What was the fate of my unhappy companions? It was impossible for me to pause to inquire. My own wretched existence was all I could think of.

Suddenly a groaning, as of fifty bears in a fight, fell upon my ears—hisses, spitting, moaning, hideous to hear—and then I saw—

Never, were ages to pass over my head, shall I forget the horrible apparition.

It was the Ape Gigans!

Fourteen feet high, covered with coarse hair, of a blackish brown, the hair on the arms, from the shoulder to the elbow joints, pointing downwards, while that from the wrist to the elbow pointed upwards, it advanced. Its arms were as long as its body, while its legs were prodigious. It had thick, long, and sharply pointed teeth—like a mammoth saw.

It struck its breast as it came on smelling and sniffing,

reminding me of the stories we read in our early childhood of giants who ate the Flesh of men and little boys!

Suddenly it stopped. My heart beat wildly, for I was conscious that, somehow or other, the fearful monster had smelled me out and was peering about with his hideous eyes to try and discover my whereabouts.

My reading, which as a rule is a blessing, but which on this occasion, seemed momentarily to prove a curse, told me the real truth. It was the Ape Gigans, the antediluvian gorilla.

Yes! This awful monster, confined by good fortune to the interior of the earth, was the progenitor of the hideous monster of Africa.

He glared wildly about, seeking something—doubtless myself. I gave myself up for lost. No hope of safety or escape seemed to remain.

At this moment, just as my eyes appeared to close in death, there came a strange noise from the entrance of the cave; and turning, the gorilla evidently recognized some enemy more worthy his prodigious size and strength. It was the huge shark-crocodile, which perhaps having disposed of my friends, was coming in search of further prey.

The gorilla placed himself on the defensive, and clutching a bone some seven or eight feet in length, a perfect club, aimed a deadly blow at the hideous beast, which reared upwards and fell with all its weight upon its adversary.

A terrible combat, the details of which it is impossible to give, now ensued. The struggle was awful and ferocious, I, however, did not wait to witness the result. Regarding myself as the object of contention, I determined to remove from the presence of the victor. I slid down from my hiding place, reached the ground, and gliding against the wall, strove to gain the open mouth of the cavern.

But I had not taken many steps when the fearful clamor

ceased, to be followed by a mumbling and groaning which appeared to be indicative of victory.

I looked back and saw the huge ape, gory with blood, coming after me with glaring eyes, with dilated nostrils that gave forth two columns of heated vapor. I could feel his hot and fetid breath on my neck; and with a horrid jump—awoke from my nightmare sleep.

Yes—it was all a dream. I was still on the raft with my uncle and the guide.

The relief was not instantaneous, for under the influence of the hideous nightmare my senses had become numbed. After a while, however, my feelings were tranquilized. The first of my perceptions which returned in full force was that of hearing. I listened with acute and attentive ears. All was still as death. All I comprehended was silence. To the roaring of the waters, which had filled the gallery with awful reverberations, succeeded perfect peace.

After some little time my uncle spoke, in a low and scarcely audible tone: "Harry, boy, where are you?"

"I am here," was my faint rejoinder.

"Well, don't you see what has happened? We are going upwards."

"My dear uncle, what can you mean?" was my half-delirious reply.

"Yes, I tell you we are ascending rapidly. Our downward journey is quite checked."

I held out my hand, and, after some little difficulty, succeeded in touching the wall. My hand was in an instant covered with blood. The skin was torn from the flesh. We were ascending with extraordinary rapidity.

"The torch—the torch!" cried the Professor, wildly; "it must be lighted."

Hans, the guide, after many vain efforts, at last succeeded

in lighting it, and the flame, having now nothing to prevent its burning, shed a tolerably clear light. We were enabled to form an approximate idea of the truth.

"It is just as I thought," said my uncle, after a moment or two of silent attention. "We are in a narrow well about four fathoms square. The waters of the great inland sea, having reached the bottom of the gulf are now forcing themselves up the mighty shaft. As a natural consequence, we are being cast upon the summit of the waters."

"That I can see," was my lugubrious reply; "but where will this shaft end, and to what fall are we likely to be exposed?"

"Of that I am as ignorant as yourself. All I know is, that we should be prepared for the worst. We are going up at a fearfully rapid rate. As far as I can judge, we are ascending at the rate of two fathoms a second, of a hundred and twenty fathoms a minute, or rather more than three and a half leagues an hour. At this rate, our fate will soon be a matter of certainty."

"No doubt of it," was my reply. "The great concern I have now, however, is to know whether this shaft has any issue. It may end in a granite roof—in which case we shall be suffocated by compressed air, or dashed to atoms against the top. I fancy, already, that the air is beginning to be close and condensed. I have a difficulty in breathing."

This might be fancy, or it might be the effect of our rapid motion, but I certainly felt a great oppression of the chest.

"Henry," said the Professor, "I do believe that the situation is to a certain extent desperate. There remain, however, many chances of ultimate safety, and I have, in my own mind, been revolving them over, during your heavy but agitated sleep. I have come to this logical conclusion—whereas we may at any moment perish, so at any moment we may be saved! We need, therefore, prepare ourselves for whatever may turn up in the great "CHAPTER of accidents."

"But what would you have us do?" I cried. "Are we not utterly helpless?"

"No! While there is life there is hope. At all events, there is one thing we can do—eat, and thus obtain strength to face victory or death."

As he spoke, I looked at my uncle with a haggard glance. I had put off the fatal communication as long as possible. It was now forced upon me, and I must tell him the truth.

Still I hesitated.

"Eat," I said, in a deprecating tone as if there were no hurry.

"Yes, and at once. I feel like a starving prisoner," he said, rubbing his yellow and shivering hands together.

And, turning round to the guide, he spoke some hearty, cheering words, as I judged from his tone, in Danish. Hans shook his head in a terribly significant manner. I tried to look unconcerned.

"What!" cried the Professor, "you do not mean to say that all our provisions are lost?"

"Yes," was my lowly spoken reply, as I held out something in my hand, "this morsel of dried meat is all that remains for us three."

My uncle gazed at me as if he could not fully appreciate the meaning of my words. The blow seemed to stun him by its severity. I allowed him to reflect for some moments.

"Well," said I, after a short pause, "what do you think now? Is there any chance of our escaping from our horrible subterranean dangers? Are we not doomed to perish in the great hollows of the centre of the earth?"

But my pertinent questions brought no answer. My uncle either heard me not, or appeared not to do so.

And in this way a whole hour passed. Neither of us cared to speak. For myself, I began to feel the most fearful and devouring hunger. My companions, doubtless, felt the same horrible tortures, but neither of them would touch the wretched morsel of meat that remained. It lay there, a last remnant of all our great preparations for the mad and senseless journey!

I looked back, with wonderment, to my own folly. Fully was I aware that, despite his enthusiasm, and the ever-to-be-hated scroll of Saknussemm, my uncle should never have started on his perilous voyage. What memories of the happy past, what previsions of the horrible future, now filled my brain!

Chapter 41

HUNGER

Hunger, prolonged, is temporary madness! The brain is at work without its required food, and the most fantastic notions fill the mind. Hitherto I had never known what hunger really meant. I was likely to understand it now.

And yet, three months before I could tell my terrible story of starvation, as I thought it. As a boy I used to make frequent excursions in the neighborhood of the Professor's house.

My uncle always acted on system, and he believed that, in addition to the day of rest and worship, there should be a day of recreation. In consequence, I was always free to do as I liked on a Wednesday.

Now, as I had a notion to combine the useful and the agreeable, my favorite pastime was birds' nesting. I had one of the best collections of eggs in all the town. They were classified, and under glass cases.

There was a certain wood, which, by rising at early morn, and taking the cheap train, I could reach at eleven in the morning. Here I would botanize or geologize at my will. My uncle was always glad of specimens for his herbarium, and stones to examine. When I had filled my wallet, I proceeded to search for nests.

After about two hours of hard work, I, one day, sat down by a stream to eat my humble but copious lunch. How the remembrance of the spiced sausage, the wheaten loaf, and the beer, made my mouth water now! I would have given every prospect of worldly wealth for such a meal. But to my story.

While seated thus at my leisure, I looked up at the ruins of an old castle, at no great distance. It was the remains of an historical dwelling, ivy-clad, and now falling to pieces.

While looking, I saw two eagles circling about the summit of a lofty tower. I soon became satisfied that there was a nest. Now, in all my collection, I lacked eggs of the native eagle and the large owl.

My mind was made up. I would reach the summit of that tower, or perish in the attempt. I went nearer, and surveyed the ruins. The old staircase, years before, had fallen in. The outer walls were, however, intact. There was no chance that way, unless I looked to the ivy solely for support. This was, as I soon found out, futile.

There remained the chimney, which still went up to the top, and had once served to carry off the smoke from every story of the tower.

Up this I determined to venture. It was narrow, rough, and therefore the more easily climbed. I took off my coat and crept into the chimney. Looking up, I saw a small, light opening, proclaiming the summit of the chimney.

Up—up I went, for some time using my hands and knees, after the fashion of a chimney sweep. It was slow work, but, there being continual projections, the task was comparatively easy. In this way, I reached halfway. The chimney now became narrower. The atmosphere was close, and, at last, to end the matter, I stuck fast. I could ascend no higher.

There could be no doubt of this, and there remained no resource but to descend, and give up my glorious prey in despair. I yielded to fate and endeavored to descend. But I could not move. Some unseen and mysterious obstacle intervened and stopped me. In an instant the full horror of my situation seized me.

I was unable to move either way, and was doomed to a terrible and horrible death, that of starvation. In a boy's mind, however, there is an extraordinary amount of elasticity and hope, and I began to think of all sorts of plans to escape my gloomy fate.

In the first place, I required no food just at present, having had an excellent meal, and was therefore allowed time for reflection. My first thought was to try and move the mortar with my hand. Had I possessed a knife, something might have been done, but that useful instrument I had left in my coat pocket.

I soon found that all efforts of this kind were vain and useless, and that all I could hope to do was to wriggle downwards.

But though I jerked and struggled, and strove to turn, it was all in vain. I could not move an inch, one way or the other. And time flew rapidly. My early rising probably contributed to the fact that I felt sleepy, and gradually gave way to the sensation of drowsiness.

I slept, and awoke in darkness, ravenously hungry.

Night had come, and still I could not move. I was tight bound, and did not succeed in changing my position an inch. I groaned aloud. Never since the days of my happy childhood, when it was a hardship to go from meal to meal without eating, had I really experienced hunger. The sensation was as novel as it was painful. I began now to lose my head and to scream and cry out in my agony. Something appeared, startled by my noise. It was a harmless lizard, but it appeared to me a loathsome reptile. Again I made the old ruins resound with my cries, and finally so exhausted myself that I fainted.

How long I lay in a kind of trance or sleep I cannot say, but when again I recovered consciousness it was day. How ill I felt, how hunger still gnawed at me, it would be hard to say. I was too weak to scream now, far too weak to struggle.

Suddenly I was startled by a roar.

"Are you there, Henry?" said the voice of my uncle; "are you there, my boy?"

I could only faintly respond, but I also made a desperate effort to turn. Some mortar fell. To this I owed my being discovered. When the search took place, it was easily seen that mortar and small pieces of stone had recently fallen from above. Hence my uncle's cry.

"Be calm," he cried, "if we pull down the whole ruin, you shall be saved."

They were delicious words, but I had little hope.

Soon however, about a quarter of an hour later I heard a voice above me, at one of the upper fireplaces.

"Are you below or above?"

"Below," was my reply.

In an instant a basket was lowered with milk, a biscuit, and an egg. My uncle was fearful to be too ready with his supply of food. I drank the milk first, for thirst had nearly deadened hunger. I then, much refreshed, ate my bread and hard egg.

They were now at work at the wall. I could hear a pickax. Wishing to escape all danger from this terrible weapon I made a desperate struggle, and the belt, which surrounded my waist and which had been hitched on a stone, gave way. I was free, and only escaped falling down by a rapid motion of my hands and knees.

In ten minutes more I was in my uncle's arms, after being two days and nights in that horrible prison. My occasional delirium prevented me from counting time.

I was weeks recovering from that awful starvation adventure; and yet what was that to the hideous sufferings I now endured?

After dreaming for some time, and thinking of this and other matters, I once more looked around me. We were still ascending with fearful rapidity. Every now and then the air appeared to check our respiration as it does that of aeronauts when the ascension of the balloon is too rapid. But if they feel a degree of cold in proportion to the elevation they attain in the atmosphere, we experienced quite a contrary effect. The heat began to increase in a most threatening and exceptional manner. I cannot tell exactly the mean, but I think it must have reached one hundred twenty-two degrees Fahrenheit.

What was the meaning of this extraordinary change in the temperature? As far as we had hitherto gone, facts had proved the theories of Davy and of Lidenbrock to be correct. Until now, all the peculiar conditions of refractory rocks, of electricity, of magnetism, had modified the general laws of nature, and had created for us a moderate temperature; for the theory of the central fire, remained, in my eyes, the only explainable one.

Were we, then, going to reach a position in which these phenomena were to be carried out in all their rigor, and in which the heat would reduce the rocks to a state of fusion?

Such was my not unnatural fear, and I did not conceal the fact from my uncle. My way of doing so might be cold and heartless, but I could not help it.

"If we are not drowned, or smashed into pancakes, and if we do not die of starvation, we have the satisfaction of knowing that we must be burned alive."

My uncle, in presence of this brusque attack, simply shrugged his shoulders, and resumed his reflections—whatever they might be.

An hour passed away, and except that there was a slight increase in the temperature no incident modified the situation.

My uncle at last, of his own accord, broke silence.

"Well, Henry, my boy," he said, in a cheerful way, "we must make up our minds."

"Make up our minds to what?" I asked, in considerable surprise.

"Well—to something. We must at whatever risk recruit our physical strength. If we make the fatal mistake of husbanding our little remnant of food, we may probably prolong our wretched existence a few hours—but we shall remain weak to the end."

"Yes," I growled, "to the end. That, however, will not keep us long waiting."

"Well, only let a chance of safety present itself—only allow that a moment of action be necessary—where shall we find the means of action if we allow ourselves to be reduced to physical weakness by inanition?"

"When this piece of meat is devoured, Uncle, what hope will there remain unto us?"

"None, my dear Henry, none. But will it do you any good to devour it with your eyes? You appear to me to reason like one without will or decision, like a being without energy."

"Then," cried I, exasperated to a degree which is scarcely to be explained, "you do not mean to tell me—that you—that you—have not lost all hope."

"Certainly not," replied the Professor with consummate coolness.

"You mean to tell me, Uncle, that we shall get out of this monstrous subterranean shaft?"

"While there is life there is hope. I beg to assert, Henry, that as long as a man's heart beats, as long as a man's flesh quivers,

I do not allow that a being gifted with thought and will can allow himself to despair."

What a nerve! The man placed in a position like that we occupied must have been very brave to speak like this.

"Well," I cried, "what do you mean to do?"

"Eat what remains of the food we have in our hands; let us swallow the last crumb. It will bel Heaven willing, our last repast. Well, never mind—instead of being exhausted skeletons, we shall be men."

"True," muttered I in a despairing tone, "let us take our fill."

"We must," replied my uncle, with a deep sigh, "call it what you will."

My uncle took a piece of the meat that remained, and some crusts of biscuit which had escaped the wreck. He divided the whole into three parts.

Each had one pound of food to last him as long as he remained in the interior of the earth.

Each now acted in accordance with his own private character.

My uncle, the Professor, ate greedily, but evidently without appetite, eating simply from some mechanical motion. I put the food inside my lips, and hungry as I was, chewed my morsel without pleasure, and without satisfaction.

Hans, the guide, just as if he had been eider-down hunting, swallowed every mouthful, as though it were a usual affair. He looked like a man equally prepared to enjoy superfluity or total want.

Hans, in all probability, was no more used to starvation than ourselves, but his hardy Icelandic nature had prepared him for many sufferings. As long as he received his three rix-dollars every Saturday night, he was prepared for anything.

The fact was, Hans never troubled himself about much except his money. He had undertaken to serve a certain man at so much per week, and no matter what evils befell his employer or himself, he never found fault or grumbled, so long as his wages were duly paid.

Suddenly my uncle roused himself. He had seen a smile on the face of our guide. I could not make it out.

"What is the matter?" said my uncle.

"Schiedam," said the guide, producing a bottle of this precious fluid.

We drank. My uncle and myself will own to our dying day that hence we derived strength to exist until the last bitter moment. That precious bottle of Hollands was in reality only half full; but, under the circumstances, it was nectar.

It took some minutes for myself and my uncle to form a decided opinion on the subject. The worthy Professor swallowed about half a pint and did not seem able to drink any more.

"*Fortrafflig*," said Hans, swallowing nearly all that was left.

"Excellent—very good," said my uncle, with as much gusto as if he had just left the steps of the club at Hamburg.

I had begun to feel as if there had been one gleam of hope. Now all thought of the future vanished!

We had consumed our last ounce of food, and it was five o'clock in the morning!

Chapter 42

THE VOLCANIC SHAFT

Man's constitution is so peculiar that his health is purely a negative matter. No sooner is the rage of hunger appeased than it becomes difficult to comprehend the meaning of starvation. It is only when you suffer that you really understand.

As to anyone who has not endured privation having any notion of the matter, it is simply absurd.

With us, after a long fast, some mouthfuls of bread and meat, a little moldy biscuit and salt beef triumphed over all our previous gloomy and saturnine thoughts.

Nevertheless, after this repast each gave way to his own reflections. I wondered what were those of Hans—the man of the extreme north, who was yet gifted with the fatalistic resignation of Oriental character. But the utmost stretch of the imagination would not allow me to realize the truth. As for my individual self, my thoughts had ceased to be anything but memories of the past, and were all connected with that upper world which I never should have left. I saw it all now, the beautiful house in the Konigstrasse, my poor Gretchen, the good Martha; they all passed before my mind like visions of the past. Every time any of the lugubrious groanings which were to be distinguished in the hollows around fell upon my ears, I fancied I heard the distant murmur of the great cities above my head.

As for my uncle, always thinking of his science, he examined the nature of the shaft by means of a torch. He closely examined the different strata one above the other, in order to recognize his situation by geological theory. This calculation, or rather this estimation, could by no means be anything but approximate. But a learned man, a philosopher, is nothing if not a philosopher, when he keeps his ideas calm and collected; and certainly the Professor possessed this quality to perfection.

I heard him, as I sat in silence, murmuring words of geological science. As I understood his object and his meaning, I could not but interest myself despite my preoccupation in that terrible hour.

"Eruptive granite," he said to himself, "we are still in the primitive epoch. But we are going up—going up, still going up. But who knows? Who knows?"

Then he still hoped. He felt along the vertical sides of the shaft with his hand, and some few minutes later, he would go on again in the following style:

"This is gneiss. This is mica schist—siliceous mineral. Good again; this is the epoch of transition, at all events, we are close to them—and then, and then—"

What could the Professor mean? Could he, by any conceivable means, measure the thickness of the crust of the earth suspended above our heads? Did he possess any possible means of making any approximation to this calculation? No.

The manometer was wanting, and no summary estimation could take the place of it.

And yet, as we progressed, the temperature increased in the most extraordinary degree, and I began to feel as if I were bathed in a hot and burning atmosphere. Never before had I felt anything like it. I could only compare it to the hot vapor from an iron foundry, when the liquid iron is in a state of ebullition and runs over. By degrees, and one after the other, Hans, my uncle, and myself had taken off our coats and waistcoats. They were unbearable. Even the slightest garment was not only uncomfortable, but the cause of extreme suffering.

"Are we ascending to a living fire?" I cried; when, to my horror and astonishment, the heat became greater than before.

"No, no," said my uncle, "it is simply impossible, quite impossible."

"And yet," said I, touching the side of the shaft with my naked hand, "this wall is literally burning."

At this moment, feeling as I did that the sides of this extraordinary wall were red hot, I plunged my hands into the water to cool them. I drew them back with a cry of despair.

"The water is boiling!" I cried.

My uncle, the Professor, made no reply other than a gesture of rage and despair.

Something very like the truth had probably struck his imagination.

But I could take no share in either what was going on, or in his speculations. An invincible dread had taken possession of my brain and soul. I could only look forward to an immediate catastrophe, such a catastrophe as not even the most vivid imagination could have thought of. An idea, at first vague and uncertain, was gradually being changed into certainty.

I tremulously rejected it at first, but it forced itself upon me by degrees with extreme obstinacy. It was so terrible an idea that I scarcely dared to whisper it to myself.

And yet all the while certain, and as it were, involuntary observations determined my convictions. By the doubtful glare of the torch, I could make out some singular changes in the granitic strata; a strange and terrible phenomenon was about to be produced, in which electricity played a part.

Then this boiling water, this terrible and excessive heat? I determined as a last resource to examine the compass.

The compass had gone mad!

Yes, wholly stark staring mad. The needle jumped from pole to pole with sudden and surprising jerks, ran round, or as it is said, boxed the compass, and then ran suddenly back again as if it had the vertigo.

I was aware that, according to the best acknowledged theories, it was a received notion that the mineral crust of the globe is never, and never has been, in a state of complete repose.

It is perpetually undergoing the modifications caused by the decomposition of internal matter, the agitation consequent on the flowing of extensive liquid currents, the excessive action of magnetism which tends to shake it incessantly, at a time when even the multitudinous beings on its surface do not suspect the seething process to be going on.

Still this phenomenon would not have alarmed me alone; it would not have aroused in my mind a terrible, an awful idea.

But other facts could not allow my self-delusion to last.

Terrible detonations, like Heaven's artillery, began to multiply themselves with fearful intensity. I could only compare them with the noise made by hundreds of heavily laden chariots being madly driven over a stone pavement. It was a continuous roll of heavy thunder.

And then the mad compass, shaken by the wild electric phenomena, confirmed me in my rapidly formed opinion. The mineral crust was about to burst, the heavy granite masses were about to rejoin, the fissure was about to close, the void was about to be filled up, and we poor atoms to be crushed in its awful embrace!

"Uncle, Uncle!" I cried, "we are wholly, irretrievably lost!"

"What, then, my young friend, is your new cause of terror and alarm?" he said in his calmest manner. "What fear you now?"

"What do I fear now!" I cried in fierce and angry tones. "Do you not see that the walls of the shaft are in motion? Do you not see that the solid granite masses are cracking? Do you not feel the terrible, torrid heat? Do you not observe the awful boiling water on which we float? Do you not remark this mad needle? Every sign and portent of an awful earthquake!"

My uncle coolly shook his head.

"An earthquake," he replied in the most calm and provoking tone.

"Yes."

"My nephew, I tell you that you are utterly mistaken," he continued.

"Do you not, can you not, recognize all the well-known symtons—"

"Of an earthquake? By no means. I am expecting something far more important."

"My brain is strained beyond endurance—what, what do you mean?" I cried.

"An eruption, Harry."

"An eruption," I gasped. "We are, then, in the volcanic shaft of a crater in full action and vigor."

"I have every reason to think so," said the Professor in a smiling tone, "and I beg to tell you that it is the most fortunate thing that could happen to us."

The most fortunate thing! Had my uncle really and truly gone mad? What did he mean by these awful words—what did he mean by this terrible calm, this solemn smile?

"What!" cried I, in the height of my exasperation, "we are on the way to an eruption, are we? Fatality has cast us into a well of burning and boiling lava, of rocks on fire, of boiling water, in a word, filled with every kind of eruptive matter? We are about to be expelled, thrown up, vomited, spit out of the interior of the earth, in common with huge blocks of granite, with showers of cinders and scoriae, in a wild whirlwind of flame, and you say—the most fortunate thing which could happen to us."

"Yes," replied the Professor, looking at me calmly from under his spectacles, "it is the only chance which remains to us of ever escaping from the interior of the earth to the light of day."

It is quite impossible that I can put on paper the thousand strange, wild thoughts which followed this extraordinary announcement.

But my uncle was right, quite right, and never had he appeared to me so audacious and so convinced as when he looked me calmly in the face and spoke of the chances of an eruption—of our being cast upon Mother Earth once more through the gaping crater of a volcano!

Nevertheless, while we were speaking we were still ascending; we passed the whole night going up, or to speak more scientifically, in an ascensional motion. The fearful noise redoubled; I was ready to suffocate. I seriously believed that my last hour was approaching, and yet, so strange is imagination, all I thought of was some childish hypothesis or other. In such circumstances you do not choose your own thoughts. They overcome you.

It was quite evident that we were being cast upwards by eruptive matter; under the raft there was a mass of boiling water, and under this was a heavier mass of lava, and an aggregate of rocks which, on reaching the summit of the water, would be dispersed in every direction.

That we were inside the chimney of a volcano there could no longer be the shadow of a doubt. Nothing more terrible could be conceived!

But on this occasion, instead of Sneffels, an old and extinct volcano, we were inside a mountain of fire in full activity.

Several times I found myself asking, what mountain was it, and on what part of the world we should be shot out. As if it were of any consequence!

In the northern regions, there could be no reasonable doubt about that. Before it went decidedly mad, the compass had never made the slightest mistake. From the cape of Saknussemm, we had been swept away to the northward many hundreds of leagues. Now the question was, were we once more under Iceland—should we be belched forth on to the earth through the crater of Mount Hecla, or should we reappear through one of the other seven fire funnels of the island? Taking in my mental vision a radius of five hundred leagues to the westward, I could see under this parallel

only the little-known volcanoes of the northwest coast of America.

To the east one only existed somewhere about the eightieth degree of latitude, the Esk, upon the island of Jan Mayen, not far from the frozen regions of Spitsbergen.

It was not craters that were wanting, and many of them were big enough to vomit a whole army; all I wished to know was the particular one towards which we were making with such fearful velocity.

I often think now of my folly: as if I should ever have expected to escape!

Towards morning, the ascending motion became greater and greater. If the degree of heat increased instead of decreasing, as we approached the surface of the earth, it was simply because the causes were local and wholly due to volcanic influence. Our very style of locomotion left in my mind no doubt upon the subject. An enormous force, a force of several hundreds of atmospheres produced by the vapors accumulated and long compressed in the interior of the earth, was hoisting us upwards with irresistible power.

But though we were approaching the light of day, to what fearful dangers were we about to be exposed?

Instant death appeared the only fate which we could expect or contemplate.

Soon a dim, sepulchral light penetrated the vertical gallery, which became wider and wider. I could make out to the right and left long dark corridors like immense tunnels, from which awful and horrid vapors poured out. Tongues of fire, sparkling and crackling, appeared about to lick us up.

The hour had come!

"Look, Uncle, look!" I cried.

"Well, what you see are the great sulphurous flames. Nothing more common in connection with an eruption."

"But if they lap us round!" I angrily replied.

"They will not lap us round," was his quiet and serene answer.

"But it will be all the same in the end if they stifle us," I cried.

"We shall not be stifled. The gallery is rapidly becoming wider and wider, and if it be necessary, we will presently leave the raft and take refuge in some fissure in the rock."

"But the water, the water, which is continually ascending?" I despairingly replied.

"There is no longer any water, Harry," he answered, "but a kind of lava paste, which is heaving us up, in company with itself, to the mouth of the crater."

In truth, the liquid column of water had wholly disappeared to give place to dense masses of boiling eruptive matter. The temperature was becoming utterly insupportable, and a thermometer exposed to this atmosphere would have marked between one hundred and eighty-nine and one hundred ninety degrees Fahrenheit.

Perspiration rushed from every pore. But for the

extraordinary rapidity of our ascent we should have been stifled.

Nevertheless, the Professor did not carry out his proposition of abandoning the raft; and he did quite wisely. Those few ill-joined beams offered, anyway, a solid surface—a support which elsewhere must have utterly failed us.

Towards eight o'clock in the morning a new incident startled us. The ascensional movement suddenly ceased. The raft became still and motionless.

"What is the matter now?" I said, querulously, very much startled by this change.

"A simple halt," replied my uncle.

"Is the eruption about to fail?" I asked.

"I hope not."

Without making any reply, I rose. I tried to look around me. Perhaps the raft, checked by some projecting rock, opposed a momentary resistance to the eruptive mass. In this case, it was absolutely necessary to release it as quickly as possible.

Nothing of the kind had occurred. The column of cinders, of scoriae, of broken rocks and earth, had wholly ceased to ascend.

"I tell you, Uncle, that the eruption has stopped," was my oracular decision.

"Ah," said my uncle, "you think so, my boy. You are wrong. Do not be in the least alarmed; this sudden moment of calm will not last long, be assured. It has already endured five minutes, and before we are many minutes older we shall be continuing our journey to the mouth of the crater."

All the time he was speaking the Professor continued to consult his chronometer, and he was probably right in his prognostics. Soon the raft resumed its motion, in a very rapid and disorderly way, which lasted two minutes or thereabout; and then again it stopped as suddenly as before.

"Good," said my uncle, observing the hour, "in ten we shall start again."

"In ten minutes?"

"Yes—precisely. We have to do with a volcano, the eruption of which is intermittent. We are compelled to breathe just as it does."

Nothing could be more true. At the exact minute he had indicated, we were again launched on high with extreme rapidity. Not to be cast off the raft, it was necessary to hold on to the beams. Then the hoist again ceased.Many times since have I thought of this singular phenomenon without being able to find for it any satisfactory explanation. Nevertheless, it appeared quite clear to me, that we were not in the principal chimney of the volcano, but in an accessory conduit, where we felt the counter shock of the great and principal tunnel filled by burning lava.

It is impossible for me to say how many times this maneuver was repeated. All that I can remember is, that on every ascensional motion, we were hoisted up with ever increasing velocity, as if we had been launched from a huge projectile. During the sudden halts we were nearly stifled; during the moments of projection the hot air took away our breath.

I thought for a moment of the voluptuous joy of suddenly finding myself in the hyperborean regions with the cold thirty degrees below zero!

My exalted imagination pictured to itself the vast snowy plains of the arctic regions, and I was impatient to roll myself on the icy carpet of the North Pole.

By degrees my head, utterly overcome by a series of violent emotions, began to give way to hallucination. I was delirious. Had it not been for the powerful arms of Hans, the guide, I should have broken my head against the granite masses of the shaft.

I have, in consequence, kept no account of what followed for many hours. I have a vague and confused remembrance of continual detonations, of the shaking of the huge granitic mass, and of the raft going round like a spinning top. It floated on the stream of hot lava, amidst a falling cloud of cinders. The huge flames roaring, wrapped us around.

A storm of wind which appeared to be cast forth from an immense ventilator roused up the interior fires of the earth. It was a hot, incandescent blast!

At last I saw the figure of Hans as if enveloped in the huge halo of burning blaze, and no other sense remained to me but that sinister dread which the condemned victim may be supposed to feel when led to the mouth of a cannon, at the supreme moment when the shot is fired and his limbs are dispersed into empty space.

Chapter 43

DAYLIGHT AT LAST

When I opened my eyes I felt the hand of the guide clutching me firmly by the belt. With his other hand he supported my uncle. I was not grievously wounded, but bruised all over in the most remarkable manner.

After a moment I looked around, and found that I was lying down on the slope of a mountain not two yards from a yawning gulf into which I should have fallen had I made the slightest false step. Hans had saved me from death, while I rolled insensible on the flanks of the crater.

"Where are we?" dreamily asked my uncle, who literally appeared to be disgusted at having returned to earth.

The eider-down hunter simply shrugged his shoulders as a mark of total ignorance.

"In Iceland?" said I, not positively but interrogatively.

"Nej," said Hans.

"How do you mean?" cried the Professor; "no—what are your reasons?"

"Hans is wrong," said I, rising.

After all the innumerable surprises of this journey, a yet more singular one was reserved to us. I expected to see a cone covered by snow, by extensive and widespread glaciers, in the midst of the arid deserts of the extreme northern regions, beneath the full rays of a polar sky, beyond the highest latitudes.

But contrary to all our expectations, I, my uncle, and the Icelander, were cast upon the slope of a mountain calcined by the burning rays of a sun which was literally baking us with its fires.

I could not believe my eyes, but the actual heat which affected my body allowed me no chance of doubting. We came out of the crater half naked, and the radiant star from which we had asked nothing for two months, was good enough to be prodigal to us of light and warmth—a light and warmth we could easily have dispensed with.

When our eyes were accustomed to the light we had lost sight of so long, I used them to rectify the errors of my imagination. Whatever happened, we should have been at Spitsbergen, and I was in no humor to yield to anything but the most absolute proof.

After some delay, the Professor spoke.

"Hem!" he said, in a hesitating kind of way, "it really does not look like Iceland."

"But supposing it were the island of Jan Mayen?" I ventured to observe.

"Not in the least, my boy. This is not one of the volcanoes of the north, with its hills of granite and its crown of snow."

"Nevertheless—"

"Look, look, my boy," said the Professor, as dogmatically as usual.

Right above our heads, at a great height, opened the crater of a volcano from which escaped, from one quarter of an hour to the other, with a very loud explosion, a lofty jet of flame mingled with pumice stone, cinders, and lava. I could feel the convulsions of nature in the mountain, which breathed like a huge whale, throwing up from time to time fire and air through its enormous vents.

Below, and floating along a slope of considerable angularity, the stream of eruptive matter spread away to a depth which did not give the volcano a height of three hundred fathoms.

Its base disappeared in a perfect forest of green trees, among which I perceived olives, fig trees, and vines loaded with rich grapes.

Certainly this was not the ordinary aspect of the arctic regions. About that there could not be the slightest doubt.

When the eye was satisfied at its glimpse of this verdant expanse, it fell upon the waters of a lovely sea or beautiful lake, which made of this enchanted land an island of not many leagues in extent.

On the side of the rising sun was to be seen a little port, crowded with houses, and near which the boats and vessels of peculiar build were floating upon azure waves.

Beyond, groups of islands rose above the liquid plain, so numerous and close together as to resemble a vast beehive.

Towards the setting sun, some distant shores were to be made out on the edge of the horizon. Some presented the appearance of blue mountains of harmonious conformation; upon others, much more distant, there appeared a prodigiously lofty cone, above the summit of which hung dark and heavy clouds.

Towards the north, an immense expanse of water sparkled beneath the solar rays, occasionally allowing the extremity of a mast or the convexity of a sail bellying to the wind, to be seen.

The unexpected character of such a scene added a hundredfold to its marvelous beauties.

"Where can we be?" I asked, speaking in a low and solemn voice.

Hans shut his eyes with an air of indifference, and my uncle looked on without clearly understanding.

"Whatever this mountain may be," he said, at last, "I must confess it is rather warm. The explosions do not leave off, and I do not think it is worthwhile to have left the interior of a volcano and remain here to receive a huge piece of rock upon one's head. Let us carefully descend the mountain and discover the real state of the case. To confess the truth, I am dying of hunger and thirst."

Decidedly the Professor was no longer a truly reflective character. For myself, forgetting all my necessities, ignoring my fatigues and sufferings, I should have remained still for several hours longer—but it was necessary to follow my companions.

The slope of the volcano was very steep and slippery; we slid over piles of ashes, avoiding the streams of hot lava which glided about like fiery serpents. Still, while we were advancing, I spoke with extreme volubility, for my imagination was too full not to explode in words.

"We are in Asia!" I exclaimed; "we are on the coast of India, in the great Malay islands, in the centre of Oceania. We have crossed the one half of the globe to come out right at the antipodes of Europe!"

"But the compass!" exclaimed my uncle; "explain that to me!"

"Yes—the compass," I said with considerable hesitation. "I grant that is a difficulty. According to it, we have always been going northward."

"Then it lied."

"Hem—to say it lied is rather a harsh word," was my answer.

"Then we are at the North Pole—"

"The Pole—no—well—well I give it up," was my reply.

The plain truth was, that there was no explanation possible. I could make nothing of it.

And all the while we were approaching this beautiful verdure, hunger and thirst tormented me fearfully. Happily, after two long hours' march, a beautiful country spread out before us, covered by olives, pomegranates, and vines, which appeared to belong to anybody and everybody. In any event, in the state of destitution into which we had fallen, we were not in a mood to ponder too scrupulously.

What delight it was to press these delicious fruits to our lips, and to bite at grapes and pomegranates fresh from the vine.

Not far off, near some fresh and mossy grass, under the delicious shade of some trees, I discovered a spring of fresh water, in which we voluptuously laved our faces, hands, and feet.

While we were all giving way to the delights of new-found pleasures, a little child appeared between two tufted olive trees.

"Ah," cried I, "an inhabitant of this happy country."

The little fellow was poorly dressed, weak, and suffering, and appeared terribly alarmed at our appearance. Half-naked, with tangled, matted and ragged beards, we did look supremely ill-favored; and unless the country was a bandit land, we were not likely to alarm the inhabitants!

Just as the boy was about to take to his heels, Hans ran after him, and brought him back, despite his cries and kicks.

My uncle tried to look as gentle as possible, and then spoke in German.

"What is the name of this mountain, my friend?"

The child made no reply.

"Good," said my uncle, with a very positive air of conviction, "we are not in Germany."

He then made the same demand in English, of which language he was an excellent scholar.

The child shook its head and made no reply. I began to be considerably puzzled.

"Is he dumb?" cried the Professor, who was rather proud of his polyglot knowledge of languages, and made the same demand in French.

The boy only stared in his face.

"I must perforce try him in Italian," said my uncle, with a shrug.

"*Dove noi siamo*?"

"Yes, tell me where we are?" I added impatiently and eagerly.

Again the boy remained silent.

"My fine fellow, do you or do you not mean to speak?" cried my uncle, who began to get angry. He shook him, and spoke another dialect of the Italian language.

"*Come si noma questa isola*?"—"What is the name of this island?"

"Stromboli," replied the rickety little shepherd, dashing away from Hans and disappearing in the olive groves.

We thought little enough about him.

Stromboli! What effect on the imagination did these few words produce! We were in the centre of the Mediterranean, amidst the eastern archipelago of mythological memory, in the ancient Strongylos, where AEolus kept the wind and the tempest chained up. And those blue mountains, which rose towards the rising sun, were the mountains of Calabria.

And that mighty volcano which rose on the southern horizon was Etna, the fierce and celebrated Etna!

"Stromboli! Stromboli!" I repeated to myself.

My uncle played a regular accompaniment to my gestures and words. We were singing together like an ancient chorus.

Ah—what a journey—what a marvelous and extraordinary journey! Here we had entered the earth by one volcano, and we had come out by another. And this other was situated more than twelve hundred leagues from Sneffels from that drear country of Iceland cast away on the confines of the earth. The wondrous changes of this expedition had transported us to the most harmonious and beautiful of earthly lands. We had abandoned the region of eternal snows for that of infinite verdure, and had left over our heads the gray fog of the icy regions to come back to the azure sky of Sicily!

After a delicious repast of fruits and fresh water, we again continued our journey in order to reach the port of Stromboli. To say how we had reached the island would scarcely have been prudent. The superstitious character of the Italians would have been at work, and we should have been called demons vomited from the infernal regions. It was therefore necessary to pass for humble and unfortunate shipwrecked travelers. It was certainly less striking and romantic, but it was decidedly safer.

As we advanced, I could hear my worthy uncle muttering to himself:

"But the compass. The compass most certainly marked north. This is a fact I cannot explain in any way."

"Well, the fact is," said I, with an air of disdain, "we must not explain anything. It will be much more easy."

"I should like to see a professor of the Johanneum Institution who is unable to explain a cosmic phenomenon—it would indeed be strange."

And speaking thus, my uncle, half-naked, his leathern purse round his loins, and his spectacles upon his nose, became once more the terrible Professor of Mineralogy.

An hour after leaving the wood of olives, we reached the fort of San Vicenza, where Hans demanded the price of his thirteenth week of service. My uncle paid him, with very many warm shakes of the hand.

At that moment, if he did not indeed quite share our natural emotion, he allowed his feelings so far to give way as to indulge in an extraordinary expression for him.

With the tips of two fingers he gently pressed our hands and smiled.

Chapter 44

THE JOURNEY ENDED

This is the final conclusion of a narrative which will be probably disbelieved even by people who are astonished at nothing. I am, however, armed at all points against human incredulity.

We were kindly received by the Strombolite fishermen, who treated us as shipwrecked travelers. They gave us clothes and food. After a delay of forty-eight hours, on the 30th of September a little vessel took us to Messina, where a few days of delightful and complete repose restored us to ourselves.

On Friday, the 4th of October, we embarked in the Volturne, one of the postal packets of the Imperial Messageries of France; and three days later we landed at Marseilles, having no other care on our minds but that of our precious but erratic compass. This inexplicable circumstance tormented me terribly. On the 9th of October, in the evening, we reached Hamburg.

What was the astonishment of Martha, what the joy of Gretchen! I will not attempt to define it.

"Now then, Harry, that you really are a hero," she said, "there is no reason why you should ever leave me again."

I looked at her. She was weeping tears of joy.

I leave it to be imagined if the return of Professor Hardwigg made or did not make a sensation in Hamburg. Thanks to the indiscretion of Martha, the news of his departure for the interior of the earth had been spread over the whole world.

No one would believe it—and when they saw him come back in safety they believed it all the less.

But the presence of Hans and many stray scraps of information by degrees modified public opinion.

Then my uncle became a great man and I the nephew of a great man, which, at all events, is something. Hamburg gave a festival in our honor. A public meeting of the Johanneum Institution was held, at which the Professor related the whole story of his adventures, omitting only the facts in connection with the compass.

That same day he deposited in the archives of the town the document he had found written by Saknussemm, and he expressed his great regret that circumstances, stronger than his will, did not allow him to follow the Icelandic traveler's track into the very centre of the earth. He was modest in his glory, but his reputation only increased.

So much honor necessarily created for him many envious enemies. Of course they existed, and as his theories, supported by certain facts, contradicted the system of science upon the question of central heat, he maintained his own views both with pen and speech against the learned of every country. Although I still believe in the theory of central heat, I confess that certain circumstances, hitherto very ill defined, may modify the laws of such natural phenomena.

At the moment when these questions were being discussed with interest, my uncle received a rude shock—one that he felt very much. Hans, despite everything he could say to the contrary, quitted Hamburg; the man to whom we owed so much would not allow us to pay our deep debt of gratitude. He was taken with nostalgia; a love for his Icelandic home.

"Farval," said he, one day, and with this one short word

of adieu, he started for Reykjavik, which he soon reached in safety.

We were deeply attached to our brave eider-duck hunter. His absence will never cause him to be forgotten by those whose lives he saved, and I hope, at some not distant day, to see him again.

To conclude, I may say that our journey into the interior of the earth created an enormous sensation throughout the civilized world. It was translated and printed in many languages. All the leading journals published extracts from it, which were commentated, discussed, attacked, and supported with equal animation by those who believed in its episodes, and by those who were utterly incredulous.

Wonderful! My uncle enjoyed during his lifetime all the glory he deserved; and he was even offered a large sum of money, by Mr. Barnum, to exhibit himself in the United States; while I am credibly informed by a traveler that he is to be seen in waxwork at Madame Tussaud's!

But one care preyed upon his mind, a care which rendered him very unhappy. One fact remained inexplicable—that of the compass. For a learned man to be baffled by such an inexplicable phenomenon was very aggravating. But Heaven was merciful, and in the end my uncle was happy.

One day, while he put some minerals belonging to his collection in order, I fell upon the famous compass and examined it keenly.

For six months it had lain unnoticed and untouched.

I looked at it with curiosity, which soon became surprise. I gave a loud cry. The Professor, who was at hand, soon joined me.

"What is the matter?" he cried.

"The compass!"

"What then?"

"Why its needle points to the south and not to the north."

"My dear boy, you must be dreaming."

"I am not dreaming. See—the poles are changed."

"Changed!"

My uncle put on his spectacles, examined the instrument, and leaped with joy, shaking the whole house.

A clear light fell upon our minds.

"Here it is!" he cried, as soon as he had recovered the use of his speech, "after we had once passed Cape Saknussemm, the needle of this compass pointed to the southward instead of the northward."

"Evidently."

"Our error is now easily explained. But to what phenomenon do we owe this alteration in the needle?"

"Nothing more simple."

"Explain yourself, my boy. I am on thorns."

"During the storm, upon the Central Sea, the ball of fire which made a magnet of the iron in our raft, turned our compass topsy-turvy."

"Ah!" cried the Professor, with a loud and ringing laugh, "it was a trick of that inexplicable electricity."

From that hour my uncle was the happiest of learned men, and I the happiest of ordinary mortals. For my pretty Virland girl, abdicating her position as ward, took her place in the house in the Konigstrasse in the double quality of niece and wife.

We need scarcely mention that her uncle was the illustrious Professor Hardwigg, corresponding member of all the scientific, geographical, mineralogical, and geological societies of the five parts of the globe.

End of the Voyage Extraordinaire

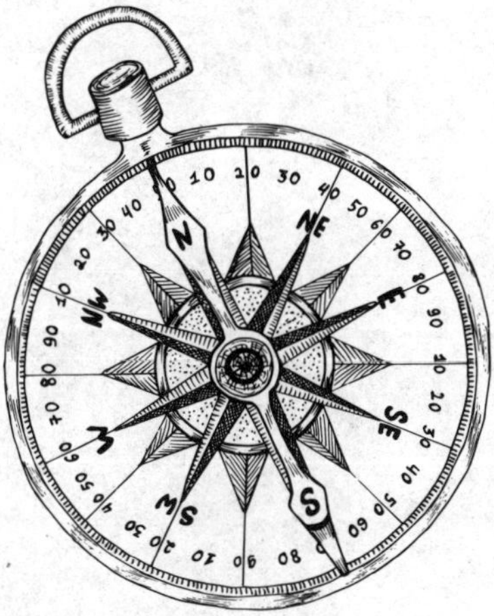
N
NE
E
SE
S
SW
W
NW